"Bernie's cakes are ~~as you are, Max. Whe~~ ...kiss me, I forget all the completely valid reasons I have for keeping my distance from you."

"There's an easy solution to that," Max said.

"What?"

"Kiss me back."

He was as tempting as the devil . . . All she had to do was walk away. She knew he wouldn't stop her. He was too much of a gentleman. But she didn't want to. Being with him, being away from her family, and her commitments for the first time in years was remarkably freeing. And why shouldn't she kiss her own bloody husband? She wasn't hurting anyone, and no one would know.

She pressed her lips against his and his arm came around her hips holding her against him from knee to shoulder.

"That's my girl."

He kissed like a dream, and she kissed him with all the enthusiasm in the world . . .

Books by Kate Pearce

The House of Pleasure Series
SIMPLY SEXUAL
SIMPLY SINFUL
SIMPLY SHAMELESS
SIMPLY WICKED
SIMPLY INSATIABLE
SIMPLY FORBIDDEN
SIMPLY CARNAL
SIMPLY VORACIOUS
SIMPLY SCANDALOUS
SIMPLY PLEASURE
   (e-novella)
SIMPLY IRRESISTIBLE
   (e-novella)

The Sinners Club Series
THE SINNERS CLUB
TEMPTING A SINNER
MASTERING A SINNER
THE FIRST SINNERS
   (e-novella)

Single Titles
RAW DESIRE

The Morgan Brothers Ranch
THE RELUCTANT COWBOY
THE MAVERICK COWBOY
THE LAST GOOD COWBOY
THE BAD BOY COWBOY
THE BILLIONAIRE BULL
   RIDER
THE RANCHER

The Millers of Morgan Valley
THE SECOND CHANCE
   RANCHER
THE RANCHER'S
   REDEMPTION
THE REBELLIOUS
   RANCHER
THE RANCHER MEETS HIS
   MATCH
SWEET TALKING RANCHER
ROMANCING THE
   RANCHER

Three Cowboys
THREE COWBOYS AND A
   BABY
THREE COWBOYS AND A
   PUPPY
THREE COWBOYS AND A
   BRIDE

Anthologies
SOME LIKE IT ROUGH
LORDS OF PASSION
HAPPY IS THE BRIDE
A SEASON TO CELEBRATE
MARRYING MY COWBOY
CHRISTMAS KISSES WITH
MY COWBOY
LONE WOLF

Published by Kensington Publishing Corp.

Three Cowboys and a Bride

Kate Pearce

ZEBRA BOOKS
Kensington Publishing Corp.
www.kensingtonbooks.com

ZEBRA BOOKS are published by

Kensington Publishing Corp.
900 Third Avenue
New York, NY 10022

All Kensington titles, imprints, and distributed lines are available at special quantity discounts for bulk purchases for sales promotion, premiums, fund-raising, educational, or institutional use.

Special book excerpts or customized printings can also be created to fit specific needs. For details, write or phone the office of the Kensington Sales Manager: Attn.: Sales Department. Kensington Publishing Corp., 900 Third Avenue, New York, NY 10022. Phone: 1-800-221-2647.

ZEBRA and the ZEBRA logo Reg US Pat. & TM Off.

First Zebra paperback: June 2024
ISBN: 978-1-4201-5498-6

ISBN: 978-1-4201-5499-3 (ebook)

10 9 8 7 6 5 4 3 2 1

Printed in the United States of America

Thanks to Sian Kaley and Jerri Drennen for beta reading this book. Thanks to Kensington for letting me write all these awesome cowboy books for so many years, and special thanks to all the readers who have supported me. I appreciate every one of you.

Prologue

Four years ago in Reno, Nevada

"Excuse me?"

Max Romero looked up from contemplating the bottom of his empty whisky glass to find a woman, with eyes the same color as his favorite drink, hovering nervously by his side. He'd already been approached by a couple of women looking for company and had politely turned them down. This one wore a flowery dress, a pink cardigan, and a strand of pearls draped around a delicate neck, which made him do a double take.

"Hey."

He was pretty sure they weren't acquainted, but he was just drunk enough not to be certain, and he'd never been one to offend a lady.

"Hi! You don't know me, but—"

He held up one finger. "You British?"

"Yes, I am, but—"

"I like your accent."

"Thank you, it's—"

"Like talking to Princess Di."

"Actually, my mother went to school with her at

some point." She frowned. "Not that she knew her well or anything."

"Like, really?"

Max made quick eye contact with the bartender who came over. It wasn't busy at the casino yet. Only the serious gamblers and drinkers were on the floor during daylight and stayed until it was dawn again. He didn't have the money to gamble, and he'd been nursing his last whisky for long enough that the guy behind the bar was giving him the stink eye. The truth was he didn't want to go out and face the real world just yet. Chatting to a sweet-faced Brit was a diversion he was more than willing to embrace.

He patted the bar stool beside him. "Do you want to sit down? Looking up is giving me a crick in the neck."

"Sorry." She blushed, staining her perfect complexion with a rosy glow. "I know I'm tall."

She took the seat and swung around to face him. Her hair was cinnamon brown and cut in a short bob, her mouth was bow shaped, and her eyes were . . . kind of sweet like a spaniel's. She looked as out of place in a Reno bar as he would look at a coronation.

"What would you like to drink?" Max asked.

"A glass of white wine would be lovely." Her quick smile transformed her face from average to pretty. "Thank you."

"I'll have a beer, thanks," Max said to the bartender before refocusing his attention on the woman beside him. "Now, tell me about your mom and Lady Di."

She fiddled with the coaster on the counter, and ducked her head, her hair swinging around to half cover her face. "There isn't much to tell, really. Just that she mentioned the school thing once."

"And you never asked about it?"

She shrugged. "It didn't mean much at the time. She went to school with all sorts of people like that."

"I guess she was posh like you?"

"I suppose she was." She paused. "One doesn't consider things like that until it's pointed out by someone else."

"One doesn't." Max nodded.

Their drinks arrived and she took a huge swig of wine, which made her cough.

"Ugh, I wasn't expecting it to be lukewarm." She shuddered and used a bar napkin to daintily wipe her mouth. "I've never understood why wine is warm here and beer is freezing."

"I guess we just like messing with your heads." Max held up his bottle and clinked it against her glass. "Here's to the differences between us."

This time he got the full blast of her smile and something inside him reacted to its genuine warmth, making him smile in return.

"Bottoms up," she said.

"Cheers."

She drank the rest of her wine in one gulp and Max wondered why she needed a jolt of courage. She didn't strike him as the kind of woman who usually approached a guy at the bar of a seedy Reno casino, but he'd learned to be open to all possibilities.

"I'm Max," he said, just in case she needed somewhere to start.

"Phoebe."

"Freebie?"

"Ha, ha, very funny." She rolled her eyes. "People have been making fun of my name since I was born. Some people call me Fee."

He was quietly impressed by her refusal to react to him. "I prefer Freebie or Furby myself."

"We had one of those. It went feral and Nanny had to hide it in the laundry room wrapped up in a towel because it wouldn't turn itself off."

"Nanny." Max took a slug of beer. "Like Mary Poppins?"

"Exactly like that." She held his gaze. "Are you always like this?"

"Like what?"

"You know—like you're teasing me all the time."

"Yeah, that's how I roll because I refuse to take life too seriously."

His day job as a Marine meant he took the life of his team very seriously indeed, but when he was stateside, he wanted nothing to do with orders, routines, or life-threatening situations. Most of his friends assumed he'd be in the thick of a loud gang of people and activities when he was on leave, but sometimes he preferred to be completely by himself. He was due to meet his two best buds in Reno before they were deployed on their next mission, but they weren't arriving for a couple of days.

The bartender placed another glass of wine at Phoebe's elbow, and she thanked him.

"Nanny made sure you had excellent manners," Max said.

"She did. My parents weren't around much so she was our rock before we went off to boarding school."

"How old were you when that happened?"

"Seven?" She frowned. "I think that was about it. I cried myself sick until I got used to it."

Max was certain that the military-style institution he'd been forced to attend by the courts as a teenager wasn't quite the same experience, but he'd cried a couple of times, too.

She cleared her throat. "Do you live in Reno?"

"Nope, I'm just visiting. I'm meeting a couple of friends here at the end of the week and we'll travel onward together."

"I ended up here by mistake." She half-smiled. "My connections got messed up due to the storm and the plane got re-routed through Reno."

"So, you're off back home tomorrow?"

"Possibly." She hesitated. "It depends."

"On what?"

She met his gaze. "You."

The man sitting beside her blinked his sapphire-blue eyes. His hair was black, he had cheekbones and dimples to die for, and he was completely in the dark about what she was about to ask him, and who could blame him, when she couldn't believe it herself. But needs must and she refused to allow the fates to destroy her. She'd been in the States to visit an old friend who had advised her to show some spirit and take command of her own destiny, so here she was, her knees shaking, taking command . . .

"Come again?"

Phoebe gripped her wineglass in her fingers. "I was hoping you might help with something."

His eyebrows rose. "Now I'm getting worried."

"But first, I need to ask you a couple of questions."

"Shoot."

She took a deep breath. "Are you married or involved with someone?"

"Nope and nope, and I'm not gay if that was your next question."

"Have you ever considered a marriage of convenience?"

He sat up straight. "A what the *hell* now?"

Phoebe's cheeks heated. "A marriage that suits both parties but doesn't necessarily involve love or a commitment to stay together forever."

He stared at her for a long moment. "Are you after a green card?"

"Goodness no!" Phoebe waved that suggestion aside with a flick of her fingers. "I just need a husband for a few months while I . . . sort out some family issues."

He studied her for a long moment, but she was encouraged by the hint of a smile on his lips. "Are you nuts?" He glanced around. "Am I about to star on some reality TV show?"

"Not at all. I'm just trying to find a solution to a problem in an amicable fashion."

"And you picked *me*?"

She shrugged. "You just looked right somehow."

She'd watched him deal with several approaches from other women with good humor and a politeness that sent them away still smiling. There was just something about him that drew her in, and she knew that when he turned her down, he'd do it nicely.

He made a sound under his breath. "Sweetheart, I am a monumental screwup. No one with any sense would want to marry me."

"Well, if that is the case, a marriage in name only might suit you rather well." Phoebe risked smiling encouragingly at him. "It really doesn't need to be for long—a year maybe? And then we can go our separate ways."

"Why do you need to get married?"

"Because—" She paused, unwilling to speak unkindly of her family, who were as tied to the stupid rules as she was. "There is a specific legal situation I need to sort out and that involves me being married.

Technically, I'm supposed to ask for permission to even *get* married, but—"

"From the king?"

She regarded him seriously. "No. May I continue?"

"Be my guest."

"I've decided that if I present my family with a fait accompli—" He opened his mouth, and she kept talking. "An accomplished fact, then they'll just have to get used to it."

"And you think that will solve your little legal problem." He studied her face. "Does it involve money?"

She hesitated. "Indirectly, but it's more about my right to live my life without interference from an outmoded, and quite frankly, ridiculous tradition that only affects the women in the family."

"Okay." He finished his beer and set the bottle down on the counter with a decisive thump. "When do you want to get married?"

Phoebe gazed at him. "You'll do it?" She might have squeaked a bit because he winced.

"Sure. Why not?" He held her gaze, her blue eyes steady. "I'm all about destroying the patriarchy."

Chapter 1

Present Day
Nilsen Ranch, near Quincy California

Max took a deep breath and went into the kitchen where Luke, his mom, Noah, and Jen were gathered around the table like a hostile jury. They all looked up at him and he had a weird flashback to the probationary courts he'd attended when he was a rebellious teen. He cleared his throat.

"I guess you all want to know where I've been."

"That would be nice," Luke, who ran the ranch, and who had been Max's team leader in the Marines instinctively took charge. "You've been AWOL for a while."

Luckily for Max, Luke had just made things work with Bernie, his longtime best friend, and soon-to-be Mrs. Nilsen if Max had anything to do with it. As Max had helped solve their problems by practically locking them in a room together, he was hoping his boss would give him a favorable hearing.

"When I first left, I wasn't sure what the hell I was doing. I just bummed around a few towns, picked up a couple of shifts on ranches, you know how it goes," Max shrugged. "Then I got a message that someone was looking for me in Reno and I went there."

"Why did you leave in the first place?" Noah asked. He was always the most direct of the three of them.

"I needed to get away."

"It left us short-handed just when we didn't need it."

"I know." Max looked down at the table. "I didn't think about that."

Noah snorted. "Typical."

"I owe you all an apology," Max continued. "I just lost it."

Now they were all staring at him like he'd gone nuts.

"You—panicked?" Luke asked. "Like, when have you ever done that? You're the coolest Marine I ever served with." He added. "Not like cool, cool, but under pressure cool, obviously."

"We knew that already," Noah murmured. His girl-friend Jen took his hand and squeezed it. "He took risks that only fools would follow through on."

"And saved your ass on at least two occasions," Max reminded Noah.

"Yeah, I know." Noah held his gaze. "I appreciate that."

Luke cleared his throat. "Can we get back on track here? Why did you have to go to Reno?"

"Because I got a message from . . . someone, that I needed to get there pronto."

"You could've told us how you were feeling before you left," Luke said. "You must have known we'd worry about you."

Max surveyed the faces in front of him and was surprised when they all nodded. He'd never thought he was accountable to anyone except his team and the Marines. Even three years out of the service, the whole civilian thing didn't sit well with him, and he didn't know what to do with people caring about what he did or didn't do.

"To be honest, I didn't think about anything but getting to Reno to assess the problem."

"What problem?" Noah asked.

"The one I'm trying to work out how to explain to you if you'd just stop interrupting me," Max said.

"Like you aren't procrastinating like hell and damn," Noah said. "I—"

"Max?" Jen was staring over his shoulder at the door leading into the rest of the house. "Who is that?"

Max rose to his feet, turned to the door, and held out his hand. "Hey, why don't you come and join us? Everyone say hi to Phoebe. We're married."

Luke was the first to recover. "That's what you were doing in Reno?"

"We . . . agreed to meet there," Max said carefully.

"We met four years ago." Phoebe raised her chin. "It's taken me this long to track him down." She smiled. "Hello, I'm Phoebe Creighton-Smith. It's lovely to meet you all."

Max pulled out a chair and Phoebe sat down, her knees shaking. She'd thought finding Max would be the worst of her problems but dealing with the aftermath felt like wandering into a minefield.

The man sitting opposite her with the kind eyes and fair hair looked like he was in charge. He offered her his hand.

"Hi, I'm Luke. I served with Max in the Marines."

Phoebe shook his hand. "Thank you for inviting me to your beautiful home."

Luke's eyebrows rose and he instinctively looked at Max before answering, which confirmed Phoebe's suspicions that Max hadn't prepared anyone for her arrival.

"You're welcome. And belated congratulations on your nuptials," Luke added. "This is my mom, Sally, who owns the ranch."

"A pleasure." Sally beamed at her with obvious warmth. "I can't wait to get to know you, Phoebe."

"Hello!" The brown-haired woman sitting next to the scowling bearded giant waved at her. "I'm Jen and this is Noah who also served with Max."

Luke smiled at her. "That's everyone except Sky. You'll meet him tomorrow after he wakes up."

"Sky's my son," Jen added.

Phoebe nodded, aware of Max's silent presence at her shoulder. She hadn't even realized she'd married a Marine until she received all kinds of correspondence from the US military because he'd named her as his next of kin. The fact that it had taken a while for the information to catch up with her in England wasn't the military's fault, but it had still taken her by surprise.

Noah cleared his throat. "Did you just imply that you got married four years ago in Reno?"

"That's correct," Phoebe said brightly.

Noah's skeptical gaze refocused on Max. "Weird that you didn't mention it at the time, bro."

Max shrugged. "I promised Phoebe I'd keep it to myself."

"Why?"

"Because it was a complicated situation," Phoebe replied to Noah who was the most intimidating of the bunch.

"Still . . ." Noah moved restlessly in his chair. "We're

supposed to be your best buds, Max. Did you even tell the marines?"

Max glared at him. "I'm not here to give you an in-depth interview about the ins and outs of my marriage. Either accept it, and move on, or shut the hell up."

Phoebe tensed, but Noah just raised his eyebrows.

"Okay, hot shot, cool your jets."

Sally smiled at Phoebe. "I do hope you'll be staying for a while."

"I believe that's the plan," Phoebe glanced at Max who was still looking rather tight-lipped. "We have a lot to catch up on."

"I'd say," Luke murmured. "Have you ever been on a working ranch before, Phoebe?"

"Not quite." She had a sense that mentioning the home farm and family estate back in England wouldn't be appropriate at this point, "I do know how to ride, though."

"English or western?" Luke asked.

Phoebe blinked at him. "I'd forgotten there were different ways."

"I'm sure Max will sort you out with all that. He's a whizz with horses," Luke said before turning to his mom. "Shall we get supper? Then these two love birds can spend some time together."

Max stood up and Phoebe instinctively joined him.

"May I help?" she asked.

Luke smiled. "That would be great. Can you set the table? Max can tell you where everything goes."

It wasn't long before they were all sitting down having vegetable soup with homemade crusty bread. Phoebe let the conversation about people and places she'd never heard about swirl over her head and only answered if someone addressed her directly. It gave

her the chance to calm down and assess her new surroundings.

The ranch was charming. A sprawling, single-story
structure built with wide-planked wooden floors and
cream-colored walls covered in family pictures that
just screamed "home." The kitchen was heavy on the
pine, but the appliances were all new, and the heating was working well enough to cut out the surprisingly cold winds coming off the distant mountain
ranges. She'd never been this far north in California
and found the immense forests and tiny towns breath-
takingly beautiful.

To be fair, she hadn't expected Max to turn up in
Reno after her ultimatum, or that she'd have to follow him back to the ranch to negotiate their future
together. But she needed this to work, and she was
determined to sort things out before another four
years elapsed. His ability to disappear had become
clearer once she'd realized what he did for a living,
but she wished he'd mentioned it at the time because not being able to locate him had been very trying.

She glanced up at him as he grinned at something
Sally said and joked with Jen. He caught her looking,
patted her thigh under the table and winked.

"You hanging in there, Feebs?"

"Just about."

"I'll take you down to the barn to meet the horses
after supper and we can talk while I do my chores."

"That would be lovely."

"Never heard shoveling horse shit described as
lovely before, but I can only hope." He finished his
soup and stood up. "I'll get the coffee on."

Phoebe raised her hand. "Do you have any tea?"

"Yup. Jen's all into that herbal stuff," Max said. "I'll bring you her magic box of potions."

Phoebe sipped her peppermint tea and briefly wished she could fall asleep right away. Jet lag was always awful, but if she went to bed too early, she'd be wide-awake and wandering the hallways at four. Something nudged her ankle, and she looked down to see a small, fluffy dog sniffing her shoe.

"That's Winky," Max said. She'd noticed he didn't miss a thing. "His sister Blinky is currently stationed by Jen hoping for fallen treats."

"I love dogs." Phoebe bent down to pet the puppy. "We have a whole crowd at home."

"Where exactly is home?" Sally asked as she added cream to her coffee.

"Suffolk."

Noah frowned. "There's a US Air Force base there, right?"

"Yes." Phoebe smiled at him, but he didn't return it. "At Lakenheath."

"That's correct. We went through there once."

"Did we?" Luke asked.

"We were on our way back," Noah said. "We weren't really taking much in. It was night and it was raining. Our plane refueled and we left without deplaning."

"Sounds about right," Luke nodded. "Is your place near there, Phoebe?"

"It's about twenty miles away so we do get planes and helicopters flying over occasionally." Phoebe half-yawned and immediately covered her mouth with her hand. "Please excuse me. The jet lag's catching up with me."

"Then why don't you and Max head out for the

barn while we finish up here?" Luke suggested. "Then you can have an early night."

Max stood, turned to Phoebe, and offered her his hand, which she took to bring herself to her feet.

"You'll need your coat."

"Then I'll go and get it and meet you out there."

As she headed back to Max's bedroom, Phoebe glanced out of the window where the sun was already disappearing behind a mountainside covered in pine trees. There was still snow on the upper slopes even though it was almost summer, and the forest looked dark and impenetrable. She grabbed her coat from the bed and went back through the kitchen. Everyone waved brightly at her except Noah, but she knew they were just waiting for her to close the outside door before they started talking about her.

Really, she couldn't blame them. The fact that Max hadn't even mentioned their marriage to the people closest to him had come as something of a surprise, but why should it? She hardly knew the man.

She hurriedly zipped up her coat and stuck her hands in her pockets as she walked along the path to the barn, which was visible from the house. The wind had a sharp edge to it that slapped at her face and made her want to hurry. Inside was refreshingly warm and well-lit. She heard Max before she saw him, as he was whistling.

"Hello?" she called out as she stepped into the welcome shelter of the old wooden structure. There were stalls on either side and a new concrete floor and drainage channel down the middle.

He stuck his head out of a door farther down and gestured toward what she assumed was the tack room.

"Would you like to help?" Max asked.

"Yes, please."

"You can refill the water buckets. Faucet's in there."

"Okay."

Phoebe had always loved helping at the family stables, so lugging gallons of water about wasn't new to her. She was also used to being around horses and knew not to startle them because they were basically big, scaredy chickens. By the time she'd finished, Max had worked his way down one side of the barn and was on the other.

She paused to admire his efficiency. He'd stripped off his jacket and hat and was shoveling straw and manure into a wheelbarrow with alarming speed. He looked up to see her watching and wiped the sweat off his brow.

"Don't let me stop you helping out here, princess."

"I was just going to ask what you wanted me to do next." Phoebe kept her reply polite. "I noted some of the feed and hay might need replenishing."

"Feel free to go ahead and do that. Feed and hay are in the tack and feed room along with each horse's schedule." Max returned to his task. "I'm almost done here."

She did as he asked and washed her hands while he took the last barrowload of manure and straw out of the barn. He joined her in the small space where he cleaned himself up. She considered herself tall, standing five foot ten, but he was at least three inches taller. He was also more muscular, and in close quarters, had the coiled energy of a big cat.

Phoebe looked over at the door, but she couldn't get out until he finished his ablutions. He glanced briefly at her as he toweled off his face.

"Thanks for helping." He set the towel on the rack. "Now, how the hell did you find me again?"

She folded her arms over her chest. "Perhaps one should rather be asking why you made it so difficult for me to find you in the first place? You basically disappeared on me."

He rubbed a hand over the back of his neck and looked charmingly rueful. "Yeah."

"That wasn't helpful."

"I get that."

She waited to hear what else he had to say, but he just stared at her.

"I think I deserve an explanation, Max," Phoebe said quietly. "You left me in a terrible pickle."

His lips twitched. "Pickle?"

She fixed him with a calm stare. "You know what I mean. I woke up to find you'd left without giving me any way to communicate with you."

His brow creased. "I thought that's what you wanted."

"How did you expect me to initiate divorce proceedings if I didn't know where you were?" she asked. "I only worked it out because the Marines sent me all that official paperwork about being your next of kin, although I didn't get a forwarding address until I received notification of your discharge."

He leaned one shoulder against the doorframe. "And it took you three years to get out here after that? Did you travel the old-fashioned way by steamship or canoe?"

"There were . . . reasons why I couldn't leave right away." She had no intention of sharing them until she reached some consensus with her soon-to-be ex. "But I'm here now."

"You look good," Max said. "Did you do something new with your hair?"

"I added highlights, but what's that got to do with—"

"Nice." He leaned in and tucked a strand behind her ear. "You haven't aged a bit. Must be all that rain."

"It's certainly supposed to be good for the complexion," she agreed. "But I didn't come all this way to talk about my hair—"

"I know," he interrupted her. "You came to talk about getting a divorce."

"That's definitely part of it." She met his gaze. "I'm just sorry it's dragged on for so long."

His dimples appeared. "Hardly your fault when I disappeared on you."

"Were you overseas?"

His expression cooled. "Yeah, but don't ask me for details because I'm not sharing anything about that shit show."

Phoebe instinctively reached out to pat his arm. "I understand. My younger brother, Arthur, is in the British Army."

"What's his specialty?"

"He's in the Household Cavalry."

"Then I guess he knows how to ride a horse." Max took her hand and led her toward the barn exit.

"Only on ceremonial occasions these days," Phoebe said as she tried to conceal a huge yawn. "He has a lovely dress unform."

"I bet." Max stopped walking and looked down at her. "Can we continue this conversation tomorrow when you're more awake? I wouldn't want you to miss anything important."

She nodded and his smile widened. "You're a smart woman, Feebs."

"Obviously not that clever because it's taken me four years to track you down," Phoebe said.

"I'm impressed you bothered to find me at all." Max held her gaze. "I mean, can't you divorce someone over the internet these days?"

"I can't say I looked into that option," Phoebe said. "I thought it polite to conclude our arrangement in person. You did me a huge favor and I'll always be grateful for that."

"How grateful?"

She rolled her eyes and started for the house. "You're a terrible flirt, Max Romero."

She had no intention of telling him that ever since she'd met him, he'd figured prominently in her most erotic dreams and fantasies and that maybe she'd just wanted to check in on him one last time and see if reality held up to her memories.

"Hey, I'm a married man." He caught up with her. "I don't flirt."

"Hmph."

"And, even if I was flirting, that would be okay since we're married."

"Incorrigible," Phoebe muttered as she went up the steps to the porch that surrounded the house.

He reached over her head to open the screen door. "After you."

"Thank you."

There was no one in the kitchen or family room and the house was quiet. Phoebe assumed they'd all retreated to their rooms to give her and Max some privacy. Max followed her down the hall toward his bedroom.

"Where is everyone?" Phoebe asked.

"Probably having an early night. They were all up at the ass-crack of dawn helping with the local humane society puppy auction at Bernie's place."

"Bernie is Luke's girlfriend, correct?"

Max gave her a smile of approval as they went into the bedroom. "You pick things up fast."

"I had to in my family."

For the first time, Phoebe looked at the queen-size bed where she'd left her suitcase.

"We share the bathroom down the hall with Noah and Jen, but they are building their own place, so it won't be like that for long." Max closed the drapes and put her suitcase on the floor. "There's plenty of space in the closet if you want to unpack."

Phoebe cleared her throat. "Is there . . . somewhere else I could sleep where I won't be inconveniencing you?"

He shrugged as he hung his jacket on the back of the door. "It's a big bed. You're not bothering me."

"But . . ." Phoebe stared at the back of his head. "I snore."

"Yeah? So do I. Maybe we'll drown each other out." He took off his fleece. "I'll go and use the bathroom while you get yourself sorted, okay?"

He left the room and her gaze traveled to the bed that looked smaller every time she looked at it. They'd shared a bed on their wedding night but as she'd immediately fallen asleep, she had no real memory of Max. She did remember waking up the next morning and finding him gone. He'd left a note on the bedside table wishing her all the best and that he'd paid for the room and extended the departure time. It had taken her several dazed minutes to realize he hadn't left his phone number or forwarding address, although she'd given him hers.

She'd then spent several fruitless minutes searching the room in case he'd been joking, but all his possessions had gone. The only evidence he'd even existed was the wedding certificate, the recently used shower, and the fact that the toilet seat was up.

Phoebe groaned and unzipped her backpack. She had her nightie, a spare pair of knickers, and her washbag to cover the essentials of traveling. She'd unpack her suitcase tomorrow. She smoothed a hand over the intricate patchwork quilt that covered the bed and wondered who had made it, and more importantly, which side of the bed Max slept on.

The door opened and Max came in wearing a towel slung low on his hips bringing a cloud of steam and the hint of pine along with him.

"All yours, Feebs. The lock works. Jen wasn't keen on me wandering in on her."

"I wonder why," Phoebe murmured as she tried not to look at his spectacular body.

Max grinned. "Towels are on the rack behind the door. Help yourself and take your time."

"Thank you." Phoebe edged past, trying not to allow any part of her body to touch his warm, wet, muscular flesh. "Please go ahead and turn the lights off. I don't want to keep you up."

"There are so many things I could say about that, Feebs, but I'm going to try and remember I'm a gentleman," Max said as she scurried away like a frightened rabbit. "As I said, take your time."

She reached the safety of the bathroom and locked the door, her breathing ragged. He was the most beautiful man she'd ever seen outside of an art gallery or museum, and he was her husband. If only temporarily.

She briefly closed her eyes, but it didn't help.

She'd forgotten how hard it was to look away from his bright blue gaze and how compelling he was in person. That's why she'd picked him to talk to in Reno. There had been something reassuring about him, but she'd still taken a terrible risk.

She eyed the shower, which, unlike the ones in Creighton Hall, was modern and easy to operate. The longer she delayed going back to Max's bedroom, the more likely it was he would be asleep. But if she loitered in the shower, *she* might fall asleep, too, and what if someone had to break down the door to get in and she'd be naked and snoring, and . . . ?

"Phoebe Margaret Elizabeth Creighton-Smith." She glared at herself in the mirror. "Get a grip."

She'd tracked him down, and that was an achievement. She tried not to think about all the time she'd spent waiting for him in Reno only for him to turn up and abruptly announce he had to leave and that if she wanted to continue their discussions, she'd have to come with him. Of course, she'd agreed. The chances of him ratting out on her again had been too high to ignore.

She stepped into the shower and closed her eyes. Despite his pretty face and gregarious manner, he'd struck her as something of a loner when they'd first met. She hadn't expected him to live in such a remote and beautiful place surrounded by people who obviously cared about him. She was glad he had that support and wished she could say the same. Despite being smothered in family, she'd always felt like the odd one out.

After reluctantly exiting the shower, she unzipped her toiletries bag, cleansed and moisturized her face, and brushed her teeth. Her nightie was crumpled from being at the bottom of her backpack, but it would have to do. She shivered as she put it on over her knickers. The air was far cooler out here than in Reno, reminding her of the big draughty nursery she'd shared growing up with her siblings in Creighton Hall. The huge sash windows had looked beautiful but were icy to the touch and prone to rattle in the slightest wind.

She put her socks on to traverse the short hallway back to Max's room. There was no light visible under the door. She breathed a silent prayer as she went in and then stopped, confronted with the pitch black of the unfiltered night. Still holding her backpack, she tried to remember where the bed was and inched slowly to her left.

"Ouch!" Her knee connected with something solid.

The bedside light went on and Phoebe stared at Max who was now sitting up. His chest was bare, and she wondered whether he was naked under the blankets.

"Sorry!" She set her backpack down on the chair and edged around to the left side of the bed. "I was trying to be quiet."

"It's not a problem." He flipped the sheets back invitingly and patted the mattress. "Hop in. I wasn't asleep anyway. I promise I won't bite."

For some reason the bed looked impossibly small with him in it.

"Is it absolutely necessary that we share a bed?" Phoebe asked. "Because on a ranch this big one might think you'd have alternate accommodation."

"How about we see how this goes before we start worrying about that." He looked her up and down. "You're exhausted. Come to bed."

With a sigh, she sank down onto the side of the mattress. "I am quite knackered."

His lips twitched. "If you say so."

"I doubt I have the energy to molest you, and if you try anything I probably wouldn't even notice."

"Hey, I don't take advantage of women, period."

She swung her legs up into the bed. "I know. It was my lame idea of a joke."

"Maybe leave the jokes to me, princess?"

He settled the covers over her and she let her head sink back into the pillow and closed her eyes. For a delicious moment, the world stopped moving and she felt herself relax. The stress of the last few weeks was still settled on her shoulders, but at least she had a place to sleep. For some reason Max Romero always made her feel safe . . .

Max eased up on one elbow to gaze down at Phoebe who had gone to sleep the instant her head hit the pillow. She'd taken off her favorite red lipstick and looked sweet as candy. He inhaled the subtle lavender scent of whatever she'd used to clean her face. He wanted to lean in and trace the curve of her lips and the line of her jawbone, but it didn't seem fair. Despite the turmoil she'd caused in his life, he didn't regret her return. It was as if he'd been waiting for her all along . . .

He wanted her wide-awake when he next touched her—and he wanted to—very much. He sucked in a breath, then released it slowly and clicked off the light. He wasn't sure if he'd be able to sleep much, which wasn't because of Phoebe, but he could watch over her, and that was kind of special.

A tiny snore escaped Phoebe and Max smiled into the darkness. She was here and despite everything he'd never been so pleased to see someone again in his life.

Ten minutes later, she turned onto her side and spooned him, making him wonder whether there was someone else she regularly shared a bed with. But he couldn't see Phoebe cheating on her marriage vows even if they hadn't consummated it. She was much too honest for that.

Ten seconds later, he opened his eyes again. Maybe that was why she'd finally come to find him. She'd met someone new and wanted to do the honorable thing.

She muttered something unintelligible and wrapped one arm around his waist, her fingers tickling the soft track of hair below his navel. His whole body came to instant attention, and he stifled a groan. He knew she wasn't doing anything deliberate, and that the problem was all him, but he wished he had the right to take her hand and direct it a fraction lower . . .

As if reacting to his dirty thoughts, she turned away, leaving him wide-awake and turned-on in a different way. He let out a slow breath and started counting backward from a thousand. If that didn't work, it might not be Phoebe who was looking for a new bed in the morning.

Chapter 2

Phoebe was certain it was still dark when Max's alarm went off in her ear. She didn't have much time to worry about it because he rolled right over her, stuck out his arm, and shut it off.

"Sorry." His voice was gravelly in the morning. "I forgot you were here."

As he was basically lying on top of her, she just stared up at him, especially when he seemed in no hurry to move.

"Am I squashing you?" Max asked.

"A bit."

"Do you like it?"

She didn't bother to reply to that, and he grinned.

"Do you want to get up and help with the barn chores or sleep longer?"

"I'll get up," Phoebe said. "I'm awake now."

"Jet lag will do that to you."

He finally moved away from her, switched on the lamp, and sat on the edge of the bed to put on his watch, confirming Phoebe's suspicions that he slept almost naked. He had at least three tattoos, includ-

ing one that disappeared beneath the waistband of
his boxers. She could also see the wounds of past battles on his back and surgery scars on his left shoulder.

She clenched her fist in an effort not to reach out
and touch him. He glanced over his shoulder and
paused.

"Are you admiring my ass or my tats?"

"They are both very nice," Phoebe said. "Do I have
to choose?"

He grinned. "Now you're being funny. I guess you're
one of those morning people I've heard about."

"I do love mornings," Phoebe agreed, averting her
gaze as Max stood and went over to put on his robe.
"So many possibilities."

"I like your spirit." Max tied the sash on his robe.
"Normally I'd run down the hall naked to the bathroom, but I'll spare you this morning,"

"Isn't it a little chilly for that?"

"I don't really notice the cold." He walked to the
door. "I'll take a shower when I come back, so I'll be
quick. I'll start some coffee in the kitchen and meet
you out in the barn."

Five minutes later, he knocked briskly on the door
to tell her the bathroom was free. She could hear
him whistling as he headed down the hallway, which
made her want to smile. He might have left the military, but like most people who'd been institutional-
ized, he was remarkably efficient.

Having grown up in freezing cold dormitories at
boarding schools with limited hot water, she was
fairly immune to the cold herself. After grabbing a
fresh jumper and a pair of clean knickers from her
suitcase she used the bathroom, put on her jeans and

thickest socks, and went to the kitchen where Jen was making something in the microwave.

"Morning, Phoebe," Jen said. "Meet Sky."

There was a small child in a highchair at the table who was regarding her with great interest. He looked nothing like Jen or Noah since he was blond and blue-eyed, but when he smiled, he was all his mother.

Sky pointed his spoon inquiringly at Phoebe.

"This is Phoebe," Jen said as she handed him a cup of milk. "She's a friend of Uncle Max's."

Sky nodded as if his mom made perfect sense and tried out the new word. "Feezies."

"Perfect." Phoebe smiled at him. "Nice to meet you, Sky."

Jen offered her a mug. "I made you hot tea."

"Gosh, thank you," Phoebe inhaled the glorious scent of black tea and milk. "I fear I'm addicted. I even travel with my own tea bags."

"I've heard that from a lot of Brits," Jen said. "There's a whole box of the stuff in the pantry, so please help yourself." Jen added milk to cool down the bowl of oatmeal along with some berries and placed it on the tray in front of Sky. "If you want something to eat now, there's bread, cereal, and oatmeal, or you can wait and have a proper breakfast when you come back from the barn."

"I think I'll wait." Phoebe blew on her tea to cool it down. "My stomach isn't sure what time it is yet."

"I know that feeling." Jen checked Sky was eating the oatmeal rather than wearing it. "I used to travel through so many time zones that sometimes it felt like I was moving backward in slow motion."

"When was that?" Phoebe asked.

"When I worked on the USNS medical ships as a

midwife." Jen smiled. "I've just completed my last tour, and I've started working with Sally at the medical clinic in town instead."

"What an interesting career," Phoebe said.

"I'll bore your ear off about it whenever you like." Jen grinned at her. "As long as you tell me how the heck you persuaded Max to get married."

Phoebe set her mug in the sink. "It's a deal. Thank you for the tea"

"You're welcome." Jen hesitated. "And I'm really glad you're here. Max needs some stability in his life."

Phoebe debated telling Jen exactly why she'd chased Max down and decided against it. If she wasn't going to be at the ranch for long, there was no point in making unnecessary waves and everyone was being so kind.

She put on her borrowed wellies, zipped up her ski jacket and went outside, gasping as the icy air sliced through her lungs. It was far colder than it looked, and she wished she'd put on her thermal underwear. She found her gloves and her knitted hat in her pockets and put them on against the chill blowing down the hillside.

The lights were on in the barn, and she could already hear the cheery banter of Max and his friends as they did their morning chores. She paused at the doorway to take off her gloves. Should she really be here?

"Hey, beautiful," Max stepped out of a stall and came toward her. He wore a thick, fleece-lined jacket, jeans, and beaten-up cowboy boots and looked good enough to eat. "I wasn't sure you'd make it."

"I said I would," Phoebe met his amused gaze. "But I'm not sure you actually need me."

"I always need you." He took her hand, his fingers warm around hers.

Phoebe sighed. "Are you ever serious?"

"Sometimes. When things are important to me—otherwise I'm a complete pain in the ass."

"I can confirm that." Luke came up behind him. He was dressed almost identically to Max except he had a beanie on his head rather than a cowboy hat. "He drives us all nuts. Morning, Phoebe."

"Good morning, Luke," Phoebe said. "How may I help?"

"We're turning the barn horses out into the pasture this morning, so if you're up to supervising that it would give us more time to shovel shit."

"Nice, boss," Max said. "Mind your language."

"I'm not offended," Phoebe hastily intervened as Max frowned at Luke. "I've heard far worse."

"Probably from Max," Noah's deep voice said from one of the stalls where he leaned on the door and joined the discussion.

"He's always behaved like the perfect gentleman toward me," Phoebe said. "My brother swears far more and even Grandmother has been known to say 'bugger' occasionally."

All three men were now smiling, and Phoebe frowned. "Did I say something amusing?"

Max wrapped his arm around her and gave her a hug. "Nah, we're just appreciating you." He turned her slightly away from the others. "Are you okay leading the horses out? They can be skittish first thing in the morning."

"I know how they feel," Phoebe muttered as she put her gloves back on. "I'd be delighted to deal with the horses. Show me where to start."

An hour later, she followed the men back up to the house and almost groaned with delight when the succulent smell of bacon wafted out from the kitchen. She hung her coat in the mudroom and stepped out of her boots. Warmth surrounded her like a blanket, and she pressed a hand to her cold cheek as she went through to the kitchen.

A stack of pancakes, a pan of eggs, and the biggest pile of bacon she'd ever seen sat in the middle of the table. Everything looked delicious. Her stomach growled and Jen handed her a plate.

"Get in there fast, Phoebe, or else the guys will eat it all."

"Surely not all of it." Even as she objected, Phoebe was doing as suggested. She hadn't survived eleven years at boarding school by being shy. "There's enough to feed an army."

"Or three cowboys, and a lady," Max said right behind her. "We get through a lot of work and a ton of calories."

Phoebe helped herself to two eggs, three pieces of bacon, and two pancakes, and sat down to eat. Max had at least twice what she had and Noah, who admittedly had a large frame, took even more. There was little to no conversation as everyone focused on the food.

Eventually Luke sat back. "Thanks for cooking, Jen."

"You're welcome." Jen brought coffee over for the guys and tea for Phoebe. "I'm heading out soon. Sally's already at the clinic."

"Is Sky still asleep?" Noah asked.

"He went for a nap after having his breakfast seeing as he was awake half the night, but he'll be up soon." Jen put her hand on Noah's shoulder. "Are you okay to get him up and keep him busy until I get back around noon?"

"Absolutely." Noah reached back and covered her hand with his own. "We might go into town and pick up the mail."

"You should take Phoebe," Jen said. "I bet she'd enjoy it."

Noah looked over at Phoebe who tried not to shrink down in her chair.

"Would you like to come to town with us?"

"That would be lovely, unless Max needs me for something." Phoebe turned inquiringly toward Max who was drinking his coffee.

"You should go. I owe these guys a couple of weeks of back chores so I'm going to be busy."

Phoebe was beginning to wonder whether Max really wanted to have a conversation with her about their current situation. She'd have to contrive a way to get him alone before she left to visit the town.

"Good," Noah nodded. "I'll give you an update on our departure time once I've dealt with Sky."

Phoebe loitered in the bedroom until Max came in from his shower.

"Hey." He smiled at her. "Aren't you going out?"

"Not for a little while. Plenty of time for us to have a chat before I leave." She sat on the bed and looked up at him. "We do have quite a lot to discuss."

He raised his arm and rubbed the back of his neck with his hand, making the knot in the towel wrapped around his hips loosen slightly. As it was on her eye level Phoebe couldn't miss it.

"Could you possibly put some clothes on first?"

"Sure, I could, but do you really want me to?"

She determinedly raised her gaze to his face. "Yes, please."

"Okay, boss."

He dropped the towel and went past her, humming under his breath as he searched the drawers for clean boxers, a long-sleeved T-shirt and then pulled on his jeans and zip up, fleece jacket. Phoebe slowly let out her breath and unclenched her fingers from the bed sheets. It really wasn't fair how attractive he was and how he made her feel without even trying.

"Okay." Max sat on the bed beside her. "Shoot."

"Originally, we agreed to stay married for as long as it took me to solve my legal issues."

Max nodded. "And then I went AWOL, and you didn't get the chance to divorce me. Although, I assumed that once you knew I was in the military, you'd establish contact and do everything by mail."

"But I didn't know if I could contact you," Phoebe pointed out. "There was nothing in the paperwork to indicate that I could do so, or how to do it."

Max frowned. "I'm pretty sure there should have been something."

"Well, if there was, I didn't receive it, and to be honest, Max," Phoebe continued in something of a rush. "I was wrong to assume our marriage would fix all my legal issues."

He raised an eyebrow. "Keep going."

"It solved one part of the problem, because my father thought marriage was a stabilizing influence on me." She shrugged. "He was very old-fashioned in that respect, but his solicitors insisted that it wasn't sufficient to break the whole entail in my grand-father's will."

"What's an entail?" Max asked.

"It's an old-fashioned provision in a will that tries to ensure that property or money stays within a family."

"Okay."

"It's possible to break an entail these days, but all the family members have to agree," Phoebe added.

"And your father wasn't having it."

Phoebe nodded. "Originally, that's how matters stood, yes."

"So, you're saying you didn't immediately seek the divorce because you needed to stay married to sort out this entail thing, and not just because you couldn't find me?"

"It was a bit of both, really." She met his blue gaze head-on. "I truly wasn't sure how to contact you, or whether you even wanted to hear from me, and I needed time to work out how I could fulfill the conditions of the will and persuade my family to honor it."

"I feel so used." Max pressed his hand to his heart.

Phoebe gave him a severe look. "You had my address. Don't forget that you could've contacted me at any point to discuss matters or divorce me."

"I was busy," Max pointed out, "trying not to get killed."

"Oh." Phoebe pressed her lips together because he was right. How on earth could she compete with that. "I'm so sorry."

Max grimaced. "Don't be. It was my choice to enlist, and I shouldn't have used it as an excuse to stop the conversation in its tracks." He reached for her hand. "Keep talking."

"I should remember that my silly little problems aren't the center of everyone else's world," Phoebe confessed. "You did me a huge favor in Reno. The onus was rightly on me to deal with the divorce, and I let you down."

He reached over and took her hand. "If we're going for honesty here, I'll admit that a lot of the time I completely forgot I was married, so don't think I was worrying about us every day. I wouldn't have been able to do my job if I wasn't one hundred percent focused."

She squeezed his fingers, and for a moment, they just looked at each other before Max cleared his throat.

"So, what's changed?"

Phoebe eased her hand free. "I'm not sure what you mean."

Max grinned. "You'd be a terrible poker player, Feebs. Why did you finally chase me down?"

"Because my father died."

His expression immediately sobered. "I'm sorry, sweetheart."

"He had pancreatic cancer, and after several years of treatment, he finally ran out of options." Phoebe tried to keep her voice from trembling. "I basically put my life on hold to take care of him since my mother died five years ago."

"That sucks," Max said.

"It was horrible watching him waste away and not being able to do a thing about it." Phoebe swallowed hard. "My siblings were present, but because they have full-time jobs, I volunteered to take on the responsibility of caring for Father. Not that I regret it. He was a wonderful man, and he deserved the best care in the world."

"Aww . . . Feebs."

Max moved so suddenly, she was wrapped in his arms before she'd taken another breath. She rested her cheek against his chest and let him hold her for a glorious moment. His heart thumped reassuringly against her ear, and she breathed in the scent of fresh laundry with an undercurrent of leather and the outdoors that she was coming to recognize was uniquely Max.

"I'm sorry." She tried to draw back, but he didn't let go of her completely. "I still get emotional about him. I know it doesn't change or fix anything."

"You can't help how you feel," Max said, his voice low and comforting. "I know I'm never going back into a war zone, but sometimes my mind and body don't believe me."

She gazed into his blue eyes, aware of the swirling undercurrents beneath his wisecracking exterior.

"I think being here surrounded by the quiet and the people who love you will help the past fade away."

"I hope you're right." Max turned his head until his mouth brushed her fingers. "Can I kiss you, Feebs?"

"What does that have to do with anything we're talking about?"

"Maybe I think we both need a break from the hard stuff."

Mesmerized by his voice, Phoebe leaned in and set her mouth against his, her whole body tensing as he sighed her name, and carefully kissed her back. He took his time until she was the one urging him on. With a low sound, he opened his mouth and let her inside and it was glorious, and hot, and . . .

With a gasp, she threaded her fingers through his short, black hair, anchoring herself against the influx of feelings for a man she really didn't know at all. His arm moved from around her shoulders to her waist so that she was pressed against his chest. She wanted to climb into his lap and push herself shamelessly against him.

"That's my girl."

Goodness, his voice was wicked. His fingers brushed her hip and she almost combusted with lust. This would never do.

"Max?"

"Hmm?"

"Can we stop for a moment?"

"Sure." He immediately released her, which only confirmed her suspicions.

"Were you trying to distract me again?" Phoebe asked. "Because it's really not fair."

"It's more fun than talking, though."

"That's true, but I'm trying to explain a very complicated situation, and now I'm all flustered."

His finger brushed her cheek. "You blush like a rose."

"Or a beetroot." Phoebe determinedly met his gaze. "May I continue?"

"Sure, go ahead."

"After my father's death, my brother, George became the head of the family."

"Okay."

"I thought he might be more amenable to breaking the legalities than my father had been, but he's remarkably stubborn and he listens to our grandmother too much."

"And Granny wasn't keen on you getting your freedom?"

"She simply believes that things should be left

alone, and that precedent and history are more important than 'my feelings'."

"Which leaves you where, exactly?" Max asked.

Phoebe took a deep breath. "As someone who needs to convince her family that her marriage isn't a sham for a start."

"Hold up." Max frowned. "Why would they even think it's a real marriage? We haven't seen each other since our wedding day. How could anyone think we had a relationship?"

Phoebe shifted uncomfortably on the bed. "Because I might have suggested we did?"

For once, Max was the one who took a moment to form a sentence. "What did you do?"

"I might have implied that you were working abroad on long-term contracts and that you weren't able to come to the UK and see me."

He nodded. "Which was kind of true."

"Yes, but I didn't know that at first," Phoebe said. "I suggested to my father that you were involved in some kind of hush-hush CIA type thing."

A dimple flicked in his cheek. "Like an American James Bond?"

"Something like that. I used to pretend to fly out to undisclosed locations to see you once a year. Sometimes I only went as far as Brighton, but my family didn't know that."

"Phoebe . . ."

"I know!" Phoebe waved her hands in the air. "It's ridiculous isn't it, and now I've created a monster, and I don't know quite how to deal with it—"

Max captured one of her hands and covered it with his own. "Breathe."

Phoebe made herself meet his gaze. "When I brought up the issue of the entail in my grandfather's will with George, my grandmother became suspicious."

"About your fake CIA husband?" Max tutted. "What a shocker."

"I didn't think she'd been paying that much attention, what with my father's death, George taking on all his responsibilities, and my sister Eugenie's upcoming marriage. But she's very shrewd despite her age."

"And now she's wondering why she's never met your husband of four years and wants you to do what—produce him out of a hat?"

Phoebe nodded. "She wants you to attend Eugenie's wedding so that she can get to know you better."

Max sighed. "You're a worse liar than me, Feebs."

"I know, it's horrible, isn't it?" She bit her lip. "You must despise me."

His eyebrows went up. "You're kidding, right? I think you're amazing."

"I lied about our marriage to my family and didn't get the divorce I promised you." There was a catch in Phoebe's throat. "How is that in any way honorable or amazing?"

"Because I admire a woman who can think on her feet?" He leaned in and kissed her nose. "I'm proud of you and I'd be cool to accompany you to your sister's wedding."

"I only started talking about you to keep my father happy when he was ill, but it got out of hand," Phoebe confessed. "He enjoyed hearing about your daring exploits."

"You made up stories about me?" Max looked absolutely delighted. "That's so cool. What did I do?"

"All kinds of things," she said. "I got the ideas from the political thrillers and spy stories in the local library."

He burst out laughing, and she stared at him in fascination. She'd expected condemnation and anger, not enthusiastic acceptance.

"Aren't you cross?"

"Hell no! This is the best thing that's ever happened to me." His smile dimmed as he looked at her. "I know it's been tough for you, but come on, Feebs, it has its funny side."

"I never thought I'd have to explain it to you, and now that I have it does seem remarkably silly," Phoebe acknowledged.

"Okay, so if I come to England for your sister's wedding and meet your family, what happens after that?"

"If my grandmother and George accept our marriage as valid, they have to accept the conditions of the new will my father made." Phoebe paused. "At least, that's the impression I got from George."

"Who you also said might not be the sharpest knife in the box."

"I did try and talk to Mr. Darby, the family solicitor, but he referred me to my grandmother."

"That doesn't sound good." Max frowned. "Maybe when we get over there, we can set things straight once and for all."

A shout came from the kitchen. "Phoebe? Are you ready to go? I'm loading Sky into my truck."

"That's Noah," Phoebe said and shot to her feet.

"Take your time. He'll wait." Max looked up at her.

"He reminds me of my PE teacher at school." Phoebe brushed her hair and found her backpack. "I don't want to end up doing extra laps of the track for being late."

"His bark is worse than his bite." Max stood up too and wandered over to open the door for her. "And he's always on his best behavior when he's around Sky."

She paused to smile at him as she went past. "Thank you for being so understanding."

"You're welcome." He winked at her. "Let me know the date of that wedding so I can square it with Luke."

"I will." She was already in motion, aware of the silent kitchen and the distant sound of a truck engine raring to go. "Is there anything you need in town?"

"If you go into the café, ask Bernie for my usual, will you? She knows what I like."

With a final wave of her hand, Phoebe rushed down the hallway, through the kitchen, and into the boot room where she put on her outdoor garb. Noah was already sitting in the driver's seat of a huge black truck and Sky was strapped into his car seat in the rear.

"Fee!" He clapped when she got in and Noah gave her a nod from behind his sunglasses.

"Don't forget your seatbelt. The driveway isn't paved."

She put on her belt and settled back into the seat, aware of the shakiness in her legs, and the relief of finally unburdening herself to Max. She'd thought he'd kick her out once he knew what she'd done, but he'd seemed entranced by the idea and had offered her his full support.

She released another calming breath. Perhaps for the first time in a long while something would go right for her, and she'd finally be able to claim what was rightfully hers.

Chapter 3

Max walked down to the barn and saddled up Bouncer, who was sulking about being abandoned for a couple of weeks and needed to be coaxed into cooperating. He took extra care with his saddle blanket and when tightening the girth until the horse stopped trying to nip him and gave him kisses instead.

"You ready to go?" Luke asked as he came out of the barn, his spurs jingling and chaps flapping like a real cowboy.

"Yes, sir."

"Boss will do." Luke gave him the side eye as he mounted his own horse. "Weather looks good for a few hours so we should be able to move the cattle to the new field."

He whistled to the dogs and headed out, leaving Max to follow along behind.

Max had to admit that it felt good to be back on the ranch he'd begun to consider home. Leaving in a huff because Luke had finally called him out hadn't been his finest hour, and bumming around taking odd jobs hadn't been as much fun as it used to be. He was secretly glad his boss had taken him back without too much hassle because he sure as hell didn't deserve it.

Sometimes stuff just came out of his mouth without him bothering to engage his brain and it wasn't okay. He wasn't a rebellious kid anymore; he was with friends, and he had to learn to keep his stupid thoughts to himself.

"Phoebe's nice," Luke said over his shoulder.

"Yeah, she's awesome." Max made sure to shut the gate behind him as they moved downslope of the ranch toward the distant creek.

"You met in Reno?"

"Yup, her plane got rerouted and we ended up in a casino bar together."

"And got married." Luke didn't look at him as he spoke. "And didn't tell your closest buds."

"I told the military. It was probably on my record if you'd looked."

"The only reason I'd be looking at that was if you'd died and I was contacting your next of kin, so I'm kind of glad it never came up," Luke pointed out.

"I didn't mention it because I promised Phoebe I wouldn't tell anyone."

"She didn't say anything to her folks when she got back home, either?"

"She did."

Luke let the silence between them grow until Max felt like he had to keep talking. "She had good reasons for doing so and I knew that when I agreed to the marriage."

"That's okay, then." Luke used his calm voice, and Max wondered what he was thinking. Sometimes he felt better when everyone was shouting at him. He knew how to deal with anger—genuine concern was another thing entirely.

"If you're wondering why it took us so long to get back together it was a . . . miscommunication."

Luke snorted.

"I had her address, and I assumed the military would give her all the stuff she needed about me, but either things didn't get through, or she didn't know how to access that information until my discharge papers came through."

"That was three years ago."

"She couldn't get away until recently."

Luke turned to look at him, his blue eyes steady. "Okay."

"It's complicated and I'm not telling you her private stuff, so just accept that it happened the way it did because there was no other choice."

"When Phoebe finally knew where you were, why didn't she come here?"

"Because this wasn't the address on record."

Luke frowned. "You had a Reno address?"

"Yeah." Max held his gaze. "That's how Phoebe ended up in Reno and I found out she was looking for me."

Max could see a thousand other questions forming in Luke's head and clicked to his horse.

"Do you want to up the pace a little? I know you said the weather looked good, but I don't want to be out here all day."

"I guess that means you've had enough of me grilling you, right?" Luke asked. "Understandable. Sometimes it's hard to get out of the habit of overseeing your life."

"I'm actually in a good place, boss," Max said.

"Yeah, I can see that." Luke nodded at the far fence. "Last one to the other side cooks dinner tonight, okay?"

Max was already on his way before Luke finished speaking.

Noah glanced Phoebe's way as they turned out onto the county road.

"It gets easier from here as the road is paved."

"Does it snow a lot in winter?" Phoebe asked.

"Yeah. Last year we got completely cut off during the storm season."

"I bet that was horrible." Phoebe looked out at the endless pine trees.

"It had its moments." Noah's quick smile was unexpected. "Jen and Sky got stuck with us for quite a while."

"That was a good thing?"

"As we're getting married, I'd say so."

"That's wonderful," Phoebe said. "Jen is lovely."

"She is," Noah lapsed into silence until they came down the mountain and reached the edge of the town. "Are you planning on sticking around?"

"That's something Max and I have to work out," Phoebe said.

"He's not always an easy person to understand, but he has a good heart."

Noah found a parking slot and angled the truck into the space. He turned off the engine, took off his sunglasses and looked directly at Phoebe.

"I don't know you, and you'll have to excuse me if this comes out wrong, but don't screw him around, okay? He's a pain in the ass, but he deserves to be happy."

Phoebe met his uncompromising stare. "I can assure you I mean him no harm."

"Some women marry military guys for all the wrong reasons. Max doesn't need that kind of hassle."

"I understand. I can only repeat that I would never knowingly hurt him."

"I guess that's a start." Noah put his sunglasses back on and undid his seatbelt. "Come on, Sky. Let's go and get you a snack at Bernie's."

Phoebe's breath whooshed out as Noah exited the truck and got Sky out of his seat. Talk about intimidating. Noah hadn't said much, but he'd made sure she knew he wouldn't appreciate her messing with Max, which was interesting when they appeared to have a somewhat combative relationship. Perhaps he was all about protecting his own—something Phoebe heartily approved of.

She stepped out of the truck and put on her sunglasses. The town had a middling-length main street with a few fine Victorian houses along one side while the shops ran along the other. She noticed the sign for a B&B and had a sudden urge to rush over and get herself a room far away from the ranch and all its occupants.

"Hey."

She squeaked and pressed a hand to her chest when Noah loomed over her.

He frowned. "Sorry, I didn't mean to scare you."

"You already did that earlier," Phoebe murmured. "Should I meet you somewhere after you've concluded your business, or would you prefer me to tag along so you can keep an eye on me?"

"Hell." Noah grimaced. "I did scare you. Jen's going to kill me. She told me not to say anything."

"It's all right." Phoebe looked up at him. "I'm sure Max appreciates having friends who are willing to speak up for him. I can only repeat that I want what's best for him, too."

Noah looked like he wanted to say a lot more and then stopped and cleared his throat. "Do you want to come to the coffee shop and meet Bernie? We can do a tour of the town after Sky's had his snack."

"That would be lovely." Phoebe blew a kiss at Sky who was waving at her from Noah's arms. "I'm looking forward to meeting Bernie."

Even though the town itself seemed quiet, the coffee shop was busy, and they had to squeeze into a corner table. Noah went to find a high chair for Sky while Phoebe looked around. Even though three people were serving at the front, there was still a line.

"I didn't expect it to be so packed." Noah frowned as he settled Sky carefully into the seat. "I don't like crowds."

"We could get our drinks to go," Phoebe offered. "It's a pleasant day and we could eat outside."

Noah shook his head. "Sky likes it here. He'd kick up a fuss if I tried to get him out before he has his snack."

The idea of the big, tough Marine bowing to the wishes of a small child made Phoebe want to smile.

"Hey, little buddy!" A red-headed woman approached, and Sky screeched and waved his hands in the air.

"Hey, Noah," the woman said, then turned her way. "What have you done with Jen?"

"This is Phoebe." Noah paused. "Max's wife."

"Hello." Phoebe smiled and offered her hand. "Are you Bernie? I've heard so much about you."

Bernie grinned. "I wish I could say the same. I didn't even know Max was married until Luke let it slip this morning when he texted me."

"We kept it quite private."

"Congratulations! Drinks are on the house—and Sky's choice of snack as well." Bernie looked pointedly at Noah. "I can't wait to hear all the details when I next come out to the ranch."

Bernie took their drinks order and offered to send a selection plate of pastries and cakes to the table, which sounded perfect to Phoebe.

Noah waited until Bernie returned to the counter before he turned to Phoebe.

"It's a small town. Better to get it out there before the gossip starts and Bernie's practically family."

"Fine by me."

Phoebe had decided to try the coffee and she wasn't disappointed. Noah took his black. Sky had some kind of juice in his sippy cup and a sprinkle cookie almost as big as his head that Noah was dishing out in very small sections.

"Bernie runs a food delivery service as well as the café," Noah said. "She's about to expand her business because it's doing so well."

"How wonderful," Phoebe sipped her coffee.

"What do you do yourself?" Noah asked.

"I'm involved in the family business." Phoebe paused. "Well, I was until my father became ill and I dropped everything to look after him."

"How's he doing?"

"He died at the beginning of the year."

Noah grimaced and met her gaze head on, which she appreciated. "I'm sorry to hear that."

"Thank you. I miss him very much."

Phoebe took refuge in her coffee and Noah let her be as he talked to Sky and dissuaded his attempts to throw his cookie around. She was surprised at his endless patience, and the calm reassurance he gave the toddler, which wasn't like his gruff persona with her at all.

He didn't know her, and he was wary of her intentions toward his friend, which spoke well of him, but made him even more intimidating. Bernie seemed nice, although her curiosity about Phoebe and Max being married was palpable. Phoebe couldn't blame her. She struggled to believe it herself sometimes.

Choosing to marry a complete stranger in a wedding chapel in Reno hadn't been clever and could've ended up very badly indeed. The thought of anyone in her family finding that out would be mortifying—although she suspected none of them would believe she'd have the guts to do anything of the kind.

As if he was connected to her brain, her cell phone buzzed with a text from her older brother, George.

Did you make it safely to Nevada?

Yes! It's beautiful here. I'll send pics of the ranch when I get a moment.

Ranch? Thought you were in Reno.

Change of plans ☺

She waited as the bubbles indicating he might be replying appeared and disappeared.

An address would be nice in case there is an emergency.

Phoebe frowned. **You have my cell number.**

Grandmother asked me to get the address. Maybe she wants to send you a birthday card.

Unlikely, unless I'm staying for six months.

She looked up at Noah who was attempting to

brush cookie crumbs out of Sky's hair. "Would it be possible to have an address for the ranch?"

"Sure. Nilsen Ranch, County Road, Quincy, Plumas County, California should work." He frowned. "Not sure of the zip. You'll have to ask Luke or check at the post office."

"I will, thank you." Phoebe tapped in the address and sent it to George who replied with a thumbs up.

Her phone went quiet, and she returned to the far more pleasurable task of sampling Bernie's cooking. The rush in the café subsided and Bernie came back. She set two boxes on the table beside Phoebe.

"Doughnuts for Max and cinnamon rolls for everyone else. Don't let Sky get into the boxes."

"Yeah, I once made the mistake of putting them beside him on the backseat," Noah said. "It was cake carnage; his sugar high lasted three days and my truck was a sticky hell."

"Max said you'd know what he liked." Phoebe got out her purse. "May I pay you?"

"They're on the house." Bernie waved away her offer. "I can't charge my family." She looked at Noah. "Did you still want to talk to me about the big day?"

Noah glanced warily at Phoebe and then at Sky. "I don't think he'll sit still long enough."

"I could take him for a walk?" Phoebe offered. "I wanted to take a look around the town anyway."

Both Noah and Bernie looked at her and Phoebe sat up straight.

"I'm quite trustworthy and used to dealing with small children."

"Sure. Okay, I won't be long." Noah fished in his pocket and brought out his keys. "You could pick up the mail from the ranch box at the post office. Sky always loves it in there."

"I'd be happy to." Phoebe took the keys.

"Brass colored key with the number on it is for the box, and if you want to dump the mail off in the truck, use the chunky key fob to unlock the vehicle."

"Got it." She held Noah's gaze. "I promise not to kidnap Sky or drive off in your truck."

"Good, because I'd hate to have to chase you down."

It took a moment for Phoebe to realize Noah might be joking.

"Best to carry him or get the stroller out of the truck," Noah advised as he handed Sky over to her.

She set the sturdy little boy on her hip and considered her options. "I'd better get the stroller because I won't be able to carry Sky and the mail together."

"I'll get it out for you," Noah took back the keys and strode off leaving Phoebe staring at his back.

"Bye-bye, Nono." Sky waved, seemingly unperturbed by his parental unit disappearing on him.

Phoebe went after him emerging into bright sunshine and the sight of Noah already opening the stroller. Sky went rigid in her arms.

"No. Walk."

"Not this time, buddy." Noah placed him in the seat. "You know it's not safe in town."

Sky's lip came out as Noah buckled him in. "Walk."

"Later, okay?" Noah crouched down to look Sky in the eye as he buckled up the harness "Be a good boy for Phoebe."

Sky looked away and Noah sighed. "Please?"

He straightened up and turned to Phoebe. "My advice is not to give in and let him out, or he'll never go back in again."

The town was charming—apart from the traffic that came through the main street. It reminded

Phoebe of Creighton village at home, which had a similar problem. Both places relied on the main road to bring in goods and people, but neither had been designed for the size and speed of current vehicles, and bypassing towns was expensive, especially when the town was planted in the middle of a vast woods.

Phoebe found the post office easily and went in through the side door to a huge hall covered in mail-boxes of all sizes. It took a few moments to find the right box and empty it into the handy bag Noah had given her. Even with five people, plus Sky, living on the ranch there was a surprising amount of mail.

She took a moment to buy some international stamps from the machine and text George the zip code. If she could find a postcard of the town to send to her grandmother, it might reassure her suspicious relative that she truly was where she was meant to be.

"Fee!" Sky waved his arms around. "Go."

She smiled down at him. "Yes, of course. Let's find something more interesting to do than look at the mail. I wonder if Noah would mind if we shared an ice cream?"

An hour later, she was in the truck with Sky napping in the back. He'd been very well behaved while she'd looked around the town and had only tried to get out of the buggy once.

"Can I ask you for a favor?" Noah's gruff voice interrupted her musings.

"Yes, of course." She turned to look at his harsh profile.

"Don't tell Jen I was talking to Bernie about the wedding."

Phoebe frowned. "I wasn't aware that you were."

"Apparently, I tend to . . . micromanage things. I was just checking in with Bernie to see that she and Jen had everything in hand for the reception." He paused. "That's supposed to be Jen's job."

"Ah. I see."

"I wasn't trying to influence anything. I just wanted to get an update—purely for my own personal spreadsheet."

"I promise I won't say anything unless she directly asks me about it."

"Thank you," Noah said gruffly. "I appreciate it."

"When is the 'big day'?" Phoebe asked.

"The end of the month." He glanced over at her. "If you're still here you're invited."

"Thank you." Phoebe nodded. "I'll discuss it with Max."

"It's at the ranch."

"How lovely. My sister is getting married in six weeks."

"I guess you'll need to be home for that." Noah signaled to turn out onto the county road. "Is Max going with you?"

"He's invited." Phoebe echoed Noah's words. "My family are looking forward to meeting him."

"None of them met him in Reno when you got hitched?"

"I was on my own."

Phoebe had a sense she should stop giving Noah information, but her innate politeness kept getting in the way.

"I thought you'd come after him to get a divorce," Noah said abruptly. "It's not as if you've spent any time together. If it were me, I'd be pretty pissed about that."

Phoebe pressed her lips together and kept quiet.

If Noah wanted any more information, he'd have to take it up with Max.

"I still can't believe he got married and didn't tell anyone. It's not like Max to keep anything quiet. Normally, the problem is shutting him up."

Phoebe smiled serenely and readjusted the boxes of cakes on her lap. Just because Noah had suddenly decided to be all chatty didn't mean she had to join in. Maybe it would be good for him to be met with silence for a change. He might be right about everything he was saying about Max, but her loyalty wasn't with Noah. It was to the man who'd agreed to marry her and that's where it would remain.

Chapter 4

"Max?"

He looked up from unbuckling Bouncer's girth to see Phoebe coming toward him. He took a moment to appreciate her beautiful face and her warm smile. He still couldn't believe she wasn't furious with him for leaving her for so long, but he guessed she'd needed him for her own nefarious schemes so maybe they were square.

"Did you have a good time in town?" He removed the saddle, slung it over one shoulder and walked toward the tack room.

"Yes, we met Bernie, and I took Sky for a stroll."

"Nice." He placed the saddle over the wooden stand and checked to see if it needed cleaning. "Did Bernie give you my doughnuts?"

"I left them in the kitchen." Phoebe smiled. "Noah was telling me that she's expanding her business."

"Yeah, she's a smart cookie."

"Max . . ."

"What's up?" He dusted off his hands and turned to face her.

"Would you mind if I took a photo of you and sent it to my family?"

"Sort of like proof of life?" Max asked. "Sure, or even better let's do a selfie together so they can see how happily married we are."

She blushed, which made him want to smile. "I'm terrible at taking those."

"I'm not. Bailey, Noah's sister is a media genius and has taught me how to do it properly." He held out his hand. "Let's put Bouncer away and then we can go outside and find a good spot."

She entwined her fingers with his. "Bouncer's the name of your horse?"

"Yup."

"I've owned several horses over the years and I've loved every one of them."

He returned to the yard, checked Bouncer's hooves, and led him back to his stall where he removed the halter. Phoebe attended to the water bucket and hay while he chatted away to his horse who always liked a nice rubdown after a ride.

When he emerged from the stall, Phoebe was standing at the entrance to the barn staring out over the forest. She looked over her shoulder as he approached.

"I can't get used to the vastness of everything here."

"It's something, isn't it?" He agreed as he joined her. "I like it."

"After what you've been through, I can understand that." She smiled. "I'm just so glad you have a home and people who love you."

Max thought about that.

"Yeah, I'm lucky." He half-smiled. "I'm not sure I

deserve it, though. I tend to make life difficult for everyone who tries to be nice to me."

"Why's that?"

He shrugged. "My naturally suspicious nature? Sometimes it's hard for me to work out whether someone is really on my side or just messing with my head."

She nodded. "I feel like that about my family sometimes. People who insist they care for me and are only doing things in my best interest sometimes aren't."

Max considered all the information that hadn't gotten from Reno to Phoebe in the UK. He'd have to have a conversation about that soon. He wasn't looking forward to it. He shook off the tension and grinned at Phoebe.

"Ready for your close-up, Mrs. Romero?"

"I usually prefer to hyphenate us."

"Like I'm Mr. Romero-Creighton-Smith now?"

Phoebe handed him her phone and followed him out into the pasture where some of the ranch horses were grazing. "I think it sounds nicer the other way around."

"Max Creighton-Smith-Romero." He tried it out. "Yeah, it definitely has a better ring to it."

"Then that's settled. Where do you think we should take our photo?" Phoebe asked.

Max clasped her hand and spun her around. "Right here. We'll do some with the forest behind us and the rest with the ranch and barn."

He gathered her close against his side and wrapped one arm around her. "Here's the secret. Hold the phone high, go for a slight profile angle, and pretend to set your chin on a ledge."

"What?"

Max demonstrated and Phoebe gurgled with laughter.

"That looks silly."

"But it works." He grinned back at her. "Try it."

He took a lot of pictures because Bailey maintained that even if someone was crap at taking them, the sheer number would produce at least a couple of good ones.

"Want to take a look?" Max suggested, aware that he still had his arm around her and that she fitted just right against his side.

"If I must." Phoebe pretended to shudder as he fired up the photo app. "Oh."

"See? You look awesome!" Max thumbed through the first dozen or so. "And we look super happily married."

"You're so pretty," Phoebe mused. "My family will never believe someone like you would take an interest in me."

"Maybe they'll see you in a different light—like a real femme fatale." He fluttered his eyelashes at her wanting to take the doubt from her face. She obviously had no idea how adorable she was and he hated them for not seeing it.

"One can only hope," she murmured and looked up at him. "Thank you, Max."

"You're welcome, sweet pea." He bent and kissed her nose and then, because he couldn't resist it, her mouth. "You taste like Bernie's coffee and cinnamon rolls" He licked her lips. "Sweet."

Her hand came around the back of his neck, holding him close and for a moment she just stared at him.

"Bernie's cakes are perfection, but not as addictive as you are, Max. When you kiss me, I forget all the completely valid reasons I have for keeping my distance from you."

"There's an easy solution to that," Max said.

"What?"

"Kiss me back."

Oh, goodness, he was as tempting as the devil. . . . All she had to do was walk away. She knew he wouldn't stop her. He was too much of a gentleman. But she didn't want to. Being with him, being away from her family, and her commitments for the first time in years was remarkably freeing. And why shouldn't she kiss her own bloody husband? She wasn't hurting anyone, and no one would know.

She pressed her lips against his and his arm came around her hips holding her against him from knee to shoulder.

"That's my girl."

He kissed like a dream, and she kissed him with all the enthusiasm in the world because he deserved it.

Behind her someone loudly cleared their throat and she stiffened.

"Hey, you're scaring the horses."

"Go away, Nilsen." Max continued to hold her close even as he spoke to Luke. "Nothing to see here."

"Except I need to get through this field to the next one and I'm not creeping around my own ranch." Luke sounded as if he was trying not to laugh.

"Then tippy toe along the fence line and keep your eyes front and center," Max said.

Phoebe started to chuckle, and Max looked down at her, his dimples deepening. "Or we could just go in and have some of those doughnuts and leave the boss to get on with his work."

"That's a marvelous idea." Phoebe realized she was the one holding onto Max and instantly stepped back. "Bernie said they were your favorite."

She didn't look directly at Luke who was grinning like a fool as they went past him hand in hand.

"I'll talk to you later, Max," Luke said.

"Not if I see you first." Max looked down at Phoebe. "We'll have to get him one of those cowbells to hang around his neck so we can hear him coming a mile away."

There was a snort from Luke as he headed for the far gate. "Bernie's coming for dinner. She's looking forward to meeting Phoebe properly."

"There's a surprise," Max said as they walked away. "I bet she nearly bit her tongue off trying not to ask you a million questions when she met you."

"She was very pleasant and welcoming."

"Bernie's a good person. You'll like her." Max was still holding her hand and he squeezed her fingers. "How long do you think we'll have to stay married to convince your family we're the real deal?"

"That's a very good question." Phoebe sighed as they mounted the steps to the house. "The thing is— if I ask them that, they'll wonder why I want to know."

"Yeah, that's tricky." Max held the screen door open for her. "I guess we'll find out more at the wedding. We can talk to those lawyers of yours."

Phoebe stepped out of her wellies and took off her coat. "I'd better send those pictures to my family. Thanks so much for helping me, Max."

"My pleasure, sweet pea." He swept her a bow. "Nothing's too good for my wife."

"You're being very nice about all of this," Phoebe said in a rush. "I don't deserve it."

He shrugged. "We're not harming anyone are we?"

"Not at all."

"Then we're okay." He winked at her. "It's my turn to cook for everyone. If you want to help, come and lend a hand when you're ready."

"I'd love to." Phoebe smiled up at him and he bent to kiss her again. "I'll just send the pictures to George and Grandmother, and I'll be right back."

She rushed away leaving him standing alone, his smile fading. He liked kissing her and she seemed to like it, too, but was she just being kind, or did she feel the same spark he had? She was kind of addictive, like Bernie's coffee. He walked into the kitchen and pulled up short when he saw Noah sitting at the kitchen table.

"Hey."

Noah looked up at him. "Why's Phoebe feeling so grateful toward you?"

Max stiffened. "Why are you listening to other people's private conversations?"

"Like you never do that. I was just sitting here minding my own business when you two came in and started talking." Noah shrugged. "If you don't want to be overheard maybe keep your private stuff to your bedroom."

"In the future I'll do that." Max walked over to the sink and washed his hands. "Where's Sky?"

"Taking a nap before dinner." Noah sipped his coffee. "Phoebe's not your usual type."

Max slowly wiped his hands on the towel and set it back on the rack.

"You used to go for big, blond, and flashy."

Max contemplated the knife block. What would it take to make Noah shut up? There was no way he'd take him down with just a punch because Noah was built like the backside of a bus.

"But now that I think about it—you didn't mess around in the last few years of our military service. You just suddenly stopped. We all thought you'd caught something nasty, but maybe it was for a different reason."

"I was married." Max finally swung around to face Noah.

"Yeah." Noah looked at him steadily, a hint of surprise on his face. "So, you were."

Phoebe came back into the kitchen and abruptly stopped. "Sorry, did I interrupt something?"

"Nope." Noah slowly stood and took his mug over to the sink. "You're good. What's for dinner, Max?"

"I've got a chicken to roast and Phoebe's going to prep the veg."

She came to stand beside him, her very presence calming him down. "I'm an excellent sous-chef."

Noah nodded and headed for the door. "Sky likes chicken. Jen and Sally will be back at six."

"That's when I'm aiming for," Max said, aware that he didn't appreciate Noah asking him personal questions and that he'd have to control his temper to protect Phoebe. He wasn't used to being the one on the defensive and he wasn't sure he liked it one bit.

Phoebe went over to the sink and washed her hands.

"Is everything all right, Max?"

"Yeah, Noah's just being his usual salty self."

"I don't want to cause problems for you." She looked at him. "If you want me to leave—"

"Definitely not. This is as much your home as it is mine." He walked over and gave her a hug. "Noah's just a pain in the ass about everything."

"He's very good with Sky."

"I'll give him that," Max said. "But don't let him rile you, okay? I'll deal with him."

"I'm quite capable of standing up for myself," Phoebe raised her chin.

"I know." He risked a quick kiss on her nose. "You tracked *me* down."

She cupped his chin. "I'm glad I succeeded."

"Me too. Now how about we start cooking this food? The chicken's going to need at least an hour and a half."

"So, come on, Phoebe. Tell us how you and Max met."

Bernie looked expectantly across the table. They'd eaten the excellent roast chicken, finished off an apple pie and were on the coffee and tea part of the evening. Jen was putting Sky to bed, but everyone else was still gathered around the table.

Phoebe glanced over at Max, a hint of panic in her eyes. "You tell them, you make it sound much more exciting."

"Sure!" Max grinned at her. "Well, I was sitting at the bar and this beautiful British woman asked if she could talk to me, and the next thing I knew, we were getting married at a wedding chapel."

Bernie looked skeptical. "There must be more to

it than that. I mean even for you; Max, that's fast work, and Phoebe seems quite sane."

"No, that's exactly how it happened," Phoebe said.

"Were you drunk?" Luke asked.

"Me or Feebs?" Max grinned. "She was stone-cold sober, and I'd had a couple of whiskys. It wasn't even lunchtime."

"So, why did you agree to marry each other?" Bernie asked, looking from Max to Phoebe.

Max held Phoebe's gaze as he replied. "Because we wanted to? We've stayed married for four years so we obviously made a good decision."

"You're only still married because you haven't been in the same country for four years," Noah piped up. "You've hardly had the chance to experience married life."

"How do you know?" Max winked at Phoebe. "Maybe my darling wife has been flying out to see me once a year and you didn't even know about it."

Phoebe's lips pursed, fighting a smile as everyone around the table suddenly looked intrigued.

"Maybe you should check out her passport stamps." Max sat back with the air of a confident man. "She's a well-traveled woman."

Noah looked directly at Phoebe. "So, you're not planning on divorcing him?"

"Noah, that's just plain rude," Sally said gently. "Even if she was, it's none of your concern."

"It just seems odd to me." Noah shrugged. "Seeing as Max didn't even give her his address here."

"I found him anyway." Phoebe was definitely holding up her side of things. "The paperwork I received must have been outdated."

Noah's gaze returned to Max. "Yeah, what's that about you having a Reno address?"

Max did a quick risk assessment and realized that if he wanted to draw Noah's fire away from Phoebe, he'd have to make a concession on something else.

"It's a family address."

Luke sat up straight. "You have family in Reno?"

"Yeah, my half sister, Maria, lives there."

Silence fell around the table.

"You have a *sister*?" Luke asked.

"News to me," murmured Noah. "But what the hell do I know about anything these days."

"Half sister. She's a lot older than me. She works at one of the casinos," Max elaborated. "She was originally listed as my next of kin. I guess when I changed the paperwork to add Phoebe some of it didn't get altered."

"Sounds about right for the military," Luke nodded.

"Which is why it took me a while to find out all the details of where Max was currently living," Phoebe added.

"Then how did you know how to find him when you came over before?" Noah asked, his fingers drumming on the kitchen table.

Max held up his phone. "Ever heard of one of these, buddy?"

"Still, you never discussed all the other stuff, like where you actually lived?"

"We weren't exactly thinking about it when we met." Max kissed Phoebe's hand. "We had better things to do."

Damn, Noah was persistent. Max should have made sure he and Phoebe had concocted a decent cover story the second she'd arrived. He'd been stupid and she was paying the price for it.

"But—"

"Noah . . ." Sally said gently. "This isn't an interrogation. Max and Phoebe look very happy together and that's enough for me."

"Thanks, Doc," Max said. "I appreciate that."

She'd always been in his corner from the very first day they'd met, as if sensing that despite his loud-mouth bravado he needed her support the most.

"Sorry." Noah looked at Phoebe and then at Max. "I'll shut up."

"Mom's right as usual." Luke held up his mug. "Congrats, Max, and welcome to the family, Phoebe."

"Thank you," Phoebe said. "You have all been wonderful."

"As are you for taking Max on." Bernie grinned at her. "He's going to need a firm hand."

"Oh, I think I can manage that."

Max winked. "Seriously, all she has to do is talk to me in that posh accent, and I'm already on my knees. I call it the Mary Poppins effect."

Bernie burst out laughing. "Oh, my goodness I love it, and I can totally see that. All you needed, Max, was a strong woman to tell you what to do all along."

"Maybe." Max grinned.

"Did Max get you an engagement ring or did it all happen too fast?" Jen, who had returned to the kitchen, sat down beside Noah.

For the first time, Phoebe hesitated. "We didn't really have time to shop, but I've been wearing this betrothal ring that came from my great-grandmother."

She held out her left hand. Max couldn't believe he hadn't noticed the ruby and diamond ring on her third finger.

He whistled. "I did good."

"You mean Phoebe did," Noah murmured.

Bernie and Jen were too busy oohing and aahing over the ring to notice that Noah was once again giving him the third degree. Max fixed his friend with a hard stare.

"Can you just lay off for five minutes and let the ladies admire the ring I didn't buy?"

"Yeah, stop it, Noah," Luke added. "This isn't the right time or place."

"Are the stones real?" Jen asked as she slipped the ring on her own finger and admired it under the lights. "That central ruby is lovely."

"I have no idea," Phoebe said. "I just inherited the thing." She squinted at it. "It definitely needs a bit of a clean."

Max noticed again how Phoebe never made a big deal out of anything. He'd bet his horse that the diamonds and rubies were one hundred percent genuine and probably worth more than he'd ever make in his life.

Bernie tried on the ring as well and glanced over at Luke, her expression dreamy before she handed it back to Phoebe. "I like that it's not just a diamond. Everyone has one of those. This is far more interesting."

"It was probably made just for her." Phoebe looked down fondly at the ring. "My great-grandfather was a bit of a perfectionist."

"I hope it's insured," Noah said.

Phoebe looked over at him. "It is, and I'm very careful with it. I don't wear it when I'm out in the barn." She paused. "But I promise I'll take extra care when I'm here."

Noah cleared his throat and Max tensed, wondering what his friend was going to come out with next.

"Seeing as we're talking about weddings, Jen has something to say."

"Thank you, Noah." Jen looked around the table. "As we're all here for once I wanted to go over the wedding plans."

"Cool." Max was relieved to be moving away from the subject of him and Phoebe. "How's it all coming together?"

"Well, Bernie's doing the catering."

"Well, of course." Bernie bowed. "We've decided to go all-day buffet style with the food rotating in and out as needed. We'll also deal with the beverage service. Rob's on that."

Sally put up her hand. "I'm organizing the setup here at the ranch, including decorations, chairs, a dance floor, and a big tent in case it rains."

"I'd love to help with that." Phoebe looked at Sally and Jen. "If that's okay?"

"We'd love to have you." Sally beamed at her. "I'm also expecting Luke and Max to act as my muscle when needed."

"I'm all yours, ma'am." Max posed and flexed his biceps and Luke groaned.

"Which leaves Noah to set up the sound system and organize the parking." Jen looked out from the list on her phone. "What have I missed?"

"Bridal flowers?" Phoebe asked.

"Oh." Jen frowned. "I hadn't thought about that. Seeing as it's only me."

"I could make you a bouquet," Phoebe offered. "I spent a year at finishing school in the Alps learning all sorts of useless skills and flower arranging was one of them."

"What's a finishing school?" Luke asked.

"You're so adorable." Bernie patted his arm. "I'll tell you all about it later."

"If you'd like to help with the flowers that would be great." Jen smiled at her and tapped something into her phone. "You're officially on my list now."

Phoebe blushed and Max realized how important it was for her to feel as if she was contributing and fitting in. He liked that about her so much and she was doing it just for him, which was astounding.

"We all good, then?" Noah looked around the table and everyone nodded. "Then I'll check on Sky."

Jen waited until he was out the door before she looked at Bernie.

"How much is he trying to interfere in the planning?"

"Just a tad, but I've been super impressed by his restraint, especially when I tell him to butt out," Bernie said. "This is a good learning experience for him."

Jen sat back. "I knew he wouldn't be able to resist building his own spreadsheets and making sure I'm keeping to the deadlines, but he's been relatively low-key about it so far."

"Then I guess we'll all just keep pretending we don't know what he's doing." Bernie looked around the table. "Unless he loses it completely and attempts a coup or something."

"Or I could just tell him to stop," Max offered.

"No," Bernie and Jen said together.

Max tried not to grin. "You sure?"

Luke gave him the eye. "Max . . ."

Max held up both hands. "It's okay. I promise I'll keep out of it. Are we doing a bachelor party, Luke?"

"Noah doesn't want one."

"So what?" Max shrugged. "We can't let him get away with being a grump over this. It's a big rite of passage."

Luke fixed him with a stare. "If you can think of something relatively low-key that we could do, then go for it. Note the words low-key, Max. No kidnapping Noah stripping him naked and taking him on a plane to Vegas, okay?"

"We've already got Jen's party worked out," Bernie said happily. "We're all going to the spa at Watermill Creek and then dinner and dancing afterward."

"Sounds good." Max looked at Phoebe. "Did you bring your dancing shoes?"

"I'm a terrible dancer," Phoebe confessed.

"But you'll still come, right?" Bernie asked. "You're part of the family now."

"And we can make up for missing your big day and party for two," Jen added.

"That's very sweet of you, but I certainly don't want to intrude on your special day." Phoebe smiled. "I'm happy just to be invited."

Max stared at her. She was a genuinely good person. He'd hit the jackpot when he'd met her in Reno.

"Max?"

He looked over at Jen. "Yeah?"

"You look all goofy when you smile at Phoebe."

"That's because she's awesome."

Bernie and Jen gave a giddy sigh and then smiled at him and Phoebe.

"I told you it was true love," Jen said. "I've never seen Max like this before."

"Me neither," Luke said. "It's weird." He stood up.

"How about we clear the table, Max, and let the ladies talk?"

"We certainly have a lot to chat about." Jen's gaze went around the table. "I can't believe I'll be a married woman in less than four weeks."

Max stacked some plates and rose to his feet. "Are we inviting Dave?"

"Hell no!" Luke said as he ran the water into the sink and started rinsing off the dishes. "That's the last thing we need."

"He's settled down with whatshername now, hasn't he?" Max asked.

"For now," Jen said, frowning. "And I did invite him. He *is* Sky's dad after all." She glanced over at Luke. "And your friend."

"Ex-friend since he acted like such a jerk," Luke muttered.

"Still a Marine, though," Max said.

"Yeah, but he doesn't deserve to be at this wedding. You know what Dave's like. He'll try to make it all about him, and Noah might murder him, which isn't a good look on your wedding day."

"It's okay, he's not coming," Jen said. "He's off skiing in Aspen or something."

"Well, thank God for that," Max declared. "Now, would you like more coffee? I can bring you some after I clean up."

"I think we're good for now." Jen pointed at the family room. "Let's go in there so we can pick out the treatments we want to have at the spa."

Max watched the ladies walk away. Phoebe was chatting amicably with Sally who was nodding at whatever she was saying. He hoped she'd be able to hold her own when the other women bombarded her with questions about their relationship. He suddenly remembered her elaborate fabrications to her family and was pretty sure she'd be okay.

"She fits in good," Luke said from behind him.

"Yeah . . . she does." Max didn't turn around. "I wasn't sure how it would go, but she's been awesome."

"I like her."

"So do I." Max picked the mugs off the table and brought them over to the dishwasher.

"I'm still not buying the how-you-met story, bro."

Max shrugged. "It's the truth. We met in a bar and got married."

"Who popped the question?"

"Ah, now that would be telling." Max went back to the table to get Phoebe's teacup and saucer. "I think it was a mutual decision."

"Sure, it was." Luke rolled his eyes. "I know it was you, dude. What I can't understand is why Phoebe was willing to go along with it."

Phoebe settled into the corner of the couch and let the spirited discussion about Jen's party roll over her. She wasn't quite sure how a traditional American bachelorette party went but she was more than willing to learn.

"Didn't you say your sister was getting married soon?" Jen asked.

"Yes, in about six weeks, why?"

"What is she doing for her party?"

"Her Hen Do?" Phoebe frowned. "She wanted an adventure weekend so we're going to be hiking, camping, riding horses, and scaling rocks."

"So, pretty much the everyday activities on this ranch," Sally said. "You don't sound very keen."

"I'd much rather be at the spa with Jen," Phoebe confessed. "I had to do all that outdoorsy stuff when I was at boarding school in Scotland and it's not my idea of a relaxing time. But Eugenie is horse mad just like me, so I'll enjoy every minute of that particular activity, which is good enough for me."

Jen passed her tablet over. "Do you want to pick your spa treatments? We've got the whole day booked out."

"I'd love to." Phoebe started to scroll through the delights on offer. "I've always wanted to try a proper mud bath."

"Trust me, I had one and it wasn't as much fun as I expected," Bernie said. "The mud was *cold*! My dad said I might as well have saved my money, gone into one of the muddy fields at home and rolled around for free."

Phoebe grinned. "Then perhaps I'll try the hot stones instead. And a facial, and a manicure." She checked the boxes and handed the tablet back to Jen.

"Sounds good," Bernie said. "And now that Max can't hear us, what really went down in Reno?"

Chapter 5

Phoebe rolled onto her back and stared up into the blackness. "

What's up?" Max's sleep-roughened voice made her shiver. "Can't sleep?"

"We really need to get our stories straight about Reno," Phoebe said. "I'm constantly worried I'm going to say something that isn't the same as you're saying."

"Valid point." Max came up on one elbow and looked down at her. "Okay, if I turn on the light?"

"Seeing as neither of us is sleeping that's fine." Phoebe sighed.

He rolled over onto his side and clicked on the lamp. "I always prefer to see someone's face when I'm talking to them."

He sat up allowing the covers to pool in his lap, set his pillow behind his head, and put his arm around Phoebe's shoulders. She leaned into his side, her cheek coming to rest naturally against his bicep. He smelled nice and she slowly inhaled.

"You sniffing me, Feebs?"

"Yes." She nuzzled his skin with her nose. "I think I'd be able to find you anywhere now."

His arm tightened briefly around her and then he chuckled. "Good to know."

"Bernie, Jen, and Sally all wanted to know what happened in Reno," Phoebe said. "I kept repeating what you'd already said, but I don't think they quite believed me."

"I've had the same grilling from the boys." Max heaved a sigh. "Luke's convinced it was all me, and Noah just thinks I'm up to no good."

"I don't mind if you tell them I proposed to you."

"Yeah, but it isn't anyone else's business, is it?" He kissed the top of her head. "If I tell them that they'll start asking you a whole load of personal questions you shouldn't have to answer."

"I don't mind."

"Maybe I do."

Phoebe eased slightly away from him so that she could see his face. He looked deliciously stubborn; his mouth set in a firm line.

"Is this really about protecting me, or more about you just not wanting to admit I was the one who made you get married?"

"You think that hurts my macho pride?"

She met his gaze. "Does it?"

His dimples reappeared. "Feebs, did you know you're fricking adorable when you get all serious with me?"

"Are you trying to change the subject?"

"Maybe. It's hard to be serious when you're glaring at me like that." His voice deepened. "I just want to kiss all that disapproval right off your face."

"Can we stay on topic, please?"

His gaze lowered to her mouth. "Sure, sweetheart, whatever you want. What was the question again?"

She tried to remember what it was herself. "I asked if you were reluctant to admit that I forced you to marry me."

His eyebrows went up. "I don't remember you holding a gun to my head."

"I took advantage of your kind nature."

He frowned. "I'm not kind. Ask anyone here. You didn't make me do anything I didn't want to."

"Then if someone asks me again, I'm going to tell them the truth. That I asked you to marry me."

"Sure." He shrugged. "I don't mind. Just be prepared for some awkward follow-up questions if you do."

"I'm not a very good liar."

"Could've fooled me. Weren't you the one making me an undercover agent?"

She felt her cheeks heat. "That was different. I was just spinning tales for my father. I didn't realize he was passing them on to the whole family until it was too late. And it's much harder to lie when I'm actually looking at someone. I don't have the right kind of face for that."

"True." He put his finger under her chin. "Don't ever play poker, Feebs."

"I won't."

He gently kissed her. "I haven't had a chance to thank you."

"For what?"

His smile was crooked. "Hanging in there with me. Being nice to my friends, making out like you're happy to be with me."

"None of that is hard, Max." Her eyes held his. "You've already done so much for me."

He kissed her again and this time she responded because she couldn't help herself. She quickly forgot about anything except the textures of his mouth, the nip of his teeth on her throat and the way he hummed his approval as she wrapped her arms around him to keep him close. His fingers moved down her spine, counting off her vertebrae until he curled one large hand over her hip and urged her closer. She came up on one knee to straddle his hard-muscled thigh and unconsciously began to move against him.

Eventually, he raised his head, his breathing as ragged as her own. "If we keep this up, I'm going to want to strip you naked and make love to you all night."

She blinked at him. "Do you think that's a good idea?"

"How the hell would I know? I can't think straight when you're kissing me."

"I feel the same," Phoebe confessed. "And technically, we *are* married for the foreseeable future, so it's all perfectly proper."

"True." He was regarding her warily.

"So, if we did make love, we wouldn't be hurting anyone." She gazed at him. "I believe it's almost expected if one is married to that person."

He groaned. "You're driving me wild, darlin'."

"But the thing is . . ." Phoebe hesitated.

He nuzzled her throat. "I promise I'll take good care of you."

"I'm sure you will, but—" She eased away from him. "I haven't actually done it before."

He went still. "Like never?"

"I know! It's so embarrassing, but I was at an all-girls school and college, then finishing school and straight into the family business. And I wouldn't cheat on you when we were married, so I never found the time to date for long enough to, to . . ." She waved her hand around. "*Do* that."

His fingers closed around hers and held them still as he continued to look at her.

She frowned. "Will you say something, please?"

"Normally you're telling me to shut up. I'm just processing here, Feebs." He slowly brought her hand to his mouth and kissed it. "I'm game if you are. In fact, I can't think of anything I'd like more."

Phoebe looked into his eyes and saw sincerity and a blaze of desire that made her insides curl with lust.

"And I can't think of anyone I'd rather have my first time with."

He swallowed hard. "No pressure, then."

"To be fair, I won't know whether you're any good because I have nothing to compare you with," Phoebe pointed out, which made him smile again. "And I'm sure you've had plenty of practice."

"Not for a few years." He held her gaze. "I kept my vows just like you did."

"Really?"

"Yeah, it was the right thing to do."

She squeezed his fingers. "I'm glad."

"Me too. We can learn together." His voice deepened. "We'll take it slow, maybe cover a couple of bases tonight and see how we feel about attempting a home run another day, okay?"

Phoebe crinkled her nose. "I didn't understand anything you just said."

He grinned. "Just that I won't do anything you're not one hundred percent onboard with. If you feel rushed or uncomfortable just tell me to stop and I will."

Phoebe nodded. "That sounds acceptable."

"Good." He patted his thigh. "Now, how about you come back over here and let's get started?"

She climbed into his lap, and he arranged her so that she was facing him, his expression serious as he ran his fingers down her back.

"This okay?"

Phoebe nodded, her attention fixed on his muscled chest and the coarse hair that covered it. She reached out her hand and tentatively stroked his skin. She wanted this—with him—because he was the only man who had ever made her feel safe and sexy at the same time.

"That's the spirit, Feebs. I think you're going to be a fast learner."

"You have to tell me if what I'm doing is okay as well," she reminded him.

"You can touch me all you like," Max said gruffly. "I love it."

Encouraged by his words, she traced his collarbones and the muscled curves of his arms, her fingers outlining his tattoos when she encountered them, making him shiver. He kept his hands loosely around her waist, his thumbs massaging her hip bones as she petted him.

Emboldened, she leaned in and kissed him, looping her arm around his neck, which drew her breasts up against his chest. It felt delicious.

"Feebs?"

"Yes?"

"Would you be comfortable taking your pajama top off?"

She glanced down at her buttoned-up, flannel, bunny-print shirt. "I am getting rather warm."

"I've got this." His fingers worked the top three buttons and then he stopped to look at her. "Okay if I take it off over your head?"

She nodded, suddenly aware that she had nothing under her top and that Max would soon be seeing her naked for the first time. She instinctively pressed a hand to her chest.

"You okay?" Max paused. "We don't have to do this."

"It's just that I'm not particularly well endowed-up top," she said in a rush.

Max regarded her seriously. "I can't say I've noticed."

"I heard Noah say you usually dated blond, curvy women."

"I might have in the past, but that's not who I married."

"What if you find me . . . repulsive?"

"Then I'll run away screaming and never be seen again," Max said. "But I don't think that's going to happen, sweetheart. And if you want to keep your top on until you feel more comfortable with me then don't stress it."

"Maybe if I just unbutton it completely and then you can take a look and see what you think?" Phoebe suggested.

Max's lips twitched. "Sure, whatever works for you,"

"My brother said I'm as flat as an ironing board," Phoebe said as she bent her head to unbutton the rest of her top.

"Your brother sounds like a dick," Max said. "I can't wait to meet him."

A gurgle of laughter found its way through Phoebe's nervousness, and she cupped Max's chin. "Thank you."

"For what? Insulting your brother?"

"For just being so nice to me." She undid the last button and raised her chin. "You can look all you want."

She closed her eyes as Max's fingers drifted over the slight curve of her breast and then returned to pluck at her nipple. She leaned into his touch, and he applied more pressure, making her shudder.

"Did you like that?" His voice was low and so sexy that she was fairly sure that if she'd been wearing knickers, they would've spontaneously combusted.

"Yes." She breathed out.

"How about this?"

His mouth fastened on her nipple, and she instinctively grabbed hold of his shoulder as he sucked and tongued her nipple into pulsating hardness. She slid her fingers into his hair and held on tight as he continued to torment her needy flesh. At some point, she got annoyed with her top getting in his way, and threw it to the floor, making him chuckle, and transfer his attention to her other breast.

She undulated against him in the same rhythm as his sucking, riding his thigh as her whole body gave into his demands. While his mouth worked its magic, he used his other hand to pinch her nipple. She started to feel hot and rolled her hips even harder until a rush of sensation took over and she shuddered to a climax.

Max raised his head and stared at her. "Damn, Feebs. If you come when I just touch your breasts what are you going to do when I go down on you?"

"Probably explode?" Phoebe gasped. "Can you try?"

"Yes, ma'am."

His smile was wicked as he rolled her onto her back and loomed over her, his gaze on her mouth, his fingers tracing the top of her pajama bottoms. Phoebe met his gaze, suddenly brave.

"You can take them off."

He let out a breath as he slowly drew her pants down over her knees and put them to one side.

"Feebs . . ." He paused. "You're beautiful. You have legs like a colt."

"Is that a cowboy compliment?" Phoebe asked breathlessly as he stroked his way down her thigh to her ankle and back again.

He bent to kiss her knee and gently moved it to one side, spreading her legs. "Okay if I carry on?"

"Yes, please."

He settled himself between her thighs, one hand cupping her hip while the other gently explored her most sensitive parts.

"You're wet for me," His voice was pure sin. "You already came for me."

She wanted to grab hold of him by the neck and place him exactly where she needed him—not that she even had a clue what she was doing—it just seemed like her body knew what she wanted better than her mind.

He dropped a gentle kiss on her mound, and she jumped as his fingers swirled the wetness around her bud.

"Okay?" he murmured against her thigh. "Pull my hair hard if you want me to stop."

She pressed her lips together since right now that was the last thing she wanted to happen. If he didn't keep going, she might expire with lust.

His tongue flicked over her most sensitive flesh, and she shuddered, her thoughts in chaos, her body responding to his every touch like she was desperate.

Even as he licked her clit, he teased one finger inside her making her gasp. At his slight hesitation, she dug her fingers into his shoulder.

"Don't stop."

Max growled against Phoebe's thigh. He didn't want to stop. He wanted to ravish her until she screamed his name so loudly that she woke up the horses in the barn. How could someone with such little sexual experience be so damn hot? He focused his attention back on her clit and added another finger, drawing them in and out in the same rhythm as his tongue.

She moaned and her hips rocked upward, making his already-overexcited dick stiffen like steel. He was glad he was wearing boxers or Phoebe would be seeing way more than she was probably ready for.

"Max . . ."

He didn't need her words to know she was about to climax again. He drove her through it, taking the opportunity to get another finger inside her where he could feel every clench of her tight internal muscles. He couldn't wait to feel her around his dick, but he would wait. He'd wait until the world was cold if she wasn't ready for him.

He raised his head to look at her dazed expression and almost came in his boxers. He'd done that. He was the one who'd put that satisfied look on her face and all he wanted to do was make sure he got to do it again and again.

Keeping his fingers embedded within her, he took his weight on his elbow and came up to kiss her mouth.

"You liking this, Mrs. Creighton-Smith-Romero?"

"It's divine," she whispered against his lips. "It's everything I always dreamed it would be."

A wave of satisfaction washed over him as he kissed her again and she wrapped her arms around him. He thumbed her clit in time to the thrusts of his fingers and tongue and she came again in long, slow, powerful waves that made her whole body arch up toward his.

He wanted to make love to her so badly he was shaking with it. But he wasn't going to rush the best thing in his life.

"Hey, sweetheart. Good so far?"

She opened her eyes and smiled at him. "Wonderful." She kissed him. "Thank you *so* much."

"Such great manners," Max murmured. "But I'm the one who should be thanking you."

"I haven't done anything for you, yet," Phoebe said. "I would like to." She studied his face. "I do have some experience with that side of things."

"I'm glad to hear it," Max said gravely. "Because I'm very fond of my private parts and I wouldn't want you to accidentally rip something off."

Her smile when she realized he was teasing her was glorious and made Max want to start all over again and give her as many orgasms as she wanted.

"Would you like me to . . . ?" She glanced at his tented boxers.

"I think that should wait until round two," Max said. "Tonight was all about you."

Her nose crinkled. "That seems remarkably unfair."

She seemed to have totally forgotten that she was naked in his bed and that she was still riding his thigh. The scent of her arousal was all around them, and Max wanted to rub his face in it and roll around for a while, which was nuts. He couldn't help pressing against her and she sighed.

"I think." Max kissed her. "You haven't finished coming for me tonight."

She blushed. "I wouldn't want to be greedy."

"I want you to be." He held her gaze. "I want you to demand I satisfy you completely so that when we do make love, I'll know exactly how to turn you on."

She stroked his cheek. "Max, that's easy. I just have to look at you."

The shy trust in her eyes made him want to simultaneously protect her from everything, and screw her brains out, and he didn't know how to deal with any of that.

He gently disentangled himself and caressed her hip. "We've made a great start. Shall we carry on tomorrow night?"

Her brow crinkled. "Did I say something wrong, Max?"

Dammit, she was way too good at reading him, too.

"Nah." He kissed her more deeply. "I really want to take this slow, okay?"

"As long as you let me have a turn tomorrow then I suppose that's all right." She kissed his nose. "If that's what you want, obviously."

"I can't wait." He sat on the side of the bed and yawned loudly. "Man, you've worn me out. You okay if I use the bathroom first?"

"Please go ahead. I need to find my pajamas and make myself decent."

He took his robe off the back of the door. There was no way he was walking down the hallway with a hard-on because he was bound to bump into someone, and it was difficult to ignore. He locked the bathroom door and hopped into the shower, keeping the temperature on the chilly side as he dealt with his dick with a few hard strokes and collapsed gasping, one hand braced against the shower wall.

She was fire and he was . . . totally enthralled, and he didn't know what the hell to do about any of it. His only thought was one of his favorite WWII quotes about when you're going through hell to keep going. He might get burned alive, but at least he'd experience something amazing.

If she wanted him to make love to her, he'd be there. Whether he'd survive the experience was another matter entirely.

Chapter 6

"Phoebe?"

She jumped as Luke spoke from the opposite side of the table. She had a feeling it wasn't the first time he'd tried to get her attention.

"Sorry! I was daydreaming." She set her mug down. It was barely six in the morning, and she had slept through Max's alarm, and woken up to an empty bed. "What is it?"

"You can ride a horse, right?"

"Yes. I believe my father put me up on my first horse before I could walk."

"Don't tell Sky." Luke grinned at her. "He's dying to get up there and Jen won't let him. She says he's too young."

He finished his coffee. "We've got to drive some of the cattle between two grazing areas about a quarter of a mile apart, and we could do with an all-hands-on-deck effort. Mom usually helps, but she's on call for the clinic, and Mano's wife just had a baby so he's at the hospital with her."

"I'd be delighted to help." Phoebe couldn't think

of anything she'd enjoy more—apart from what Max had planned for her that night . . .

"Awesome." Luke stood up. "You can choose your own horse, or I can saddle up my mom's mare for you."

"Whichever is easier," Phoebe said. "What time are we leaving?"

Luke consulted his phone. "In about half an hour?"

"Should I make some sandwiches and a flask of tea to bring for everyone?" Phoebe asked.

"I think Noah's already got that covered, but you might need to make your own tea. There are plenty of flasks in the cupboard above the range." Luke headed for the door. "Bring a raincoat as well as a hat. The weather can change real fast out here."

"I will," Phoebe called after him as she went to rinse out her mug and make herself a flask of tea. She'd already eaten some toast, and she'd check the pantry to see if there were any nutrition bars to bring along with her hot drink.

She went back into Max's room to make the bed and smiled foolishly at the disordered sheets. Her trust in Max had only increased tenfold. He'd made what had felt like an embarrassing failure on her part into a thing that didn't matter at all. He'd treated her like a princess and slept with his body curved around hers all night long.

She plumped up the pillows and set them back on the bed along with the top quilt. At one point she'd sensed his slight withdrawal but assumed he'd been trying to be respectful with her person. Not that he'd needed to be. She'd loved everything he'd done to her and wanted so much more . . .

She put on a thicker pair of socks and found her hiking boots and waterproof wax jacket. The thought of helping out on a real cowboy ranch was exhilarating. Seeing Max work with his friends was also a treat, although she sensed some tension with Noah who wasn't as easy to get along with as Luke and the rest of the gang. But she'd seen how Noah was with Jen and Sky, and knew he wasn't as gruff as he appeared, and despite his appearance, he definitely looked out for Max.

She also reminded herself that she'd only seen the best of Max and that, like Noah, he was a far more complex person than he let on. She occasionally sensed a wariness from everyone when Max opened his mouth, which spoke of past tensions. And apparently, when he'd come to Reno to find her, he'd left without explaining where he was going, which had put Luke in a difficult position.

But wasn't everyone more complicated than they appeared? Phoebe grabbed her hat and walked to the door. In all her dealings with Max and her family she certainly had stretched the truth somewhat. Her cell buzzed as she reached the kitchen, and she took the tea bags out of her tea. She checked her messages, saw something that looked rather long from her brother, and decided to read it when she got back.

She had work to do and she didn't want to hold anyone up or embarrass Max. She screwed the lid tight on her flask, put a handful of granola bars in her pocket along with tissues, lip balm, and her phone, and went out. The air was colder than she'd expected and coming straight off the distant mountains.

There was a group of cowboys gathered in the paddock in front of the barn. Phoebe recognized some of them, but others were new to her. Max waved as she came toward him. He wore his usual cowboy uniform of jeans, spurs, chaps and boots, a thick fleece-lined jacket and his white Stetson.

"Hey, Feebs. I hear you're coming out with us today."

"If that's okay." She smiled as he looped an arm around her shoulders and kissed the top of her head.

"Can't think of a better way to spend my day." He grinned. "I'd rather look at your face than Noah's."

"Right back at you," Noah called out from somewhere.

Max turned to the two guys he'd been talking to. "*Esta es mi esposa*, Phoebe."

He turned back to her. "Feebs, meet Luis and Paolo, two of our best hands."

Phoebe stuck out her hand. "A pleasure."

"You're married?" Luis looked at Max. "Since when?"

Max shrugged. "Four years now, isn't it, Feebs?"

"Yes, indeed." She smiled brightly at both men. "I'm very lucky."

Max nodded and took her hand. "I have to introduce Phoebe to her horse, guys. I'll check back with you later."

They strolled away and Phoebe sighed.

"What's up?" Max looked down at her.

"It's just that everyone looks so horrified when they meet me."

"Sweetheart, that's not about you. It's just that no one ever thought I'd get married so they're wondering if you're a saint."

"Or a fool," Phoebe said gloomily.

He stopped and turned to her so that she could look up at him.

"There's only one fool in this marriage and I can

one hundred percent guarantee that it isn't you." He paused. "I could stop telling everyone. Would that help?"

"No! I'm perfectly fine with being married to you."

His eyes crinkled at the corners when he smiled down at her. "Good."

"Not again . . ." Luke spoke from behind her. "Could you two stop cooing at each other so we can get going?"

"Have you seen yourself with Bernie?" Max looked over at Luke. "I'm just showing Phoebe her horse."

Luke pointed over his shoulder. "Macy is tied up right outside the barn in completely the opposite direction to where you're heading."

"Thanks for the input," Max nodded. "Come on, Feebs, we'd better get you mounted up before Luke loses it completely."

He walked her over to the barn and spent a few minutes talking her through Sally's horse's habits while she got acquainted with the lively mare. He helped her up into the massive saddle and made sure her stirrups were at the right length before handing her the two reins.

"Remember, hold 'em like an ice-cream cone in one hand, use them like a rudder on a boat, and don't kick too hard or she'll buck you off."

"Got it." Phoebe gathered the reins and felt the horse's instant response. She'd only ridden western style once before. If she wanted to be useful, she'd have to get up to speed pretty quickly. None of the cowboys had time to worry about her.

Luke came over and smiled at her. "Looking good, Phoebe. Just follow me or Max and you'll be fine."

"I'll do my best," Phoebe said as she settled into

the worn leather saddle that offered far more support than her usual English one. The hint of cold in
the air vanished as the warmth from Macy's flanks
crept up Phoebe's thighs. She made sure her hat was
well fixed on her head and followed the rest of the
riders out through the gate, and toward the foothills.

Macy picked her way through the coarse clumps
of grass and old tree stumps like a pro, meaning
Phoebe got the chance to look around and enjoy the
magnificent setting. There was obviously a waterfall
somewhere as she could hear a consistent roar. They
seemed to be skirting the ever-encroaching trees and
working their way toward the west. Several dogs ran
with the horses, tongues hanging out, tails wagging
as they made the occasional sideways quest to investi-
gate an interesting scent. The cold air scented with
pine stung her face, but she didn't care.

Being on a horse had always been a way to escape
her stifling home life, and the horrors of boarding
school, and nothing had changed that. Max kept
pace with her, which meant she got to admire his su-
perb horsemanship and the way his body moved ef-
fortlessly with his mount. Occasionally, he whistled to
the dogs or grinned at her, but he let her ride free.

Luke, who was leading the group, stopped, and
waited for them to gather around him. He split them
up into teams to work to get the cattle out of the one
field, across two others, and onto an unpaved road
and down into the valley. Phoebe was teamed up with
Max, Luis, and Paolo to guard the right side of the
gate while Luke and his team rounded up the cattle
and drove them out of the field.

The dogs stopped fooling around and became all
business, getting in close, circling the cattle, nipping
at their heels, and making the cowboys' work a lot

less dangerous. Phoebe watched everything with great interest, Max at her side.

"Don't you normally do this bit?" she asked.

"Sometimes." His smile was a delight. "Today it's all on Noah." His gaze shifted past her to Luke. "Get ready. They're gonna come our way and we need to stand firm, so they'll head toward the left and away from the forest."

"Got it."

Phoebe copied the cowboys' stance and arranged her horse at an angle toward the approaching cattle blocking any escape. Macy didn't seem bothered at all, her ears flicking to dislodge the inevitable flies, her placid gaze on the cattle. One thing Phoebe did know about horses was that they were usually fine, until they weren't, and that even the quietest pony could get freaked out by the strangest things.

She gathered her reins and focused on the cloud of approaching dust and the whooping cowboys pushing the herd toward the narrow point of exit at the gate. As the dust reached her, she wished she'd brought a bandana to cover her mouth and nose because it was suddenly hard to see. She blinked and set her hand on Macy's neck while she murmured for her to stay calm.

There were a lot of cattle—far more than Phoebe had expected, as she was used to smaller English farms. She tried to count them but gave up when the total went over a hundred, and simply held her station. They streamed by, the dogs at their heels, the cowboys whistling and urging them through the open gate and out into the wider pasture next door.

"Good job, everyone!" Luke yelled. "Let's keep 'em moving across this field toward the far corner."

Max grinned at Phoebe as he rode past. "You're

doing great. Just stay in line and walk Macy toward
the far gate. If any of the cows make a break for it, try
and head them off, or whistle and one of us can lasso
them."

"I wish I knew how to do that," Phoebe said.

"I'll teach you."

He turned his attention back to the cattle who
were moving in the right direction, if somewhat reluctantly. The cowboys had fanned out around them
in a semicircle and were slowly closing them in and
moving them down the slope. It reminded Phoebe of
watching her father's prize sheep dogs work the
sheep.

There were gaps between the riders and occasionally a rebel steer tried to change direction and make
a break for freedom. So far none of them had made
it farther than a few steps before one of the dogs or
the cowboys had stepped up and stopped them.
Phoebe was impressed by the efficiency of the opera-
tion. It took a skilled workforce to keep the cattle
calm while still getting them moving toward the gate
and Luke's team had it down.

While they waited for Luke to open the gate into
the next field, Max moved closer to Phoebe.

"The next part is the longest and the land spreads
out so there's more chance some of the cattle will
wander off."

"Okay." Phoebe nodded.

"Just take it slow and watch what the rest of us are
doing and you'll be fine. You're a great rider."

She shrugged. "My father insisted upon it."

"Did you hunt?"

"Like, foxes?" Phoebe shuddered. "No, I couldn't
bear it. I got a lot of stick for not joining in, but I'm
glad I didn't. It's heavily restricted now, which was a

tremendous relief. I did compete in three-day eventing for a while."

"What's that?"

"It's a combination event where you compete in show jumping, dressage, and cross-country all on one horse, and in three days."

Max whistled. "That's a lot of different skills for a person to learn, let alone a horse."

"I loved it," Phoebe said. "The winner had to be good at all three." She bit her lip. "I was once asked on a trial for the British Olympic team, but I had to turn them down."

"Why?"

"I didn't have time to train properly after Father became ill, so I sold my horse."

"Sorry to hear that, Feebs."

She smiled. "That's life. When did you learn to ride?"

His smile was wicked. "You won't like the answer to that."

"Try me."

"I'd sneak into people's fields and ride their horses bareback when they weren't around. I fell off a lot and had a few concussions, but I taught myself the basics." He paused. "When my dad found out, he got me lessons and came with me, which was great."

Phoebe chuckled. "That doesn't surprise me in the least."

"Not a lot of horse ownership in my neighborhood."

"Which is a shame because learning to look after a horse is such a confidence-building experience. If I had the time and the money, I'd love to run that kind of event for disadvantaged children. It's one of the reasons why I'm so determined to break the terms of this will—" Phoebe broke off and looked toward Luke. "I think we're about to get our orders."

"Yeah, Luke loves bossing people around. He did it a lot in the Marines," Max said.

"Because he was your superior officer." Noah came up on the other side of Max. "And a damn good one."

"We all got out alive, so I'd have to agree," Max said. "Can't deny he enjoys it, though."

Both men looked at Luke who stared right back at them.

"What?"

"Just admiring your ability to command, boss," Max said.

"Sure, you are," Luke said. "I'm going to open the gate and we'll let them through as slowly as we can, so they won't have time to spread out too fast. Everyone got it?"

They all nodded, and Luke whistled to the guy on the other side of the gate. "Open it up and then file through and fan out so we cover as much ground as possible."

Max couldn't stop glancing over at Phoebe as they progressed through the sloping meadow. Her face glowed with excitement, she rode like a dream, and she seemed to be having the time of her life. He envied her ability to live in the moment and embrace what was going on around her with such enthusiasm. He felt better just being with her, which was a first. He wasn't great at trusting anyone, but he knew she had his back just like Luke and Noah did. *Why* she supported him was still a mystery, but he wasn't going to knock it.

"Max! Look out!"

He jerked his attention away from Phoebe to find a steer coming straight at him. At least Bouncer had the sense to get out of the way, but it meant the steer was past him, and heading for the forest at an ungainly gallop.

"Yipee!" Phoebe turned her horse on a dime and set off in pursuit with Max right behind her.

"Keep him away from the trees!" Max shouted as he fumbled to release his lasso.

Phoebe immediately moved to his left, coming up almost alongside the steer and changed its trajectory, which gave him the space to spin out his rope and neatly capture the steer around the neck. He eased Bouncer through the gears and down to walk allowing the animal to slow down with him and not get panicked.

"Nice catch!" Phoebe grinned at him. She'd lost her hat, and her hair was windswept and wild.

"I shouldn't have let him get by me in the first place," Max said ruefully. "Let's get him back where he's supposed to be."

"Were you taking a nap?" Phoebe teased as she turned her horse around.

"I was too busy looking at you," Max confessed.

She went even pinker than she already was, and a shy smile hovered on her lips. "You're such a joker, Max."

She set off back toward the lower pasture and Max followed more slowly with the steer. Luke gave him the eye as they approached.

"What's with you, today?"

Max shrugged and leaned down to release his rope. "Sorry about that."

"No harm done, and Phoebe seemed to enjoy the chase."

Both men glanced over at Phoebe who was chatting to Luis as if they'd known each other for years.

"Always good to have someone watch your back," Luke said as if he'd been reading Max's mind.

"It sure is."

"Will you act as my rear guard?" Luke asked. "I need to get back to the sharp end."

"Sure, boss."

Max made certain that this time he was in the right position as they persuaded the last few steers to pass through the gate. They had to get the cattle across the unpaved ranch road, over the rock-strewn dried out creek, and into the field in the shade of the pine trees. It would take at least another hour and the sun was now overhead. He took a moment to drink some water and looked around to find Phoebe to remind her to drink as well, but there was no sign of her.

Noah saw him looking and called out. "She's gone ahead." He paused. "Probably good for your concentration."

Max wasn't sure he liked how everyone knew he was fixated on Phoebe, but there wasn't a lot he could do about it. He raised his hand in acknowledgement and put his flask away.

"She's a good rider," Noah carried on talking. "I'm not worried about her taking a more forward position."

"Damn straight." Max shut the gate behind him and made sure it was locked in place. "She's doing fine."

He waited until Noah loped off to take up his position in the middle of the pack and followed along behind, mopping up strays and keeping everything moving in the right direction. Being at the back meant he received more than his share of kicked up cow shit and dust, but he figured he deserved it. He put his sunglasses on and zipped his fleece over his mouth and nose and kept it together until Luke finally called for a halt.

The redwood trees provided some much-needed shade. There was still a trickle of water coming down the creek for the horses, which kept the whole pasture moist for the cattle to graze on. He found Phoebe chatting with Luke under the trees while she helped set out the lunch Noah and Luke had brought in their saddlebags.

"Hi!" She smiled at him. "I was just telling Luke how you roped that steer in one try. It was most impressive."

He handed her his water flask. "I bet you've forgotten to drink anything."

"Correct. I was having too much fun." She turned to Luke. "The distances you have to cover with your cattle are huge."

Luke raised his eyebrows. "That was just a quick change around. In the fall we do a three-day drive to get them closer to the ranch for the upcoming markets and the winter."

"Three days?" Phoebe asked.

Luke shrugged. "It's a big place."

"We have to extract them from all the hills and valleys, which takes time even with sat-nav imagery and tags," Max added. "We start out on the farthest boundaries with the all-terrain vehicles and move inward, camping overnight when the light goes."

"I can't even imagine." Phoebe looked over at the swiftly rising ground of the foothills. "There can't be much grass up there."

"Not much, but there's water running down from

the snowcap on the mountains and cattle need that to survive, too. They find the good grazing spots and stay there until we come by and encourage them to leave." Luke took out a large container. "Can you put that on the table, please?"

"Yes, of course." Phoebe set the box down alongside the other two. "Do you think there's enough for everyone here?"

"I've got more." Noah's deep voice came from behind them. He put a set of bulging saddlebags on the bench, "There's a bunch of fried chicken, rolls, and fruit in here as well as some beverages."

"I'm starving," Phoebe said. "It must be all that fresh air."

"You did good." Noah nodded to her.

"Thank you."

"I'd hire you as a working hand."

"That's the nicest thing you've ever said to me," Phoebe stuttered and immediately went red. "I mean, not that we've had that many conversations, but—"

Max took pity on her and patted her hand. "How about I do the unpacking and you check on the horses? I think I forgot to loosen Bouncer's girth."

"I'll go and check." Phoebe turned toward the forest, Max's flask still in her hand. "Do they need water?"

"Luis is taking care of that," Max reassured her. "But if you see any of the guys, tell them it's time to eat."

"Will do." Phoebe walked off leaving Luke, Noah, and Max at the table.

Noah unbuckled the bag. "I packed everything in tight so I'm not expecting too much damage. Can you start on the other one, Max?"

"Sure." Max complied.

"I meant what I said about Phoebe," Noah set a large foil package full of chicken wings on the table and Max's stomach growled. "She'd be a great hire. Shame she won't be sticking around."

"You don't know that." Max looked up from his task.

"Aren't you going back to England for a wedding in a few weeks?"

"Sure, we are, but that doesn't mean we aren't coming back."

"You think she'd live out here?" Noah looked around the shady glen.

"Jen did."

"She did it for me," Noah said. "And Bernie's from around here and she gets it."

Max set a bottle of iced tea on the table with great precision. He was having an amazing day; the sun was shining, and he wasn't going to let Noah spoil it. "Do you want me to put all the beverages out, or should I leave some in the cooler bag?"

"Nothing to say about Phoebe?"

Max looked at him. "Nothing I want to say to you, bro."

Luke cleared his throat. "Can we focus on the food here?"

"Happy to, if Noah would just get off my back for five minutes." Max set the cooler on the ground.

"I'm just making conversation," Noah said. "The trouble with you, Max, is that you're great at dishing it out, but not so good at taking it."

Max took a long, slow breath and met Noah's gaze head on. "Maybe you're right." He turned to Luke. "I'm going to check in with Phoebe and call the rest of the guys over for lunch, okay?"

"Thanks, Max." Luke was looking at him oddly. "That would be great."

He walked away, staring into the shallow creek in need of some space between himself and Noah who might be one of his best friends, but sure knew how to needle him. But that's what happened when you let people in. They worked out your weak spots and exploited them, and you couldn't do anything about it because you were friends . . .

"Max?"

He looked up and smiled as Phoebe came through the trees to join him. Her hair had curled in the heat, and she'd caught the sun on the tip of her nose.

"Is everything okay?"

He shrugged. "Yeah, it's great."

She touched his arm. "I overheard a bit of what Noah was saying to you."

"Which bit?"

"When he suggested that I wouldn't be coming back here with you after the wedding."

"Oh, right. The good bit." Max managed a smile. "It's none of his business, Feebs. Just remember that."

"I suppose he thinks that because you are friends, he can be nosey," Phoebe said. "My sister's the same. She seems to think I owe her an explanation for everything I ever do." She paused to link her fingers with his. "But you're right. We don't have to explain ourselves to anyone."

"Except each other," Max said. "And I've done a piss-poor job of that so far."

"Well, that's where you're wrong." Her smile was so sweet it made him catch his breath. "I think we've been communicating really well recently."

"Yeah?" He stroked his thumb over her mouth.

"What if I tell you that was just the start of the conversation? We haven't even gotten onto the important stuff yet."

"I think this stuff—the talking, the kissing and the just being together is pretty amazing myself." Her smile widened. "But I'm such an amateur."

"A gifted one."

"Thank you." He loved the way she blushed. "Maybe you bring out the best in me."

He kissed her, enjoying the warmth of the sun on her lips and the hint of pine sap he could smell in her hair "I think you've got that the wrong way around, Feebs. You bring out the best in me."

She went on tiptoe to wind her arms around his neck and kissed him and he forgot about Noah and just lived in her world for a blessed moment.

"We should eat." He reluctantly let her go.

"I'm starving." She grinned at him. "This has been so much fun."

He took her hand, and they started walking toward where the others were gathered.

"Especially the bit when you roped that steer on your first try."

Luke looked up as they approached.

"Next he's going to claim that he only let the steer through so he could show off for you, Phoebe."

"You took the words right out of my mouth." Max winked at Phoebe. "Now, what would you like to eat?"

As they packed up the meal, Luke asked him to carry one set of the saddlebags over to his horse. Max obliged and buckled them in place while Luke dealt with the other set.

"Thanks for not going off at Noah," Luke said, his

attention still on securing the bags. "All I can think is that he's suffering from wedding jitters and doesn't know where to direct that anxiety."

"I don't appreciate constantly being called out. But I'm trying to be a better person here."

"I noticed," Luke said. "And if that's the effect Phoebe has on you, I'm one hundred percent behind her sticking around."

"We haven't talked about it, yet." Max was more willing to discuss this with Luke who, as his boss, needed to know his future plans more than Noah. "We're still working things out."

"I can see that." Luke patted his horse's rump and checked the girth was tight. "I just want you to know that if you do want to live here, you're both very welcome."

"Thank you." Max held Luke's gaze. "Considering all the crap I've dragged you through, I . . . appreciate that."

"Semper fidelis, right?" Luke made a face. "Apart from Dave, obviously."

"Always faithful," Max echoed his boss's words. "I'm trying, boss."

"I know." Luke punched him gently on the shoulder. "Now, why don't you go and see if Phoebe is ready to leave and if she's game for a gallop across the meadow with you."

"I'm on it," Max went to turn away and then asked. "You got another cap in your saddlebags?"

Luke rummaged around and handed him one. "Here you go."

"Thanks."

Max walked over to where Phoebe was already mounted on her horse.

"Hey." He held up the cap. "Put this on, would you?"

"Am I burning?" Phoebe took the hat and studied it "I wasn't sure if it was just embarrassment, what with me putting my foot in it every time I talk to Noah."

"Nah, it's definitely the sun." Max shaded his eyes to look up at her as she smoothed down her hair and put the cap on. "It suits you."

She fluttered her eyelashes at him. "I'm very glad to be representing Al's Feed Store. Are we heading back to the ranch now?"

"Yeah, but it should take a fraction of the time we took getting here." He nodded at Macy. "She likes a good gallop."

Phoebe visibly brightened. "She does?"

Max mounted Bouncer beside her. "Do you want to race me to the top gate?"

Phoebe gave him a seductive up and down glance. "Is there a prize?"

"I'm the prize." He waggled his eyebrows.

"How does that work exactly?"

He lowered his voice so that no one else could hear him. "You win, you get to tell me what to do tonight. I win, I get to tell you."

"Sounds fair." She nodded. "See ya."

She was gone so fast he almost swallowed his tongue.

"Hey! That's my trick!" Max yelled.

He set off after her, Bouncer's longer strides eating up the ground between them, but he couldn't quite get in front of her—wasn't even sure if he wanted to. She was riding low in the saddle like a jockey, her head almost touching Macy's neck as she allowed the horse to dictate the pace.

She reached the top gate about half a length in front of him and punched her fist in the air with triumph. "I beat you!"

"Only because you cheated." Max grinned at her as he unlatched the gate and they both went through. "But that's okay. I've been known to do that myself."

"Just so we are clear, I get to tell you what to do for the rest of the day?"

He grinned. "Nice try, but the deal is you get to be the boss in the bedroom once we're alone tonight."

She wrinkled her nose. "Are you sure it isn't for the rest of the day?"

"One hundred percent sure. Why?"

"Because if I were calling the shots, I'd be asking you to kiss me right now."

"On horseback?"

"Anywhere really." She met his gaze, her brown eyes shining. "I'm having such a lovely day, Max. I don't want it to end."

She clicked to her horse and set off again. This time Max made no effort to chase after her because he already knew she'd be right there waiting for him when he got back to the barn.

Chapter 7

Once she'd showered and changed into fresh clothes, Phoebe reluctantly checked her phone and read the long, pompous message from George, which included references not only to the entail she was currently trying to dismantle, but all the reasons he and her grandmother were using to justify not breaking it. At the end, he did try to suggest a compromise, but Phoebe wasn't impressed.

After reading the message a dozen times to make sure she understood it she sent her reply.

Offering me a different property In Scotland isn't going to work, George. I want what was left to me and I want it without any legal entanglements. Why is this so difficult to understand? I've fulfilled the conditions of Grandfather's stupid will by marrying and that's all there is to it. If you won't accept this, I will be looking for legal advice of my own and I don't care if I bring 'shame on the family' by exposing our dirty laundry. I deserve to be happy. If you keep this up, I certainly won't be bringing Max over for the wedding to justify your unnecessary curiosity.

She pressed SEND and briefly closed her eyes. All she wanted was the opportunity to use her inheritance to do some good in the world. Neither George nor her grandmother would be happy with her refusing their offer, but they were far away, and she refused to let them ruin her time with Max.

She sighed. The freedom of being on the ranch, of not having to think about her every word, was intoxicating. And Max . . .

He was wonderful.

As if she'd conjured him in her thoughts, he came through the door. His black hair was damp from the shower, and he'd put on a clean, blue T-shirt that stretched nicely across his chest and matched his eyes.

"Hey, Annie Oakley."

"Wasn't she a sharpshooter?" Phoebe asked as he came to sit beside her on the bed and took her hand.

"Yeah, I guess that's not really your thing, is it?"

She looked at him. "You think I don't know how to shoot a gun?"

His slow smile was a thing of beauty. "You do?"

"My father taught us all how to shoot when we went up to Scotland for our holidays."

"What kind of shooting?"

"Game mainly." She shrugged. "Things we could eat. I refused to stalk any stags. Oh, and clay pigeons. I was quite good at that."

"You're a woman of hidden depths, Feebs." He squeezed her fingers. "Why were you looking so thoughtful when I came in?"

"I had a text from my brother, George. He was being obnoxious again."

"Makes sense," he nodded. "I did say he was a dick."

"He's trying to fob me off."

Max frowned. "What the hell does that mean?"

"He wants to substitute what I want for something else."

"Like a bait and switch?"

"I suppose so. I told him it wouldn't be acceptable and that if he keeps me from having what is rightfully mine, I'll seek legal advice."

"Sounds expensive. But you're right to stand up for yourself." Max paused. "Are we still going back for this wedding, because it doesn't sound like it's going to be much fun?"

"I have to." Phoebe sighed. "I'm Eugenie's maid of honor." She managed a smile. "But you don't have to come."

"If you're going, so am I." He met her gaze. "We're in this together, right?"

"I hope we are, but I'd totally understand if you wanted to avoid all my family drama."

"I live for drama," Max reassured her. "Usually, I'm the one creating it, so it's interesting to watch it play out as a bystander."

"I don't know why you think you're such trouble, Max. You've been incredibly sweet to me."

"Which is not how I am to most people." He sighed. "I really am a pain in the ass, Feebs. I have a big mouth, poor impulse control, and a sack full of military trauma to process."

"Luke said you were one of the most efficient team members he'd ever worked with."

He raised his eyebrows. "You've been chatting to Luke about me?"

"I chat to everyone and they're all dying to give me their opinion of you. It's almost as if they're warning me off."

"Because they know what I'm like, and they don't want you to get hurt." Max looked grim. "I . . . lose it sometimes."

Phoebe stared at him. "Okay."

"And I don't want to hurt you."

"You won't." She leaned in and kissed him gently on the mouth. "Shall we go and eat? I'm really looking forward to my dessert."

Max looked around the table and then back at Phoebe who was chatting earnestly to Jen about flowers, or something else wedding related. She'd caught the sun today and her skin was glowing. He kept trying to tell her he wasn't a good man, but she didn't want to hear it. And if he was being honest—something he'd been working on recently—he didn't want her to look at him with disgust when he inevitably did something to horrify her.

He wasn't good at relationships. His parents had handed him over to the authorities to deal with when he was a troubled teen. After that, he'd been on his own except for Maria who'd been the only one in the family to offer him a place to lay his head when he returned from deployments.

He turned to Noah. "Hey, would it be okay if I invited my sister to your wedding?"

Noah looked intrigued. "Fine by me. But check with Jen."

"About what?" Jen asked.

"Whether I can invite my sister Maria to your wedding," Max said. "I'll take care of all the details, so you won't have anything to worry about."

"I'd love to meet her." Jen smiled. "Go for it."

"Thanks." Max smiled back. "I'm not sure if she'll be free, but I'll ask."

"She can stay in one of the new cabins if you'd like," Luke suggested. "There are a couple that are ready to be occupied and she can give us some feedback."

Luke had recently started converting some of the old ranch hand buildings and stables into smaller, self-contained apartments. His theory being—and Max didn't disagree with him—was that it might encourage people to come to live and work out in the wilds where accommodations could be pricey or nonexistent. As a construction crew had already been on the ranch building Noah and Jen's new house, it had proved a good use of their extra time. The cabins could also be used for holiday rentals if things really took off.

"I'll talk to her," Max said. "And let you know as soon as possible."

"The nice thing about having a buffet-style wedding is that you're not agonizing so much over the price of each plate of food," Jen said. "And, after seeing Bernie's menus, I think we'll be able to feed the whole town."

"Bernie sent you menus?" Noah looked up.

"Yes, because I'm in charge of that part of the wedding, remember?" Jen smiled brightly at Noah. "If you are very good, I might even share them with you, and get your opinion on the options she's offering."

"I'd appreciate that." Noah said gruffly.

Luke winked at Jen as Noah's fingers drummed on the kitchen table and he frowned into his coffee.

Max thought about saying something to rile Noah up but he couldn't be bothered. His friend was suffering enough having to relinquish control over something he desperately wanted to micromanage the hell out of. It spoke volumes about how much he loved Jen that he was willing to even try and control his worst impulses.

Jen reached over and set her hand over Noah's restless fingers.

"It'll be all right, Noah. Bernie's good at this." She squeezed his hand. "I'll show you the menus after Sky goes to bed, okay?"

"I can wait. There's no rush."

Max couldn't help grinning at that pile of horseshit, and Noah, of course, noticed.

"What's so funny?"

"Nothing." Max stood up. "Anyone want more coffee?"

Phoebe yawned and hastily covered her mouth. "Please excuse me. I had a wonderful day, Luke. Thank you for including me."

"You earned your keep," Luke said. "You're more than welcome to come out with us whenever you want."

"I heard you saved Max's bacon, Phoebe," Sally said as she accepted her refilled coffee mug from Max.

"She did." Max grinned at Sally. "And Luke's beef."

He turned to Phoebe. "I'm going to call my sister and then I'll be out at the barn if you need me."

Phoebe nodded. "I think I might turn in early, tonight. It's been a long day and I'm not used to so much exercise."

"You might be stiff tomorrow." Sally was still a physician at heart. "Get Max to rub some emu cream over your joints before you go to sleep. It does wonders."

"Oh!" Phoebe looked interested. "I've never heard of that."

"Sally forgot to mention that it's also known as the passion killer," Max said as he put his mug in the dishwasher. "So maybe wait until the morning, Feebs, and when you're out in the fresh air because it stinks to high heaven."

"I think I'll pass." Phoebe chuckled and everyone around the table joined in as she stood up. "I'll wish you all good night. I promise I'll be up bright and early to help with the barn chores."

"Not if I have anything to do with it," Max murmured in her ear as she went past him, which made her go pink. "You're going to be sleeping like a baby because I've worn you out."

He went outside and found the best cell reception spot behind the barn and called his sister's number.

"*Hola, Maria.*"

"Max!" There was a torrent of Spanish before she slowed down and remembered how badly he spoke it and resumed in English. "How are you? Did Phoebe find you okay?"

"You met Phoebe." Max nodded even though she couldn't see him. "Of course you did."

"How do you think she knew how to contact you and get you to meet her in Reno? We had a very nice visit."

Max frowned. "I guess because she wasn't at your place when I arrived. She was at the hotel where we first met. And I was so surprised to see her that I didn't get into the specifics about how she'd gotten there at all, which was stupid of me."

"Well, she turned up on my doorstep. When she told me her name, I knew who she was, because I'd seen it on some of the paperwork the Marines sent me years ago." Maria paused to take a breath. "You didn't mention anything about her to me, Max."

"I know . . . I should have told you."

There was a long silence. "I know how hard it is for you to share things, but I've always been on your side."

"You're right, I'm sorry."

"Phoebe said she'd asked you to keep everything secret, but still it would've been nice if you'd told me yourself."

"I messed up. It all happened so fast. I barely remembered to tell the Marines. I didn't mention it to Luke and Noah, either, but that's no excuse. They had a hell of a surprise when I turned up with Phoebe at the ranch this week."

"I bet they did," Maria said. "She seemed very nice. Not at all what I was expecting. She's not as flashy as some of your other girlfriends."

"She's awesome."

"I was so surprised that you were still married. Phoebe said she hadn't been sure how to contact you. She came to my house since it was the only address she had. I felt awful about that because it was my fault. A few years ago, one of the government letters said they'd added a new name and address in England, which was a surprise, so I forwarded one of the letters on to that address with a nice note. When I didn't hear back, I assumed there had been a mistake and I'd done something foolish. I didn't want to be sending any more personal information about you to someone who didn't need it, Max."

Max shoved a hand through his hair and slowly ex-

haled. It certainly explained why Phoebe had only received the basic paperwork and hadn't known how
to reach him.

"You're not to blame, Maria. I created this mess. If
I'd been straight with you from the start, it could all
have been avoided."

She surprised him by laughing. "Max, isn't that
the story of your life? If you'd ever listened to anyone's opinion apart from your own, you wouldn't
have ended up in so many scrapes."

"Okay, you got me," Max conceded. "Now, can we
talk about something else?"

"Of course."

"My buddy Noah is getting married at the end of
the month. I wondered if you'd like to come to the
ranch for the wedding?"

The silence went on for so long that he thought
they'd lost the connection.

"Hey? You still there?"

"Yes, I am. "

"I'll organize everything. All you have to do is put
on your best dress and turn up."

"You . . . want me to be there?"

He grimaced at her incredulous tone.

"Yeah, you're my family."

"Then I'd love to come." Her voice was a little
shaky. "If this is what marriage to Phoebe has done to
you, Max, I'm all for it."

"I'll email you all the details, okay?" Max said.
"And I'm really sorry, for everything."

"*Te amo, mi hermano.*"

She sounded as if she was about to burst into tears.

"Love you, too, Maria."

Max ended the call and just stood there staring out over the forest. He sucked at relationships. He'd taken his sister's love for granted and she'd ended up apologizing when the fault was all his. He didn't know how to deal with people who cared about him. Like a stray dog begging for scraps and affection, he was always anticipating the next kick and getting the nip in first.

And now he had Phoebe right there, in his bed, waiting for him to come to her so that they could make love for the first time, and he didn't want to mess that up.

"Hey." Luke came up alongside him. "You okay?"

Max put his cell away. "Just contemplating what a monumental screwup I am."

"It's good you realize that's what you are."

Max gave him the side eye. "Thanks?"

Luke shrugged. "Understanding who you are means you can start fixing what's wrong. Ask me how I know."

"Bernie's been getting at you?"

Luke smiled. "Bernie told me to get my ass to a therapist months ago. I ignored her and everyone else until I had no choice."

"What made you change your mind?" Max asked.

"Because I couldn't fake it anymore," Luke said simply.

"I don't need therapy. I know who and what I am, and it ain't pretty." Max let out a breath.

"You're not that bad, Max."

"You have no idea what I did before I joined up."

"Actually, I have some idea." Luke held his gaze. "I did get access to your records when I was recruiting our specialist team."

"And you still picked me?"

"Yeah, because you're a badass. And every team needs one of those to make it tick."

"You had Noah."

"He's a different kind of ass entirely. He's an intimidating control freak."

"Whereas I'm just a freak."

"You saved all of us on several occasions by thinking outside the box and daring to be different, so don't ever think you're not valuable." Luke punched him gently on the arm. "I'm proud to have served with you. You drive me nuts, but you still make me think and do stuff I don't necessarily want to do."

"Like tell Bernie you love her?"

Luke grinned. "I owe you big time for that, bro."

"Nah. Sometimes things are just obvious to everyone except the people involved." Max sighed. "I'd better go in before I start sobbing on your shoulder, boss. Sorry for the pity party."

He started to walk away, and Luke kept talking.

"You still don't get it, do you?"

Max looked over his shoulder. "What?"

"That this is a safe place for you. That whatever you do you'll always find a home here."

"Thanks. I appreciate that." Max said.

Luke half-smiled. "Hell. I suppose that's a start. Maybe one day you'll actually believe it."

Phoebe sat up in bed and looked at her watch. Max was taking an awfully long time to come to bed. Had she misread his intentions and scared him off with her too-obvious enthusiasm? Eugenie always said she was like an over-eager puppy too desperate for affection and George called her naive. Maybe Max had believed her when she said she was worn out from the days excursion and was waiting until she dropped off before he came to bed.

Should she text him? Even as she glanced uncertainly at her phone, which was charging on the dresser, the door opened, and Max came in.

"Hey." He smiled at her. "Not asleep, yet?"

"I—" Phoebe looked at him carefully. "Is everything all right? Did you speak to Maria?"

He took off his jacket and sat down on the side of the bed. "I didn't realize you two had met."

"It was the only address I had for you. I don't know which of us was more surprised when I rang the doorbell expecting to see you."

"I lived with her when I wasn't away with my unit." Max bent to take off his socks. "She's the only person in my family who still talks to me."

"That must be difficult," Phoebe said. "My family are incredibly exasperating, but I can't imagine life without them."

"I wasn't an easy kid to have around. I got into trouble at school and on the streets, and my parents didn't know how to stop me going down the wrong path."

"Did they try?"

"Oh, yeah. My poor mama . . ." Max shook his head. "I made her cry so many times and I pretended I didn't care. My dad hated that."

Phoebe reached for his hand, and he let her take it.

"I ended up in a gang, and then I ended up in juvenile court, and eventually I got sent to one of those military schools to teach me some manners. It kind of worked and at least it gave my parents a break."

"How old were you when that happened?"

"Thirteen or fourteen, maybe?" Max shrugged. "Old enough to know better and to understand what I was putting my folks through."

"I'm so sorry."

"Don't be. The school straightened me out and gave me a way to channel all that anger into something useful by joining the military."

"I bet your parents were proud when you did that," Phoebe said.

"They sent me a card with a hundred bucks in it, so I guess so." He started to unbutton his shirt. "They didn't come to see me graduate from boot camp, although I made sure they were invited. I wrote a couple of times when I was deployed, but I didn't hear back. Maria was the only person who bothered to keep in touch." He smiled. "She's my half sister, but she lived with us and practically brought me up."

"She was very kind to me," Phoebe said. "Once we got over the whole surprise part. She felt bad about not forwarding all the correspondence, and I felt bad because I didn't respond to her original letter."

"Why didn't you do that?"

Phoebe sighed. "Because I was too busy arguing with my family, and the whole marriage thing felt like a dream, and subconsciously I suppose I was trying not to deal with it."

"Understandable."

"Not really." She met his blue gaze. "But there are a million reasons why people don't reply properly to someone, and communications break down."

He flicked her nose. "Are you trying to make me feel better about my parents, Feebs?"

"I'm trying to remind you that we all make mistakes and have regrets." She hesitated. "Have you ever tried to get in contact with them again?"

"Nope. I figured that their lives were probably way better without me."

"You don't know that."

He put two fingers under her chin and held her gaze. "If they wanted to talk to me face to face, they could always ask Maria, and they have never done so. I respect that because I don't believe in happy endings for everyone."

"You're basically telling me to keep out of it, yes?"

"Got it in one, Feebs." He leaned in to kiss her.

"Okay."

His smile returned. "I don't for one moment believe that."

"I can't help myself," Phoebe confessed. "I always want the people around me to be happy."

"I am happy." He kissed her again. "I'm right here with you."

"That's a really sweet thing to say, but have you ever thought about, maybe . . ."

He reached across, scooped her up, settled her in his lap, and kissed her until she forgot what words were, and only wanted more of him. When she managed to pull back, she was breathing hard.

"That's not fair."

"Like I care?" He ran his fingers down her spine. "I like this game much better."

"Only because you always win," Phoebe complained. "And I don't know what I'm doing."

"For someone who says that you sure drive me wild."

"I do?"

He rolled his eyes. "You know you do, and stop wriggling on my lap."

Phoebe gave another experimental wiggle. "Oh."

"Now, seeing as you're in the driver's seat tonight, do you want to fool around a little or do you want to take a rain check and go to sleep?"

"A rain check?"

"Like a promissory note."

"Ah, an IOU." Phoebe nodded. "No, I'm quite awake now, thank you, and I'd like to proceed."

"Okay, how do you want me?" Max looked at her expectantly.

"I'm not sure." She nibbled her lip. "Maybe with less clothes on?"

"I can do that."

He finished taking off his shirt and stood up to unbutton his jeans. His boxers were navy blue and tight. He glanced inquiringly at Phoebe.

"On or off?"

"On for the moment?" Phoebe was fairly sure her voice had gone up an octave. "There's a lot of you to take in."

He opened his mouth and then closed it again.

"What?"

His dimples emerged. "I was about to make a joke that you might not understand until tomorrow morning."

Phoebe mentally reviewed their conversation. "Oh. That."

"Yeah." His smile was wicked. "I definitely want to see you do that."

She reached out her hand and ran a finger over the prominent bump in his boxers.

"I am not entirely ignorant of the male anatomy, Max."

"I'm glad to hear it." He rolled his hips, which made her fingers dig into his hardening flesh.

"When I've gone out with men in the past, I've generally found that they have expectations of what I should do for them but aren't quite as willing to reciprocate."

"I've no idea why. Going down on a woman is the best thing ever."

Phoebe cupped his balls and his breath hitched.

"Would you lie down on the bed for me, Max?"

"Sure thing, sweet pea. On my back or my front?"

"On your back, sitting up against the headboard."

He did as she asked and grinned expectantly up at her. "Are you going to hogtie me to the bed?"

"Maybe next time," Phoebe said, her gaze on his abs and the visible muscles in his arms. "Riding a horse is very good for the physique."

"So I've been told. Are you joining me or are you just lollygagging?"

She sat on the side of the bed. "I'm just appreciating you, like a fine piece of art."

"I know you're the boss, but I'd appreciate a more hands-on approach."

"I'll get there." Phoebe let her gaze linger on the breadth of his shoulders and the dark hair on his chest. "You're just so pretty to look at."

He flexed his arm muscles and placed his hands on the headboard behind him. "How about I promise not to touch you without permission?"

"I'd like that." She crawled toward him, her nightie catching on her knees. She straddled his lap and met his suddenly attentive gaze.

"You're naked under there."

"Yes." She settled against the hard bulge in his boxers. "I am."

"Nice."

"May I kiss you?" Phoebe asked.

He nodded.

She cupped his chin, gently set her mouth over his, and kissed him. He let her take her time exploring his mouth and she adored him for that. He murmured her name as she drew back and kissed her way down his throat, pausing to nip his ear, and trace her tongue along the line of his collarbone. She used her hands as well, learning the shape of him, working out what made him shiver and murmur her name under his breath like a curse. She wanted to rip off her nightie and rub herself shamelessly against him, but if she did, she wasn't sure whose control would snap first.

She looked up at him, one hand on his shoulder. "There was one man I went out with, who . . ."

Max's whole body went rigid. "What did he do?"

"He mistook my amateur enthusiasm for experience, and tried to go too fast, and scared the bejeebers out of me."

"Is he coming to your sister's wedding?"

She frowned. "I don't think so."

"Does he live nearby because I'm more than happy to go and teach him how to respect a woman."

Phoebe rolled her eyes. "I don't need you fighting my battles, Max, it was years ago." She hesitated. "And I think I was slightly to blame because I did respond to him at first and, as you know, I'm quite enthusiastic about this, and maybe he misinterpreted that."

Kate Pearce

"Stop right there. You were not to blame." He held her gaze. "He was an inconsiderate ass."

She stroked his stubbled cheek. "I know that, but what I'm trying to say is that ever since then I've worried that I'm too much of a contradiction for any man to understand."

"I understand you."

She smiled. "You don't think it's weird that someone can be so turned on that they climax before they've even had proper sex?"

"I think you just needed to meet the right man." He kissed her hard, deep, and dirty. "And, in case you've got any doubts, that's me."

She kissed him back, one hand in his hair the other roaming freely down his back, her breasts squashed against his chest. She rolled her hips, and he groaned as she moved on his cotton-covered shaft.

"You drive me wild, Mrs. Creighton-Smith-Romano. You know that, right?"

She clambered off his lap and pushed his thighs wide, her color high, and her heart thumping like a drum. She yanked at his boxers making him yelp and slowed down so she could peel them off him to reveal the hard length of his cock.

"Oh . . ." Phoebe sighed. "You *weren't* joking. There really is a lot of you to take in."

Holding his gaze, she leaned forward and licked his crown tasting the salty wetness and feeling the pulse of his heartbeat in his heated flesh.

"Feebs . . ."

"Hmm?"

"Please keep going."

She settled between his thighs, grasped the base of

his shaft, and gently squeezed. "How beautiful you are, Max."

She took her time testing him with her tongue and her fingers, working out what he loved by the hitch in his breathing and his muttered curses. As her confidence grew, she gradually sucked more of him into her mouth. And it was so easy, and natural, and deeply gratifying to *get* those reactions from him that she forgot about being nervous and just enjoyed him.

"Let me touch you, sweetheart," Max said. "Let me make you feel good."

Phoebe shook her head making him groan.

"At least take that damn flowery nightdress off."

Phoebe ignored him, her interest entirely on the fascinating feeling of his stiff flesh between her lips and how every suck made her smooth-talking cowboy lose the ability to speak at all. She loved being in control, which was exactly what Max had given her.

"Sweetheart . . . if you keep that up, I'm going to come."

She already sensed that in the way he was desperately trying not to push more of himself down her throat. He grabbed her hand and wrapped it around the base of his shaft, his fingers covering hers.

"I'm gonna . . ." He growled her name and his hand tightened around hers stopping all movement, his body rigid, his heart pounding.

"That's—" He breathed out hard and suddenly relaxed, his gaze up at the ceiling as the first tremors rippled through him.

Phoebe waited until he released her hand and flexed her fingers as she eased back.

He made a face. "Did I crush your hand?"

"It's okay. I didn't notice at the time." She pushed the hair out of her eyes and grinned at him. "That was lovely!"

"Yeah, well, not as great as this is going to be." He reached for her and rolled her onto her back, one thigh between her legs.

She held him off, her palms flat on his chest and laughed up at him.

"Back off, cowboy. Remember who's in charge? This was all for you tonight."

He raised his eyebrows, one hand stealing up inside her nightie to caress her bottom. "I can't let you go unsatisfied, sweet pea, that wouldn't be right."

"Watching you was very satisfying, I assure you."

His hand wandered between her thighs, and she tried not to moan.

"I guess, I mean here you are, all worked up, and wet for nothing?" His thumb grazed her clit and she jumped. "When you have a man right here who wants to make you scream in ecstasy?"

She regarded him seriously. "But it isn't fair."

"You're the boss tonight. You decide what's fair." Max bent his head to kiss her mound. "It just seems like such a waste not to give you what you need."

"As long as you don't think I'm taking advantage of you," Phoebe said demurely.

He looked up and frowned. "I never feel like that."

"Then, maybe just a quick one? I must confess that it won't take long for me to . . . climax."

"That's because you're a very sexy woman, Feebs." Max grinned at her and then returned his attention between her thighs. His tongue flicked over her needy bud, and she bucked her hips and grabbed his head.

His laughter vibrated against her skin setting off a wave of sensations that made her cling to him like a vine as he licked and fingered her to another roaring climax. He briefly looked up as she regained her senses and met her gaze.

"You can stop now if you like," Phoebe croaked. "We're definitely even."

"Nah." He slid another finger inside her. "You're not done yet."

"How do you know?"

"Because I promised you'd scream and that hasn't happened yet, so lie back and enjoy."

Phoebe covered her eyes and pretended to sigh even as her body readied itself for even more excitement. "If I must."

"Oh, you must. Because next time we do this I'm going to be inside you for real, so we need to practice."

He pushed her left knee wide and tugged at the skirt of her nightie. "Can we get rid of this, now?"

"And be naked together?"

"We're married."

It was her turn to grin at him. "That's right. We can do anything we want to each other."

She undid the two buttons and pulled the garment over her head. The sensation of her bare skin touching Max's was so intense she shivered. She wanted to rub herself all over him like a cat.

"Are you cold?" Max asked.

"Can you just hold me a moment?" Phoebe asked. "All of me?"

"I can do that." He stretched out over her, his hands braced on either side of her head, his knees outside hers and gently rolled them both onto their sides. His arms came around her and she tucked her head under his chin.

"This okay, Feebs?"

She nodded, caught up in the delight of finally being naked with him, and how she didn't care whether she wasn't as perfect as she thought she should be. She drew her right leg over his hip, and felt his cock harden against her stomach.

"Max . . ."

"Hmm?"

"I've been on birth control for years to control my periods. I have an implant thing."

"Yeah?"

"Which means that I won't get pregnant when, I mean, if we make love."

"We'll be making love." He kissed the top of her head. "And I'll be using protection as well."

"That's very sweet of you." Her eyes were already half-closed as he smoothed one hand up and down her back.

"Not sweet." There was a hint of steel in his voice. "When I was young and stupid, I nearly married a woman I'd met at a bar who said I'd gotten her pregnant."

"And had you?" Phoebe opened her eyes.

"No, but it taught me a valuable lesson."

"Which was?"

"Always use protection unless you are one hundred percent committed to being a father."

"Okay"

He paused. "What did you think I was going to say I learned?"

"Not to pick up strange women in bars?"

"Hey." He eased back so that she could see his face. "You picked *me* up, remember?"

"So I did." She smiled at him, and he kissed her forehead.

"Just so we're clear."

"Absolutely." She yawned, snuggled back under his chin, and closed her eyes. "Good night, Max."

"Night, Mrs. CSR."

She chuckled. "I like that. Sounds like a crime show. Much easier to say."

"You know the military. We love an acronym."

"Is that what it's called?"

"According to Luke it is. You can ask him in the morning if I got it right."

She nodded and let herself fall asleep, safe in Max's arms.

Chapter 8

Max patted Bouncer on the rear and sent him out into the pasture before closing the gate. He leaned on the fence and watched his horse graze. It was still early, and a mist hung over the forest and the foothills closing the valley in. He breathed in the sharp, pine-scented air and found himself smiling. Life was good. Phoebe was . . .

"Hey, dreamer."

He turned his head to find Luke coming down the path from the barn. "Just taking it all in, boss. You should try it sometime."

Luke stopped beside him, his gaze trained on the trees.

"I still look for snipers."

"So do I." Max sighed. "We're screwed, aren't we?"

"Probably, but we'll be heroes when the zombies turn up."

Max turned back toward the barn and Luke followed him. "Have you come up with any ideas for Noah's bachelor party?"

"Yeah, I have, actually." Max grinned. "I think Noah is going to love it."

"Maybe it would be best if you tell me about it first," Luke suggested. "Since I am his best man."

"I'll email you the details. It's not that far from here, and I promise there will be no alcohol, no strippers, and no bad surprises—except I can't wait to see Noah's face."

Luke groaned. "He's so strung up about this wedding that he might just walk out."

"He won't be able to leave if we drive him there blindfolded."

"Max . . ."

Noah came out of the barn and stared at them. "What's going on?"

"Nothing." Max gave him a bright smile. "Just talking about your big day."

"You probably know more about it than I do." Noah glared at Luke. "Jen's making sure I don't interfere."

"Then why not lie back and let her take care of things for you?" Max asked.

"Because . . ." Noah shook his head as if Max was an idiot. "*I'm* the one who should be taking care of her."

"But she's enjoying it, and if you take over, you'll spoil it for her."

"Who made you the expert on what Jen wants or how she thinks?" Noah demanded.

"No one," Max said patiently. "I'm just saying—"

"Then maybe stop talking? I don't need any advice from you on how to manage my relationship."

"There's no need to get salty, Noah," Luke intervened. "I happen to agree with Max."

"Just because Max is 'married', he's suddenly thinks he's husband of the fricking year." Noah jabbed a finger in Max's direction. "And yet he's too scared to ask Phoebe what the hell she's doing here, and whether she plans to come back or will drop him when she gets to England."

Max held Noah's stare and took a couple of deep breaths.

"Don't take your wedding jitters out on Phoebe, okay? She's been nothing but nice to you since the day she arrived."

"And why is that, Max? Don't you think it's weird how she's suddenly turned up here?"

"She has her reasons and she's a far better person than either of us." Max pushed past Noah. "I've got to get going. Go kick a rock or something and come back in a better mood."

He walked away, his hands clenched into fists, a red mist obscuring his vision. He and Noah had always had a contentious relationship and he could deal with that, but he wasn't going to let Noah insult Phoebe.

"Hey."

Noah's voice came from behind him, and Max quickened his stride.

"*Hey*!"

"What." He looked over his shoulder as Noah strode up the path toward him.

"I apologize."

"Did Luke send you after me?"

"No!"

Max stopped short and just looked at Noah.

"I was out of line going after Phoebe."

"Damn straight." Max held his gaze. "Shit-talk me all you like but leave her out of it."

"Understood." Noah grimaced. "I guess I'm wound up tighter than a clock over all this wedding stuff."

"I guess you are."

"I'm . . . not good at giving up control. But I'm trying to be better for Jen."

"Then *trust* her, okay?" Max said. "She loves you and wants the best wedding for both of you."

"Yeah." Noah swallowed hard. "I know that." He half-turned away. "Anyway, seeing as you picked up the early shift, I'll get back to work."

Max nodded and watched his friend head back down to the barn. He took a moment to compose himself before he headed up to the house to get some breakfast. Phoebe was way too good at sensing his feelings and he didn't want to worry her over Noah's stupid comments. He knew Phoebe wasn't screwing with him and nothing Noah could say would change that.

He hesitated at the front door. She hadn't said anything about coming back to the ranch with him after the wedding. But had they ever actually discussed it? Most of their conversations were about how Phoebe could get around her brother's legal blockades while they were in England. Should he ask her?

Annoyed with Noah for putting the thought in his head, he immediately dismissed it and went into the house where Phoebe was in charge of cooking breakfast for everyone. He paused at the entrance to the kitchen to watch her. She was peering into the oven, her ass up in the air, and muttering to herself, which was never a good sign.

"Boo!" Max said.

She jumped and straightened up clutching her chest. "Don't do that!"

"Sorry." He walked over to give her a kiss. Her cheeks were flushed, and she smelled like bacon and maple syrup. "What's up?"

"I'm keeping the bacon warm in the oven, and I've started the eggs, but I'm not sure how to make the pancakes. Should I start now? Do they keep?"

"They're pretty resilient." Max turned the griddle on. "Where's the batter?"

"Here." She offered him a large jug. "I just made it."

"Then how about I take care of the pancakes while you focus on the eggs?" Max suggested. "Noah and Luke won't be long."

"That would be most helpful." She smiled at him, the relief in her brown eyes obvious. "I was worried I'd mess everything up."

Max tested the heat on the griddle and started to pour circles of batter in regular intervals over the heated surface. Phoebe seemed to have forgotten the eggs and was just staring at him.

"What?"

"You're really good at that."

"I've worked in a few kitchens." He found a spatula in the drawer and tested the first pancake to see if it was ready to flip. "Can you get me a plate so I can start stacking them up?"

After breakfast Phoebe went into the bedroom and checked her phone but there was nothing from George. He hadn't contacted her since she'd rebuffed his offer and threatened not to bring Max to England with her. There was a reminder from Eugenie that if Phoebe failed to turn up for the wedding, her sister would personally fly across continents to make her sorry and haunt her in the afterworld.

Since Phoebe adored her bossy, younger sister, she wasn't worried by the threats. She texted back, reassuring Eugenie that she'd be there and that she'd be bringing Max.

What happened after that she wasn't certain. She couldn't deal with the idea that she might fail to break free of her family's outdated inheritance laws. But was she being fair dragging Max into it? He'd certainly done enough to help her already. She sank down on the side of the bed and smoothed her hand over the sheets, remembering their nights together.

He was an amazingly patient teacher and she so looked forward to his attention. He was the one insisting they didn't need to rush and that half the fun was getting to know each other. She trusted him to make things right for her and that was a beautiful thing.

She looked up as the door opened and Max came into the bedroom. He'd stayed in the kitchen to help with the washing up while Phoebe took a shower.

"Hey, sweet pea. Breakfast turned out great."

"Mainly thanks to you."

His eyebrows went up. "You did all the prep; you made the bacon, eggs, and pancake batter. All I did was pour a few circles and flip 'em."

"Maybe we're just a good team."

"You got that right." He went over to the closet and took out a rain jacket. "Any plans for the day or are you coming out with us?"

"I'm going with Jen to look at some wedding flowers."

"Sounds fun."

"She said there's a good wholesale supplier near Reno." Phoebe watched as Max put the jacket on. "Sally's home and she offered to take care of Sky."

"Which means you and Jen can have a nice day out and not worry about rushing back."

"Max, do you think Jen would be offended if I offered to pay for the flowers?"

"I'm sure she's budgeted for them, but I don't think she'd be offended if you asked," Max said. "I bet they can get expensive."

"That's true. I organized Eugenie's, and even though we're doing most of the arrangements ourselves, I was surprised at the cost."

He returned to sit next to her. "I know it's none of my business, but I don't want you to spend money you don't have just to be nice, Feebs. I mean it must have cost you a lot to come all the way out here to find me."

Phoebe stared at him. "I have money, Max."

He frowned. "I thought it was all tied up in this inheritance thing?"

"Oh, no," Phoebe waved her hand. "That's a different matter entirely. That's more about property. I have a monthly income from a trust set up by my great-grandparents, and then there's the bequest from my godmother I received when I was twenty-five, and a couple of minor family trusts. Also, I live and work at home, and I've saved most of it for years."

"Okay, excuse me if this sounds rude." Max looked like the whole idea of inherited wealth was a mystery to him, which she supposed it was. "You get money every month for doing nothing?"

Phoebe made a face. "That's one way of putting it, yes. It's not uncommon for families like mine to have provisions for family trusts that go back generations. Of course, sometimes the income is significantly smaller than it would have been when the trust was started."

"Sure." Max nodded like he was in a trance.

She sighed. "I suppose it still sounds awful however hard I try to justify it. Eugenie gives most of hers to charity because she earns a great salary and so does her future husband. Most of mine has ended up in the bank so coming to find you wasn't a problem."

He regarded her seriously. "It's okay."

"When I say it out loud it sounds dreadful, like I'm an entitled ninny."

"I don't see you like that."

"I forget how lucky I am sometimes," Phoebe confessed. "I'm so busy fighting to be free of the rest of it that I forget to be grateful for everything else." She paused to breathe. "I do have plans to use the money for good purposes, but a lot of that depends on the outcome of my current dispute with my brother over my property rights."

"I think you're doing okay." Max took her hand. "I'm glad you came to find me."

She met his gaze. "I'm glad, too."

"So, if Jen's all right with it, buy her all the damn flowers you want." He raised his hand to his lips and kissed her palm. "You're a good person, Feebs."

He got up and went toward the door. "I'd better get out there before Noah starts shouting at me."

"Was he okay today?" Phoebe asked. "He barely said a word at breakfast. I was worried he hated my cooking."

"He's just stressing about the wedding," Max said easily, but there was something in his eyes that told her there was more to the story than he was letting on. "Seeing as he ate enough for three, I don't think your food was a problem. I hope he said thank you."

"He did."

Max nodded and blew her a kiss. "Have a nice day, Mrs. CSR. Don't rush back and don't forget to buy yourself something pretty."

"Like what?" Phoebe asked.

He waggled his eyebrows. "Something soft and silky and easy to remove?"

"Oh!" Phoebe's cheeks heated. "I'll definitely look into that."

His laughter followed him down the hall. Phoebe sat on the bed until she'd stopped blushing, gathered her things, and went to find Jen.

They stopped on the outskirts of Reno at a wholesale flower nursery where they had a wonderful time walking through the aisles with an employee experienced in weddings. Phoebe wasn't surprised that practical Jen liked simple arrangements and classic flowers and that she did indeed have a budget for what she could afford in her wedding spreadsheet. After an hour of looking, they sat down in the local café to discuss their options. One of things Phoebe liked most about Jen was her straightforwardness, which allowed Phoebe to be equally direct.

Jen flicked through the photos she'd taken on her tablet and sighed. "I guess I got a little too carried away. We can't afford half of this."

Phoebe looked at the pictures. "You'd be surprised what we can do with amazing greenery and a few standout flowers."

"You're the expert." Jen smiled "Thank you for

coming with me. I wouldn't have known where to start if you hadn't asked all the right questions."

"I'm just thrilled that one of the most useless years of my life spent at a finishing school finally came into play." Phoebe took a quick breath. "If I offered to make up the difference in your budget as a wedding present to you and Noah, would you be okay with it?"

Jen looked at her for a long moment and then slowly nodded.

"Only if you promise me, you won't go mad and put yourself in debt."

"I won't. I was trying to explain to Max earlier, I'm relatively comfortable financially."

"I can't say I'm surprised." Jen grinned. "That ring you wear is probably worth more than Noah's and my savings put together."

Phoebe glanced down at her betrothal ring. "It's just because I've been lucky enough to inherit things. I've done nothing to earn them."

"That's not your fault." Jen said. "I'm only a teensy-weensy bit jealous."

"I'd quite happily swap places with you, but—" Phoebe paused. "Then I'd have to marry Noah, and I don't think that would work at all."

Jen reached over and hugged her. "Phoebe, you are wonderful, and if you want to buy some of our wedding flowers, please be my guest."

Phoebe returned the hug. "Just promise me that you won't tell Noah until it's too late for him to object."

"Don't worry about that." Jen waved her hand. "There are a whole lot of things that are going to come out in our post wedding financial debriefing that will blow his mind."

Phoebe finished her tea. "Do you want me to go and talk to the wedding coordinator about the flowers while you plot our next stop? I was wondering if there were any department stores, we might visit."

"I'll get on that," Jen promised. "And I'll check in with Sally that all's well at the ranch and that Sky is behaving himself."

Phoebe walked back across the street to the wholesalers as the sun shone down on her. It was much warmer away from the forests surrounding the ranch and she appreciated the nonstop, dazzling brightness at least for a little while. She had Jen's budget in mind alongside her vision of how the wedding should look, and for the first time in ages she felt genuinely excited to create something. She'd coordinated large events at her father's house for years and that experience stood her in good stead.

She paused at the entrance to the main shop. Was it possible she could have a business out here as a wedding and event coordinator? Was there even a need for that in Plumas County? Max hadn't really said anything about whether he wanted her to come back to the ranch with him after the wedding, but she hadn't exactly brought the matter up, either.

The sales assistant they'd spoken to earlier spotted her in the doorway, waved, and came over.

"Hi, Phoebe. Have you and the bride made any decisions?"

"Yes, we have." Phoebe said and flipped open the tablet. "Shall we start with the greenery and move on from there?"

Half an hour later, flushed with success, she came back to Jen in the café.

"It's all sorted."

"That's wonderful." Jen looked slightly relieved. "I must confess I've been dreading this task."

"Why? You had a clear vision for what you wanted, and you were able to convey that concisely to the wedding coordinator and me." Phoebe grabbed her water flask and took a long drink. "I hope you're going to love it."

"Can I see what we bought?" Jen asked.

"It's up to you, but I'd love for it all to be a surprise," Phoebe said. She didn't really want Jen to know that she'd practically doubled her budget. "I'll settle up with you after the wedding."

"You must." Jen held her gaze. "Thank you for being so kind and so gracious."

"Thank you for letting me feel part of your wedding," Phoebe replied.

Jen stood up. "I've checked in with Sky and he's having a lovely day with Sally, so there's nothing to stop us heading to the nearest mall."

"Excellent." Phoebe grabbed her handbag and gave Jen the tablet. "I'm a little short on clothes and I'll definitely need something to wear for the wedding."

"And I need a going away outfit and something beachy to wear on my honeymoon," Jen said.

"Where are you going?"

"Hawaii."

"I hear it's beautiful there."

"It is. You should get Max to take you on your delayed honeymoon."

Phoebe thought about Max in his swim shorts slowly tanning in the sun and almost swallowed her tongue.

Jen glanced at her as she unlocked the car. "You really like him, don't you?"

"Yes." Phoebe held her gaze. "He's amazing."

"I'm glad that Max has someone like you in his corner," Jen said as she hastily turned on the AC in the hot car. "He's so much happier with you around."

Phoebe got in and gingerly put on her seat belt, trying not to touch anything metal.

"I mean, I'm sure you know he's had his ups and downs with Luke and Noah, but hopefully that's all in the past." Jen adjusted her sunglasses and waited for the navigation system to load before leaving the parking lot. "He's always been very sweet to me, but he and Noah are like two prickly hedgehogs trying to play nice sometimes."

"I've noticed." Phoebe sat back as Jen turned right and headed for the freeway. "I was slightly disconcerted when I first heard them sniping at each other."

"Me too, but I know that if it came down to it, Noah would do anything for Max and vice versa. They just have a funny way of showing it."

Phoebe chuckled. "That's definitely true. I still have a lot to learn about Max."

"Don't we all." Jen increased her speed as they joined the freeway. "None of us knew he had a sister until recently."

"He told me he doesn't have any other contact with his family," Phoebe said.

"I didn't know that either, but it explains a lot. Families are complicated. I lost most of mine when I was fostered out, and I don't really have strong enough ties with any of them to want them at my wedding." Jen glanced at Phoebe. "At least it keeps the guest list down because Noah has three sisters and a mom he adores."

"I live and work with my family and sometimes it gets very claustrophobic," Phoebe said. "I spent three years caring for my dying father and hardly ever left his side."

"That must have been hard."

"I wanted to do it because I loved him very much, but it *was* hard." Phoebe let out a breath. "And sometimes I felt like I couldn't breathe without someone telling me I was doing it wrong. I lost myself somewhere."

"That doesn't sound like much fun."

"It wasn't. The longer I spend apart from my family the better I feel, and then I have guilt because I know that in their hearts, they think they know what's best for me, and they can't understand why I won't just fall in line and do my duty."

"Sounds like you could do with putting some space between you," Jen said. "Or, as my therapist used to say, establishing some boundaries."

"I'm trying," Phoebe said, shifting in her seat. "I'm just not very good at it yet."

Jen reached over and patted her clenched hands. "You're here with Max. I'd say that was a good start."

"Yes." Phoebe found a smile. "I suppose it is."

Chapter 9

"Max? Can I have a word?" Luke poked his head out of the ranch office as Max went past.

"What have I done, now?" Max asked as he changed course and went into the office.

Luke closed the door and went to sit behind his desk. From what Max could tell nothing had changed in the room since Luke's grandad had decorated it back in the 1950s. There were pictures of Luke and his dad excelling at everything at school and college and loads of family photos. Max kind of understood why Luke didn't want to change anything. It was like he was surrounded by his family cheering him on.

Luke tapped his laptop screen. "This plan for Noah's bachelor party."

"It's great isn't it? It's local, there's no hard liquor involved, no women, and definitely no gambling."

"When the hell did Olly become involved in the entertainment business?"

"He didn't." Max sat down and crossed one ankle over the other. "He's merely the facilitator of the forest space we'll be occupying."

"Do his bosses know he's doing this?"

"Yup, it's all sanctioned by the authorities. Olly said it's some kind of pilot program to help them make money in an environmentally conscious way."

"By letting us have a bachelor party in the middle of their forest?" Luke looked unimpressed, but Max was enjoying himself.

"Is this skepticism because Olly dated Bernie?"

Luke frowned. "It's got nothing to do with it. We hardly know the guy and it just doesn't sound legit."

"I've talked to Olly, his boss, and the service providers involved, and everyone is on board with it. And we got a great rate because we're their first customers. All we have to do is provide some feedback after the event and we're golden." Max sat forward. "Come on, Luke. It's going to be fun."

Luke studied his keyboard as if he'd forgotten how to type. "I've . . . been having some trouble getting away from the ranch."

"I noticed that." Max aimed for a neutral tone. It was not the time to crack a joke.

"I guess that's what's bothering me—that I'll get there and lose it or something. But I want to do it for Noah. I'm his best man." Luke finally looked up at Max. "I just can't be one hundred percent certain I won't panic."

"Maybe you should take your own truck, so that if it gets too much, you can leave," Max suggested. "I can take over. Noah would understand."

Luke sighed and stretched his arms over his head. "I guess. Bernie thinks it would be good for me to try."

"And she knows you better than anyone, boss."

Max was quietly impressed Luke had even admitted that he had a problem. One of the reasons why

Max had recently left so abruptly was because of Luke's refusal to acknowledge his PTSD. It wasn't the only reason, but he'd certainly gotten tired of being told he was the one with the problems while his two best buddies were busy screwing up their own lives.

"Okay," Luke said. "Let's do this."

"Awesome." Max rubbed his hands together. "Now, all we have to do is persuade Noah to let us take him somewhere mysterious in my truck."

Luke groaned and put his hands over his eyes.

Max was still smiling when he left the office. He went outside just as Jen's truck pulled up and stopped to welcome the ladies home.

"Max!" Jen grinned at him. "Did I ever mention how great Phoebe is, and how lucky you are to have her?"

"Nope, but you're right." He glanced over as his wife came around the truck. "Hey, sweet pea, did you have fun?"

She walked into his arms as if it was the most natural thing in the world and kissed him. She wore a new red lipstick and smelled as if she'd been trying on a few perfumes in a store.

"We had a lovely day."

"Can you help with some of the bags?" Jen asked as she raised the tailgate to reveal a mountain of purchases.

"Holy cow," Max whistled. "You girls really did go to town."

He stood patiently while Jen loaded him up like a pack mule. Even then there was still enough for both women to carry multiple bags.

"I had to get a few things for my honeymoon," Jen explained she grappled with the screen door, one bag held in her teeth. "Is Noah around?"

"Nope, he's in town at the feedstore." Max stuck the toe of his boot in the door so that they could all get through.

"Good," Jen said. "Although I'm not sure how I'm going to hide all these bags from him."

"Ask Sally. She's got plenty of space."

"Space for what?" Sally came into the kitchen holding Sky on one hip. "My! You have been busy!" She smiled at Jen. "You can use my extra closet to store anything you'd like."

"Thanks." Jen grinned and turned to Sky. "Hey, buddy! Did you have a good day?"

"Es." Sky nodded.

"I can't wait to hear all about it."

Jen and Sally went off together with Max following along behind. Phoebe turned into their bedroom with her bags after the rest of them went by.

"You can set them down here, Max. Thank you," Jen said.

Max pretended to stagger as he put down the multitude of bags and groaned when he straightened up.

"What have you got in there? Pure gold pants?"

"Yes, that's exactly what I got, Max. Noah's going to love them." Jen patted his arm. "Could you possibly make me a cup of coffee? I could use a jolt of energy."

"Sure." Max closed the door and went down the hall to his bedroom. He looked inside to see Phoebe with her head in one of her bags.

"Hey, would you like a drink?"

She looked up. "Yes, please. I'm parched. Jen really knows how to shop."

"No kidding. Did you have fun, too?"

"Yes, I bought something to wear for the Hen Do, the wedding, and a couple of other things."

"You can give me a fashion show after dinner if you like." Max did a double take. "Hold up. What's a Hen Do?"

"It's what they call a bachelorette party in England."

"Okay, so does that mean a bachelor party is a cock a do?"

She grinned at him. "Funnily enough it doesn't. It's called a stag night."

"Makes total sense—not." He nodded. "I'll get you some tea. Sally's cooked lamb for dinner. It's roasting in the oven along with the veg and potatoes and will be ready when we are."

"Thank you, Max."

"Did it go okay with the flowers?"

"Yes. Jen was very open to the idea," Phoebe said. "She let me pick from her selections. I'm just hoping I can do her and Noah justice."

"I'm sure you will."

Max continued along to the kitchen, whistling as he went. He liked seeing Phoebe in his bedroom. When she'd arrived back at the ranch with Jen and come over to hug him it had been the best feeling in the world. She fitted in well as if she'd always lived there. He reminded himself that it was an illusion and that her real home was thousands of miles away in a different country and probably a different world.

Why would she want to move in with him and live in one room on a ranch someone else owned when she probably had a huge family home to float around back in England? He couldn't compete with that or her money. For the first time he wished he could, but they'd agreed to a no-strings marriage and an amicable divorce once Phoebe's legal issues were sorted out. He had no claim on her, and she certainly hadn't talked about them having a future together beyond that.

And why should she?

Max paused as he reset the coffee to run, put on the kettle, and got out some mugs. What the hell was he thinking anyway? He'd never wanted to be tied down by anyone or anything. Even living at the ranch with people who tolerated him got claustrophobic sometimes and he had to get away. Would Phoebe let him come and visit her in England when they were no longer married?

"Hey."

He looked up to see Noah staring at him.

"Hi." Max held up a mug. "Do you want coffee?"

"Sure." Noah came closer. "I see Jen's back."

"Yeah, she's just chatting to Sally about Sky's day. I said I'd take her some coffee."

"I can do that."

"Sure. I've got to make Phoebe some tea, which takes longer."

He went into the pantry to find a tea bag. When he returned Noah was watching the coffee drip through with great concentration.

"You okay?" Max asked.

"I was just about to ask you the same thing. You looked like your favorite horse had died when I came in. I was wondering if Phoebe had left you."

"Not yet. She definitely came back with Jen." Max got the milk out of the refrigerator.

Phoebe had given him a long, earnest talk about the proper preparation of a cup of tea, which included on-the-boil water from a kettle, *never* microwaved, a significant pause for the tea to brew before removing the bag, and a dash of milk to complete the process.

"It's okay to worry about what's going to happen between you in the future, Max," Noah said.

"I'm not worried."

Noah just looked at him. "Dude, you like Phoebe, you want her to stick around, and you don't know how to deal with it."

"I think you're talking about past you and Jen, bro." Max waited until the kettle whistled, took it off the range, and poured the boiling water over the tea bag. "And, hey, even you worked it out in the end, so if I wanted to do something, it can't be that hard, but I don't. Phoebe and I understand each other and we're both getting exactly what we need from our relationship, okay?"

"If you say so."

"I do." Max made himself hold Noah's skeptical gaze. "I'm not like you, Noah."

"Ain't that the truth." Noah picked up the mug of coffee. "I'll take this to Jen. Where is she?"

"Last time I saw her she was talking to Sally." Max stirred the tea bag in the approved manner. "Just listen out for Sky and you're sure to find them."

Noah actually smiled. "We're taking a walk over to the new house after dinner. Do you and Phoebe want to tag along?"

"I'll check with Feebs, but I know she's been looking forward to seeing your new place so assume it's a yes."

Noah nodded and walked away, leaving Max staring at the brewing tea. He squeezed the tea bag against the side of the mug with a spoon and dumped it in the compost bucket. He added a dash of milk, as Phoebe called it, and took the mug to his bedroom. If he was being honest, he was getting pretty damn tired of his friends constantly questioning his relationship with Phoebe. He tried to remember they were coming from a place of concern, but he'd never taken well to being questioned or doubted. It just made him want to do something stupid.

"Here you go. It's hot and—" He grinned as he saw his lovely wife had fallen asleep on top of the patchwork quilt, her legs sprawled out like a newborn colt. "It will keep."

He set the mug down beside her and quietly left the room. He'd wake her up in time for dinner. He was already looking forward to walking through the forest with her to see Noah and Jen's new house. And *he* wasn't going to question why such a simple thing made him feel so happy. Sometimes it really was easier just to live in the moment.

The wind was already murmuring through the trees with a rising note of complaint and Phoebe decided to tie her hair back before they left for, what Max assured her, was a short walk through the forest. She came out of the bathroom and went to collect her thickest sweater from the bedroom. She'd discovered that when the sun went down behind the towering mountain ranges the temperature dropped off alarmingly.

"Hey!" Max was also there putting on a fleece over his T-shirt. "I almost forgot. I got you something when I was in town the other day."

"You did?" Phoebe went still when he offered her a small jewelry box.

"Yeah." He was looking anywhere, but at her. "I had this gold nugget I found in a creek once, and I got the jeweler to make you a wedding ring."

She slowly opened the box. "Oh, Max . . ."

"I know you have your other fancy ring, but I wanted you to have one from me." He cleared his throat. "It's yours whatever happens, okay?"

She swallowed hard and turned toward him, her voice shaking. "Will you put it on my finger for me, Max?"

He took the ring and gently slid it home. "Here's to you, Mrs. CSR."

"It's beautiful. I'll treasure it for the rest of my life." She looked up at him and was caught by the intensity of his stare. "Max . . ."

He smiled and turned away from her. "I got you something else, too.

Phoebe fought to regain her composure and accepted the bulky box he handed her. She tried to match his casual tone. "Two gifts in one day?"

"You'd better see what it is before you get too excited," Max said. "But if you're gonna be a real cowgirl you need one of these."

She opened the box and found a white, straw cowboy hat with a teal band.

"It's beautiful, Max."

Phoebe took it out of the box and turned to the mirror in the front of the old oak freestanding wardrobe. She set it carefully on her head and stared at her reflection.

"If it's too big, or you don't like it, you can exchange it at the store." Max came up behind her, put his arms around her waist, and rested his chin on her shoulder. "You look great. I figured you needed something to keep the sun out of your eyes when you're getting your cowgirl on."

She studied her reflection and that of the smiling man behind her and swallowed hard.

"It's perfect. Thank you."

"Hey." He met her gaze in the mirror. "Don't cry, sweet pea. It was supposed to make you happy."

"I am happy." She tried to smile. "It's just that no one's ever given me such a thoughtful present before."

She turned in his arms, looped her hands around the back of his neck and kissed his mouth.

"You really are the sweetest man, Max." He went to speak, and she put a finger on his lips. "I don't want to hear you telling me that's not true."

She kissed him again and this time, although he muttered something under his breath, he kissed her until a shout from the kitchen made him ease back.

"Noah's ready to go."

Phoebe smiled up at him. Was it wrong of her to wish Max wanted more from her? She'd set the rules for their relationship, and he'd played along with grace and good humor. He liked her, but, as for anything else, she had no right to even ask.

"My hat stayed on." Phoebe touched the brim.

"Which means you're the real deal, Phoebe." Max winked. "But you might want to substitute a beanie for this trip. It's getting windy out there."

Phoebe carefully set the hat back in its box and put on the beanie Max offered her. He held out his hand and they went to the kitchen where Noah and Jen were waiting for them.

"I thought you'd changed your mind." Noah was already consulting his watch.

"Nah, Phoebe was kissing me, and I had to hang around for that," Max said.

"That's correct," Phoebe said. "He got me a beautiful cowboy hat."

For some reason it felt too personal to mention the ring,

"How sweet!" Jen grinned at Max. "I never realized you had it in you to be so thoughtful."

"She kept borrowing mine," Max didn't miss a beat. "I had to do something."

Noah was already heading for the door. "Shall we get going? None of us want to be out in the forest at dusk."

Jen touched Phoebe's shoulder as she went by. "I really hope you like what we've done."

"I'm sure it will be lovely," Phoebe said as she put on her ski jacket and borrowed wellies. Max and Noah had picked up large flashlights in case they were needed for the return journey and were waiting for them outside.

"It's not far," Noah said. "And once we get the driveway paved it will be a lot easier."

"When's that being done?" Max asked as Phoebe came up alongside him.

"Next week. Just before the wedding." Noah grimaced. "Not ideal but you know how hard it is to get contractors to come out here."

He set off, adapting his long stride to match Jen's, who hung on his arm, their heads close together as they talked.

"Luke's not coming?" Phoebe asked Max.

"He's keeping an eye on Sky." Max paused. "He's also not a fan of being out in the forest in the evenings."

Phoebe thought about all the implications of that simple statement. "But you're okay with it?"

"Mentally I'm still anticipating an ambush at any point, but I think I have it in hand. Last winter, we had terrible snowstorms. Luke fell off his horse and broke his arm. We were lucky to find him before he froze to death."

Phoebe shivered. "The poor man."

"He was stuck in the snow for hours. I think it stirred up his worst memories," Max said. "He's been struggling ever since."

"Is he . . ." it was Phoebe's turn to pause. "Getting help for that?"

"He is now. Bernie persuaded him it would be a good idea to stop talking about doing it, and actually find a therapist."

"Thank goodness." Phoebe glanced inquiringly at Max.

"I don't need therapy, Feebs. I've been fighting all my life. I know what I went through and why it still pisses me off sometimes." He shrugged. "My problem is learning how to deal with my big mouth and how it affects my buddies in peace time."

"You can hardly blame yourself for what happened to Luke in a snowstorm," Phoebe pointed out.

"Sure, I can." His smile was tight. "He wouldn't have been out in the middle of a snowstorm if it hadn't been for me. I went AWOL."

"He didn't have to go out, Max," Phoebe said gently.

"He still thinks of himself as my commanding officer so of course he did."

"And that's not on you, either."

Max came to a stop and looked down at her. "You don't have to fight my battles, Feebs."

"And you don't get to tell me what I can and cannot do, Max."

For a moment, they locked gazes and then Max looked past her down the path.

"We better catch up."

"Fine." Phoebe started off again, aware that she had bumped up against one of Max's invisible boundaries and that she didn't have the right to demand answers from him. "I can't wait to see the house."

She stomped off ahead of him, her gaze fixed firmly on Noah and Jen. To her surprise, the path opened up to a sizable clearing surrounded by a timber fence where a brand-new, single-level ranch house constructed from wood and stone now stood. It was square shaped with four windows on either side of the front door and appeared to widen at the back.

"It's amazing," Phoebe called out to Jen as she slowly spun around to get the full effect. "It looks like it belongs here."

"It kind of does," Jen said. "We used reclaimed redwood and pine from the forest around us to build it, which made it much more affordable."

Noah actually smiled at Phoebe. "We were lucky that this pad was cleared years ago when Luke's great-uncle had a house here. It meant we didn't have to take out any big trees since they'd already been removed."

"Can we go in?" Phoebe was aware that Max had come up behind her, but for some reason she wasn't ready to speak to him yet. "Is it all finished inside?"

"I hope so," Jen said. "Seeing as we're planning on moving in when we get back from Hawaii."

"It's pretty much done," Noah opened the front door and stood back to let Phoebe go ahead of him. "Just some of the carpet and the electrical items left to install."

Jen snapped on the lights and Phoebe caught her breath.

"Oh, my goodness." She walked toward the vast floor-to-ceiling window at the rear of the house that looked over the foothills, the forest, and the mountains beyond still capped with snow. "This is *amazing*."

"Probably not the best idea in the winter, but we wanted to look at something pretty," Jen said. "And it's all triple glazed and very well insulated." She glanced over at Noah. "I told you it would be worth the cost."

"And you were right," Noah said, his gaze not on the spectacular view, but firmly on Jen. "As always."

Max snorted. "The power of love never ceases to blow me away." He came to stand beside Phoebe and looked out at the astounding view.

"Shut up, Max," Noah said without heat.

"Do you like it, Feebs?" Max asked as he drew her into a side hug.

"I love it."

She really had to get over being disappointed about something she hadn't asked for or earned. One day, Max would meet someone who would make him feel like Noah felt about Jen and she would be the first to congratulate him. The only reason he'd agreed to marry her in the first place was because he had no intention of settling down. He'd done it because he appreciated a good joke and that was it.

While Max and Noah talked construction, Jen walked Phoebe through the four bedrooms, utility room, and back into the large kitchen/ family room talking about all the things they'd tried to include within their budget and their plans for the future. At one point, she stopped and grinned.

"I guess I'm gushing, but this is so special to me. It's the first time I've ever had my own home." She shrugged. "I got shuffled all over the place when I was in foster care. I never had a sense of place or that I was safe."

Phoebe hugged her hard. "It's amazing, Jen. I can't think of anyone who deserves it more, or who will make this into as an extraordinary home."

"Thank you," Jen said in a muffled voice. "Now, try and persuade Max to build you a house next door and we can bring up our kids together."

Phoebe glanced over her shoulder, but Max and Noah were out in the yard and couldn't hear them.

"You should, Phoebe." Jen eased back to look at her. "Shall I ask him for you?"

"I don't think Max and I have that kind of relationship yet," Phoebe said carefully. "And I don't want to scare him off."

Jen grinned. "Max is known as the great escape artist."

"What are you saying about me, Jen?" Max had come back in.

"Just the truth," Jen said.

Max's blue gaze met Phoebe's. "Don't believe a word of it, sweet pea. Get your information straight from the horse's mouth,"

"Horse's ass more like," Noah muttered. "With your amazing ability to disappear, you're a whole circus all by yourself."

Max grinned. "Your house is awesome, Noah. You must be very proud."

Noah looked at him for a long moment. "Yeah, I am."

"Did you know Max did a lot of the carpentry, Phoebe?" Jen spoke into the sudden silence. "He hand-finished all the kitchen cabinets for us."

"They look amazing." Phoebe ran her fingers over the rippling wood panel of one of the doors.

"It sure saved us a lot of money," Noah added.

"Yeah, because you didn't have to pay me," Max said.

"When did you learn that skill?" Jen asked.

"Military school. It was that or the mechanics shops, and I was banned from touching any cars after I hot-wired a couple and took them out for a spin."

"Sounds about right for you." Noah grinned.

Max nodded. "Saved our bacon a couple of times on tour, too." He swept his hand over the kitchen countertop. "I enjoy working with wood. It's relaxing."

"I hadn't noticed," Noah said. "You were cursing up a storm every time I saw you in here."

"That's because I'm a perfectionist," Max replied, his gaze lingering on Phoebe who pretended not to notice. "When I do something, I like to get it right."

Phoebe turned to Jen. "Is it okay if I go out to the garden before the light fails?"

"Go ahead." Jen paused. "Actually, I'll come with you. I'd love some advice as to what to plant where. You already know that's not my strength."

Max stayed where he was as Phoebe and Jen went out into what would become the garden. The sun was hovering over the top of the distant mountains and would drop behind them in the next half an hour. He knew Phoebe wasn't happy and that bugged him far more than it should. He didn't like her thinking he was some kind of hero when he absolutely wasn't, and yet he didn't want to do anything that made her think less of him.

If he hadn't been in Jen's new kitchen where he'd painstakingly finished the cupboards himself, he would've kicked something. And why did it matter what Phoebe thought of him? He was doing her a no-strings-attached favor and that was all there was to it.

Behind him Noah cleared his throat.

"Max . . ."

"You know how you're always telling me to keep my mouth shut?" Max said without turning around. "Can you apply it to yourself?"

"There's another pad to the right of this one where Luke's great-uncle had his barn," Noah said. "It would make a great spot for a house."

Max briefly closed his eyes. "Thanks, I'll bear it in mind."

"For the record, I think Phoebe's good for you. Jen really likes her."

"Jen likes everybody." Max paused. "Except Dave, obviously."

"She's a good judge of character and if she says Phoebe's okay, I'll go along with that."

"Whoop-de-do," Max said. "Thanks for nothing."

He turned around to see Noah was smiling, which was unnerving.

"*What?*"

"You're totally into her." Noah nodded. "Why didn't I see it earlier?"

"Because there's nothing to see, and even if there was, it isn't any of your business."

"It's kind of amusing." Noah picked up his keys.

"Not half as amusing as watching you fall flat on your face for Jen," Max retorted.

"Ah, so you admit the situations are similar?"

"Hell no!" Max made himself smile. "Phoebe and I are an old married couple, not like you two newbs."

Jen came back in with Phoebe and shut the sliding door behind them. The temperature was dropping rapidly as a faint mist crawled over the snow-covered summit and crept into the valley.

"When's your anniversary, Max?"

He looked at Phoebe who rolled her eyes.

"He never remembers. One year he sent me flowers two weeks early."

"It's the time zones. I get confused." Even though he knew Phoebe was making stuff up to defend him, Max kept it going. "I do know it's coming up soon, right?"

"Yes, it's a few days after your wedding, actually, Jen," Phoebe said.

"Then you can celebrate in peace," Jen declared. She wagged her finger at Max as she went past him. "You'd better take her somewhere nice this year to make up."

"I'm working on it." Max waited for Phoebe to exit before he followed her out. "I hear that new chef at Lucy's B&B is excellent."

"She is," Jen said. "Noah took me there a few weeks ago when he asked me to marry him. Not that I remember much about the food, I was too stunned when Noah got down on one knee in the middle of the dining room."

"Didn't he wait until you'd finished eating?" Max asked.

"You know what he's like, Max." Jen grinned. "He wanted it all done before we'd even ordered."

They walked back along the gravel driveway and Noah put on his flashlight. Max drew Jen back and linked his arm through hers.

"Any ideas how I can convince Noah to come out for his bachelor party?"

"Apart from knocking him unconscious?" Jen asked.

"Luke says I can't do that."

"Hmm, I'll have to think about it. He's not very keen on the idea of *me* going out, let alone him."

"What if I suggested a quick drink at a bar, just the three of us?"

"That might work." Jen didn't sound convinced. "Although, he's so uptight about the whole wedding day that he might not want to risk any alcohol beforehand."

Max sighed. "I can hardly ask him to accompany me to an opera or a jazz concert. He'd never believe that for a second."

"I'd get Luke to handle it. Noah listens to Luke."

"True, and Luke *is* his best man." Max nodded. "But try and get him into the right frame of mind, would you? It would really help."

"I'll do my best." Jen agreed. "Now, I'd better go and talk to him because he's looking suspicious."

Max looked up to see Noah glowering in his direction. He held up his hands.

"Nothing to see here, bro."

Noah only broke off his gaze when Jen slipped her hand into his and directed his attention at her. Max let out his breath and went to find Phoebe who was staring back at the skyline.

"We'd better get a move on before it gets dark and the mountain lions get hungry."

"You have real lions out here?"

Max shrugged. "So I've been told."

"Then, we'd definitely better get going." She sped up to match his stride. "The house is lovely."

"Yeah, and so convenient for work."

She glanced over at him, her usual calm smile back in place. "You should build one for yourself. Jen was saying there's plenty of space on the ranch and that Luke would be delighted if you settled here."

"Did she now."

He found his flashlight and turned it on, illuminating the clouds of small flies that followed them everywhere.

"It's a wonderful spot, Max."

"You don't have to convince me."

"I've always lived in old houses. I can't imagine how nice it would be to decide exactly where you want everything to go and then build it."

For a second, he wondered whether she was making a pitch to design a house with him, but instantly shut it down. He was a coward. He didn't want to have that conversation and hear her say she was never coming back.

"How old is your dad's place?"

She didn't reply immediately and looked down at her boots.

"Is it a century house?"

"That's not old, Max." She paused. "The main part of the house—the bit when it was just a castle and keep—dates back to Norman times."

"Which was when exactly?"

"Around 1070? It's listed in the Doomsday Book. The theory is that one of William's knights built a defensive motte and bailey on the land he was given by the king, and then constructed the stone castle and moat over a period of ten years."

"Wait." Max stopped walking. "You live in a fricking *castle*?"

"Well, one wing does contain the original tower and the medieval hall was incorporated into the later rebuilds, so I suppose you could say that." She wrinkled her nose. "The rest of it is just a house that has been redesigned for centuries and now looks like a Georgian mansion in the Palladian style."

"Do you have pictures?"

Phoebe looked at him. "Yes, but can we wait until we get inside? It's getting rather chilly out here."

"Sure, yeah, of course." He took her hand and started walking again.

The only sign of Noah and Jen was the beam of light dancing over the trees and path ahead of them and the gentle murmur of their voices.

Phoebe was grateful to reach the house and they hurried inside, shedding their coats and boots in the mudroom before gathering in the kitchen where Luke was organizing coffee and hot chocolate. He reported that Sky had gone to bed without any issues.

"Phoebe lives in a castle," Max said.

"Like a real one?" Luke asked as he poured the coffee into mugs and handed them to Max and Noah.

Phoebe considered what to say. She'd grown used to downplaying her background because a lot of people thought she was boasting or treated her differently when they knew. She hoped that none of the people on Nilsen Ranch would be like that.

"As I explained to Max, the original Norman keep was absorbed into the house and forms one wing of the whole thing."

"Norman?" Luke asked. "That's eleventh century, correct?"

"Yes. Our family has been there a long time." Phoebe accepted her mug of hot chocolate from Luke with a grateful smile. "Obviously there have been some hiccups along the way when they supported the wrong king or pretender to the throne, but we managed to survive." She sipped her drink. "Family policy was for one son to support one party and the second to support the other, which generally meant the house and land stayed in family hands."

"That's fascinating," Luke said. "I can't even imagine one family living in one place for so long."

"It's a lot of history on one's shoulders," Phoebe said. "I'm glad I won't inherit because it's getting harder and harder financially to maintain the place."

"It's like in *Downton Abbey*, right?" Jen said. "One guy inherits everything?"

"Yes, that would be my oldest brother, George."

"Lucky old George," Noah muttered.

Phoebe sat at the table and got out her phone. "Would you like to see a couple of pictures I took on my birthday last year? We had a small party in the rose garden."

Everyone, including Noah, gathered behind her chair as she found the photos on her phone. Seeing her home looking so glorious gave her a twinge of homesickness.

"Here we are on the croquet lawn. You can see the castle turret and the side of the main house behind us."

She flipped through a few of the photos and Jen and Luke asked a million questions she tried hard to answer.

"Is that your sister?" Jen asked. "She looks like you."

"Yes, that's Eugenie and her husband-to-be, Anthony. He works at the same IT consulting firm as she does. They are very well matched. My younger brother, Arthur was away with his regiment when I took these photos."

"And that's your granny?" Jen smiled. "She reminds me of Noah."

"Same intimidating expression," Luke murmured.

"She looks like she's the boss to me," Noah said.

"She is," Phoebe said. "She loves to tell everyone, especially my brother George, what to do."

She studied the faces of her loved ones, all smiling determinedly at the camera, and for the first time in her life tried to view them dispassionately. There was an empty chair at the table, which was hers, and yet her family looked complete without her. And why was she the one taking the photos when it was supposed to be her birthday? She tried to remember if anyone had bothered to take a picture of her.

Forgetting she had an audience, she flicked forward on her phone and found one picture Eugenie had sent of her blowing out the candles on her cake.

Max cleared his throat. "You look beautiful, Feebs."

"Thank you, Max." Phoebe set her phone face down on the table, her thoughts swirling in a conflicted mess. "Now, I really should drink my hot chocolate before it gets cold."

Chapter 10

Phoebe undressed slowly and got into bed, leaving the lamp on beside her. She still hadn't heard back from George, which was most unusual, and she needed to know whether to book Max a ticket to England or not. She grabbed her phone and typed fast.

George. I need a decision from you regarding my return for the wedding. Please get back to me ASAP. Thanks x.

She hit SEND and waited to see if the message was delivered, or if George was going to respond, and then remembered the time difference and set the phone down. He'd see it when he got up and hopefully, he would get back to her soon.

She lay back against the pillows, appreciating the quiet now that she was safely inside, and wondered what Max was doing. She'd left him in the kitchen talking to Luke. Was he asking for permission to build his house next to Noah's as Jen had suggested? Phoebe tried to imagine a life on the ranch, working the cattle surrounded by friends and family who cared about you.

But Max hadn't suggested she share that dream with him. In fact, he'd changed the subject when she'd referred to it even obliquely. It seemed clear that neither of them wanted to talk about what might happen after the visit to England. It was all well and good living in the moment and enjoying each other's company, but at some point, they needed to have a serious discussion. One she was dreading, because the thought that he'd just wave goodbye and never think of her again was excruciating.

Max came in and halted at the door.

"I thought you'd be asleep."

"Would you rather I was? I can pretend if you like," Phoebe said a tad sharply. "We're supposed to be friends. You don't have to talk to me if you don't want to."

Max raised his eyebrows. "What's up, sweetheart?"

"Me, obviously, when I was supposed to be asleep."

Phoebe was aware she sounded a little snippy, but she'd had an unexpectedly emotional day.

Max sat on the bed and looked at her. "You seem upset."

"Why on earth would I be upset? It's not as if you just told everyone I live in a bloody castle and now they all think I'm a snob."

She wasn't sure where that had come from, but it would do.

"I . . . didn't realize it was a secret. I'm sorry." He looked down at the floor. "I guess I was just surprised, and I thought it was cool, so I blurted it out like an idiot. I told you I had a big mouth."

Phoebe pressed her lips together.

"For the record," Max said in a gentle tone, "I

don't think anyone here thinks less or more of you for where you were brought up."

"So, you're implying that the only snob here is me."

He exhaled. "Phoebe . . . all I'm trying to say is that stuff is seen differently in the US than from where you're from."

"It's fine. I just hate having to . . . explain everything."

"Are you trying to pick a fight with me?" Max asked cautiously. "Because if I've screwed anything else up, I'd rather you just told me to my face."

Phoebe had never been good at arguing, which was why she always ended up on the losing side of most of them. She shook her head.

"I'm the one who should be saying sorry. I don't really know what I'm cross about and, you're right. It's not fair to take it out on you."

Max studied her carefully and then reached for her hand.

"Do you want to talk it out?"

"I don't expect you to listen to my silly problems, Max." Phoebe hated the catch in her voice as she responded to his kindness. "And it's just family stuff that I don't understand myself or know how to unravel."

"Then how about you try things the Max way, and just let me hold you so you can cry it out, fight me, or kiss me?"

She stared at him. "I believe that's the Max way of avoiding the tough questions, isn't it?"

"Maybe." He smiled. "But it works."

"You are incorrigible."

"I'm a 'live in the moment' kind of guy, Feebs. I don't think it's healthy to worry about things you can't change or get your panties in a wad about the future. A lot of people get so hung up on those things that they forget the whole appreciating being alive part."

"But don't those things impact who you are today?" Phoebe asked.

"Sure, they do, but I deal with problems if they pop up, and don't worry about them if they don't."

Phoebe stared at him. Was he giving her a clear warning not to bring up their future? "I can't imagine living my life like that."

"That's because you belong to a family that's tied to the past big-time."

She looked down at their joined hands and took a quick breath. "Sometimes I don't think they like me very much."

He didn't say anything, but she saw the sympathy in his eyes.

"For example, for the birthday party in those pictures last year I had to organize the party, bake the cake, make the sandwiches, remind everyone to turn up and then clear it all away when they all had more important things to get on with. They barely spent two hours with me, and most of that time was them 'joking' about how I'd never had a real job, had an imaginary husband, and that I'd basically better resign myself to being Grandmother's companion when she needed me. Ha, bloody ha."

"That sucks," Max said. "You deserve better."

"But they're my family and they *are* supposed to know me best, so am I that useless a person?" She swallowed hard. "Is supporting everyone else the only thing I'm good at?"

"Sweetheart . . ."

She threw herself toward Max and he gathered

her into his arms, his hand stroking her hair as she pressed against him.

"Your family are missing out if they don't see what an amazing woman you are, Feebs," he said quietly in her ear. "You're kind, you're funny as hell, you're a really good person, and I feel privileged to have gotten to know you even a little bit."

She slowly raised her head and looked into his eyes.

"Hey." He stroked a tear from her cheek. "Can't have my best girl crying."

She cupped his face in her hands and kissed him hard. It took him less than a second to respond, his fingers caressing her scalp, his arm tightening around her hips. Ten minutes later they were both breathing hard, and Max's hand was inside her top.

Phoebe sat up and pulled her nightie over her head, leaving her in just her socks, which she wiggled out of.

"Okay." Max leaned back against the headboard, a half smile on his lips. "We're getting naked now?"

She raised her eyebrows. "Well, I am."

"I'm not stopping you, sweet pea."

She held his gaze and climbed back onto his lap. The feeling of his cotton T-shirt and jeans against her bare skin was surprisingly erotic. His breath hitched as she kissed him again. After a moment, she drew back and frowned at him.

"Put your hands on me."

"You sure about this?" he asked. "Because if I start kissing you, I'm not going to stop until I'm buried deep inside you making you scream, and I don't want you regretting that—ever."

"Why would I regret it?" Phoebe asked.

"Because you've got a big mad on about your family and I want you to do this for the right reasons, not to get back at them."

The silence after he spoke seemed to go on forever. Phoebe bit her lip. "It's okay, Max. You can just say it."

"Say what?" His brow creased.

"That you've changed your mind about it all."

"I've changed *my* mind? You're the one sitting naked on my lap."

Phoebe scrambled off and grabbed the sheet to cover herself. "About me, about everything. I mean I should've realized that you saying you wanted to take it slow meant you were having second thoughts, and who could blame you? It's not your job to educate me. I'm sorry I forced you into this embarrassing corner."

She set her feet on the floor and looked around for her nightie, which had ended up draped over the vanity.

"Nope, stop right there." Max's voice held a note of steel she rarely heard directed at her. "We are *not* going to do this. We're going to talk it out like adults."

"I am not doing that naked," Phoebe said.

"Fine, get your clothes on and we'll take it from there."

Max remade the bed and sat on the patchwork quilt while Phoebe put on her nightwear and briefly disappeared to the bathroom. When she came back, he patted the space beside him.

"Sit down."

She regarded him warily; her eyes were puffy as if

she'd had a quick cry in the bathroom. She did as he asked and crossed her arms over her chest.

"I'm sorry—"

"Let's consider the apologies a given, okay, and try and get to the bottom of why you're yelling at me when you're naked because I'm not sure I understand your reasoning."

She looked down at her lap. Max waited a moment, but she didn't speak.

"I don't want to make it all about me, but it feels like you're mixed up about your family and you're taking it out on the wrong person. I gotta say, Feebs, that doesn't feel good on my side."

She finally looked over at him. "I didn't mean to make you feel like that, Max. I know you were just trying to help me sort things out, and throwing myself at you in the middle of the conversation probably wasn't helpful."

"Okay, so we got our wires crossed. Now, how can we untangle them?"

She took a shaky breath. "I suppose I should stop assuming you feel the same way about me as my family do?"

"I already told you that, sweet pea." He met her gaze. "And I meant every word."

"I think I panicked," Phoebe said slowly.

"Yeah?"

"I thought I could forget about them by losing myself in you, and then you called me out on it, and I assumed you were rejecting me, too, so I said all those horrible things to make you feel as bad as I did."

"I just wanted to make sure we were both on the same page," Max said simply. "I don't want either of us regretting anything we choose to do together."

"I don't regret a moment I've spent with you, Max."

He could only manage to nod, held in thrall by the sincerity in her brown eyes.

"Then will you forgive me for the things I said?" Phoebe asked.

He shrugged. "What things?"

She took a quick breath. "That's lovely but I don't want you to feel obliged to make love to me."

"Feebs, when have I ever looked like I don't want to get into your pants?"

"You . . . slowed everything down and then stopped." She worried at her lip.

For once in his life, Max took his time forming his answer because he really wanted to get this one right.

"I guess, I scared myself." Even admitting that made him want to run into the forest and never come back.

"About what?"

"How much I wanted you." He held her gaze. "I'm not . . . usually that kind of guy."

Her slow smile was like a sunbeam. "Do you re-member telling me that you were the right man for me?"

"Yeah, because it's the truth."

"Then maybe I'm the right woman for you." She paused. "At this particular moment and with this par-ticular set of needs that you alone can solve."

"That's a lot of add-ons, Feebs."

Her gaze was clear. "Because I know you don't like to be caged in and I don't ever want you to feel like that."

A jolt of what should have been alarm shot through him. The weird thing was that for the first time in his life he didn't feel caged, and he didn't know what to do with that feeling. He reminded himself to concentrate on the problem in front of him and let the future take care of itself. Phoebe obviously didn't want to talk about their next steps and he was just fine with that.

"Maybe we're both scared," Max said.

Phoebe nodded.

"And maybe that's okay." He smiled at her and gently cupped her chin. "Kiss and make up?"

She leaned into his caress. "Yes, please."

They both moved at the same time but Max won, gathered her in his arms, and kissed her like he meant it.

After a long while, she eased back and smiled at him.

"Can we go to bed and just sleep? I'm an emotional wreck."

"Absolutely." He drew back the covers. "Why don't you get started on that while I use the bathroom?"

"I won't try and stay awake this time, Max." She got between the sheets and yawned. "I'm absolutely knackered."

He thought about asking what that meant, but her eyes were already closing. He knew from experience that she went out like a light when she was tired. His smile disappeared as he closed the door and headed for the bathroom. Had he gotten things right with her, and why did it matter so much that he did?

She wasn't putting any pressure on him, which was his preferred way of handling relationships, and they were trying to be honest with each other, that was probably a first for him. He realized he was too restless to sleep and went into the kitchen to make himself something to drink.

To his surprise, Sally was there stirring something

on the stove. She looked up as he came in and held up the pan.

"Want to try some spiced chai?"

"Sure."

He sat down at the table and resisted the urge to drum his fingers on the surface. Sally came to join him, and they sat together sipping their drinks in companiable silence. Her hair was darker than Luke's and streaked with grey, but she had the same blue eyes and easy smile. They'd gotten along well from the first day they'd met. Sally just seemed to accept him for what he was, and she wasn't constantly on his back like his buddies. She was the closest thing to a mother he'd had since his parents exited his life.

"It's good," Max said. "For tea."

"It helps me sleep." Sally inhaled the steam. "I think it's the spices. I notice you've been sleeping better since Phoebe got here."

"Yeah, I have." Max considered that. "I hadn't thought about it."

"She seems to have a good effect on you, generally."

"That's because she's awesome."

"So, what got you pacing the halls tonight?" Sally asked in her forthright way.

Belatedly, Max remembered she'd been the community physician for thirty years and had no problem being direct.

She poked his sleeve. "If you want to talk about anything, Max, I'm the soul of discretion. I know secrets about everyone in this valley that would shock you and I've never shared any of them."

"Good thing I never pursued that career because I'm indiscreet as hell." Max drank more of his chai, appreciating the subtle aromas. "You should write a book."

"Maybe, when I fully retire." She winked at him, reminding him of Luke. "It would have to be written anonymously, or I'd get sued."

Max wrapped his hands around his mug and considered what to say. "Phoebe and I had a bit of a misunderstanding."

Sally shrugged. "Happens in all relationships. It's how you deal with it that makes the difference."

"I think we sorted it out."

"You don't sound like you believe that sweetie."

He shoved a hand through his hair. "I'm not good at this relationship stuff."

"Gosh, Max, that's totally surprising. In all the years I've known you, you've never had a proper girlfriend."

"I was married, remember?"

"Even before that." Sally gave him an amused look. "You've always been a loner."

"A loser," Max corrected her.

"Not at all."

"Hey, I'm the life and soul of the party, everyone knows that."

She patted his hand. "Don't be silly, Max. You do that to keep everyone from getting to know the real you. What you're finding out now when you're sharing a bed with Phoebe, is that the rules have changed, and when you want to be honest with her you don't know how, and that scares you."

"Yeah." He sighed. "I'm really trying, Sally, but I don't know if I'll ever get the hang of all this sharing and caring stuff you Nilsens are so good at."

"The fact that you're willing to try says a lot about

how you feel about this girl." Sally paused. "She's good for you."

"It's not her job to be good for me. I've got to be good enough for her," Max stated.

Sally sat back and grinned at him.

"What?"

She rose to her feet and dropped a kiss on the top of his head. "I think you've got this, Max. Now, why don't you go back to bed and get some sleep?"

Max crept into the bedroom and took off his clothes, listening to Phoebe's even breathing and the stillness of the house surrounding him. He got into bed and Phoebe turned toward him, her arm sliding behind his neck and her body pressed against his. Tentatively, he put his hand on her hip, and she murmured his name, her fingertips caressing the short hair at the nape of his neck. It felt right being with her. He dropped his face into the hollow of her shoulder and kissed her skin, his body hardening as she moved against him.

"Phoebe," he murmured against her throat. "Are you awake?"

"I might be," she whispered. "If it would be helpful."

He rolled her onto her back and looked down into her whisky brown eyes. For some reason he didn't want to put on a light and destroy the sense of closeness.

"Do you want me?"

She nodded, her gaze clear. "I do."

"Just for me?"

"Absolutely." She kissed him gently on the lips. "And for myself."

He took his time kissing every inch of her with a

reverence that soon had her pulling his hair and demanding more. When he palmed her between the legs, she was already wet, he slipped two fingers inside her to bring her to her first climax. She wasn't being passive; her hands were moving over him and at one point she wrapped her fingers around his dick and almost made him come himself.

He slowed down and experienced the joy of Phoebe, her taste, the sounds she made when he touched her, and the way her body writhed on the sheets beneath his. Her fingernails bit into his scalp as he used his mouth on her clit, and she screamed into her pillow.

"You want all of me?" he asked as he slicked a hand over his hard cock. "Because I'm ready if you are."

She smiled at him. "Yes, please."

"So polite." He opened the bedside drawer and took out a condom. "Want to put this on me?"

"I'd rather you did it in case I made a mistake in the dark," Phoebe said. "But I'll watch and take notes for next time."

He eased back and covered his cock, breathing out slowly through his nose as his need to be inside her grew as desperate as his dick.

"Max . . ."

He looked down at Phoebe and she smiled, opened her arms, and that was all he needed. She drew him down toward her. In one easy motion, he angled his hips and pushed inside her.

"Oh."

He immediately went still. "You okay?"

"That's . . ." She wiggled a bit and put her hand on his ass. "Different."

"Different good or bad?"

"Interesting different." Her fingers pressed against his buttock. "Is there more?"

Max glanced down at his barely sheathed cock. "Yeah."

"I'd like more."

"Good." Max rocked his hips and gave her more until he was fully inside her, and she was coming around him so fast he barely managed to keep it together. "Jeezus."

"Is that bad?" Phoebe gasped. "Because you feel wonderful."

"Oh, it's all good." Max slid one hand under her ass and smiled into her eyes, "Hang in there, sweet pea. We're only just getting started."

Chapter 11

Luke came into the kitchen where everyone except Sky was having their breakfast.

"Do you guys remember Fittori?"

Noah looked up. "Fred Fittori?"

"The very one." Luke took his seat at the table and piled his plate high with pancakes.

"I remember him," Max said. "Great shot, fast talker, and a wow with the ladies."

"Yeah, you two had a lot in common," Luke said deadpan. "I just got a text from him. He's passing through our neck of the woods, and he wondered if we'd like to meet up."

"When?" Max asked, like he didn't already know. "We've got a lot coming up what with the wedding, Jen's bachelorette party . . ."

Luke consulted his phone. "Friday night."

"That's when we'll be out partying." Jen looked at Sally and Phoebe. "You guys should meet this Fittori guy and maybe have a little celebration of your own."

Everyone tried not to look at Noah and as if they

were just considering the idea and hadn't set the whole thing up two days previously.

"It would be nice to see him again," Max said. "I wonder if he's settled down like me?"

"He's got a full-time job, so I guess he's making progress," Luke said. "How about it, Noah, you in?"

"I'm not sure I want to be out drinking two days before I get married."

"You don't have to drink," Luke said. "We'll go out to dinner like grown-ups."

Jen touched his shoulder. "You should go. I hate to think of you sitting here all lonely while I'm having the time of my life."

"Just dinner?" Noah looked at Luke. "And are you sure you want to go out in the evening?"

Max leaned forward and caught Noah's eye. "I think it would be great for us to do that *with* Luke, don't you, Noah?"

"I guess." Noah still didn't look convinced. "Whereabouts was he planning on meeting us?"

"He's at some kind of conference up here. I'm not sure exactly where, but I think he was hoping we could meet near his location." Luke looked at his phone. "I'll check and get back to you and maybe you could make a final decision then?"

"Okay." Noah nodded. "Let me know. Now, does anyone want the last strip of bacon? Because if you don't, it's all mine."

Phoebe, who was getting ready to join the rest of the crew for a day rounding up strays, drew Max aside when he came into the mudroom.

"Do you think he bought it?"

"Noah? Hard to tell. He's a suspicious bastard."
Max touched Phoebe's nose. "Don't forget your sun-
screen, Mrs. CSR."

"What did you call her?" Luke stopped midstride
toward the door.

"It's our last name, doofus. Creighton-Smith-
Romano," Max replied.

He could still hear Luke cackling as he went out
the door and down toward the barn.

"Not sure what he's laughing about, Feebs." Max
winked at her. "He's probably jealous."

"It *is* a big responsibility," Phoebe agreed. "Having
all those hyphens to live up to."

She zipped up her jacket and put her new hat on
her head. She still hadn't heard from George, and
she was starting to worry. If he didn't contact her by
the end of the day, she'd have to speak to her grandmother and that rarely went well.

"You okay, Feebs?" Max asked as they walked out
to the barn together.

"I'm fine!" she said brightly. "Just thinking about
the flowers from the wholesalers. I don't want them
arriving too early or too late. I think I'll have to speak
to them again to make sure we're on track."

"The good news is that if they don't turn up the
wedding can go ahead anyway," Max reminded her.

"But I bet Jen and I would still be stuck with the
bill."

"Not if we sent Noah down to talk it through with
them. I've seen him make grown men weep in car
dealerships as he screwed every penny out of them."

"I call that good business practice," Noah spoke
from behind them. "A well-prepared spreadsheet will
never let you down." He glanced over at Phoebe as

he went past. "If you have any problems with the flowers, talk to me, okay? I'll deal with them, so Jen doesn't have to worry."

"Yes, of course." Phoebe was now speaking to his back. "Thank you."

She looked up at Max. "For a big man he's very quiet on his feet. Do you think he heard the first part of our conversation?"

"He was nowhere near us or Luke when we were talking, and you barely mentioned him. And being Noah, if he *had* heard anything, you'd be hearing about it right now." He looked down at her as he opened the mudroom door. "You still don't look happy."

"I'm trying to talk to George about some family issues and he's not answering me." Phoebe went for the truth.

"Is this about the wedding or the legal stuff?" Max asked as they went down to the barn.

"Everything really." She sighed. "I . . . had a little falling out with him."

"About me?"

She gently punched his arm. "Not everything is about you, Max, but you are part of the issue at hand."

"So, it is all about me. What's the problem?"

"George is trying to fob me off with some property in Scotland in exchange for my inheritance on the estate."

"Okay, so how do I fit in with that?"

Phoebe rolled her eyes. "George is trying to wriggle out of giving me what I am legally owed. I told him it wasn't acceptable and that if he kept it up, I wouldn't dream of bringing you with me to England."

"You don't want me to go with you?"

She stopped so that she could look at him properly. "I don't want you walking into a family ambush. It isn't fair."

He shrugged, his expression hard to read. "I've lived through a few ambushes, Feebs. They don't scare me."

"It's bad enough that I've had to give into their pressure and ask you to accompany me in the first place without them complicating matters even more."

"I already told you I'm okay with that." He held her gaze, a smile hovering on his lips. "They don't scare me."

She raised her chin. "Then maybe they should."

"They're just people, sweet pea."

"People I know far better than you do." He opened his mouth, and she held up a finger. "Please don't tell me to relax or chill out or any other such nonsense."

"I was going to say that family can be tough and that sometimes a little perspective from someone not directly involved can help make sense of things."

Her instinct was to hotly deny that, but she tried to be reasonable.

"Yes, that is a possibility."

This time he did smile. "You need to work on your delivery, Feebs. Your mouth's saying one thing while your eyes are still glaring at me."

"I am trying, Max." She sighed. "I've been fighting this battle for years all by myself. Sometimes I feel like I'm going mad, and that they must be right simply because they all agree that I'm wrong."

He leaned in, angled his head around the brim of her hat, and kissed her cheek.

"You're a strong woman, Phoebe Creighton-Smith-Romero. You'll win."

"I wish I had your confidence,"

"That's exactly why you need to keep me around and take me to England," Max said. "You don't need to do it alone, sweetheart. You've got me."

Later that evening, Phoebe finally saw a reply come through from George. She excused herself from the dinner table and went into Max's bedroom to read his message.

Please call me.

Annoyed that she'd have to pay for the international call, she found his number and waited for the call to go through.

"Phoebe."

George sounded even more clipped over the phone.

"George."

"About all this nonsense. Grandmother isn't pleased with you."

"Oh, dear, my life is ended."

There was a slight pause. "There's no need to be sarcastic. Grandmother only has the best interests of this family at heart. She truly believes that your attempt to dismantle the estate would set a dangerous precedent."

Phoebe sat on the bed. She was certain her grandmother was sitting right next to George, dictating what he was supposed to say. For a moment she imagined her grandmother frantically scribbling on giant cue cards and flashing them at George, which made her want to smile.

"Well? What have you got to say about that?" George demanded.

"I'd say that ignoring the legal wishes of the former owners of the estate would set a dangerous precedent."

"It's not that simple and you know it."

Phoebe took a slow breath. "Have you anything new to discuss with me, George or is this just another attempt to bully me into doing what you want?"

"I am not—"

Phoebe spoke over him. "Yes, you are, and I don't appreciate it. Now, have you anything useful to say, or can I go and finish eating my dinner?"

There was some whispering and then George spoke again.

"I'm not sure what kind of company you are keeping, Phoebe, but you are being remarkably rude. We insist that you bring yourself and that mythical husband of yours to meet us and do what is best for your family!"

"I have been remarkably patient with you and Grandmother for years, George, and I've had enough. When I come back for Eugenie's wedding, I will be finding my own legal representation and taking you to court." She paused as he started to splutter. "And I will not be bringing Max."

"You can't—"

"I bloody well can," Phoebe said. "Regards to all the family. I'll see you in a couple of weeks."

She ended the call and stayed where she was taking long, slow breaths. She was still staring at the door when Max came through it.

"I'm guessing it didn't go well." Max looked at her.

"It depends how you define 'well'. I told him to go stuff himself."

Max nodded. "Fair enough"

"And that I'll be seeking legal counsel when I get back to England."

"Also, good." He raised his eyebrows. "So, why aren't you celebrating?"

"Because they still want to use you to control me and I'm not having it." She met his gaze. "I'm not going to let you come to England with me."

She saw in his eyes when that hit home and wanted to cry. She gripped hold of the quilt in one shaking hand.

"Max, I know you probably have a strong opinion about why I'm wrong about this, but I really can't deal with it right now."

"Okay." He half-turned to the door. "Do you want me to bring your dessert in here for you? Sally made a great apple pie."

Phoebe rose to her feet. She wanted to ask him to hold her but didn't have the nerve when she knew she'd hurt him.

"That's very kind of you, but I'll come and eat at the table."

"That's my girl." He held the door open for her but didn't try and touch her as she went past. "Don't let the Brits grind you down."

Max shut the stall door and took the last barrow of manure out to the pile before returning to the tack room where he sorted out a few tangled halters and bridles. He was just looking for something else to do when someone cleared their throat behind him.

He turned around and nodded at Luke. "Just making sure everything's shipshape, boss."

"I appreciate that." Luke looked around. "I think you've done all my chores, too."

"Well, I still owe you a few weeks work," Max said as he went into the feed room to make sure he hadn't missed anything.

Luke followed him. "Everything okay?"

"Why wouldn't it be?"

"Because you're out here past your bedtime practically shining the floors of a horse barn," Luke said. "That usually means you're trying to avoid something or getting ready to leave."

"I'm not leaving anytime soon." Max shut the door with something of a bang. "You can depend on that."

Luke hadn't been officer material for nothing, and Max could see him making the connections in his brain.

"What about the wedding in England?"

"I'm surplus to requirements."

"Phoebe's changed her mind?"

Max deliberated telling his boss to take a hike and then paused. He'd been banging on about Phoebe getting some perspective on her problems. Maybe it was time for him to bite the bullet and do the same.

"It's a long story," Max said.

"I have the time. We can stay out here or go up to the office." Luke paused. "There was something I wanted to talk to you about anyway."

"Let's go inside before I start polishing the roof tiles," Max said. "Everyone's gone to bed, so it'll be nice and quiet."

Ten minutes later, they were tucked away in the office with fresh coffee, a closed door, and a silent house around them.

"How are the finances looking?" Max asked, knowing he was prevaricating, but happy to go along with it.

It had been a brutal winter and they've lost a third of their herd, which had destroyed all the progress

Luke had made since retiring from the Marines to make the ranch his full-time job.

Luke made a face. "Better than I feared but it's still not easy." He patted a pile of files on his desk. "This is all the paperwork for grant applications, federal farm aid, tax loopholes and bank loans for this year."

Max whistled. "That sucks. Noah's been helping you out with it all, right?"

"Yeah, he knows his way around a spreadsheet and it's better than bothering Mom. She used to do all the books while working full time at the clinic."

"Sally's a goddess."

"Truth." Luke looked at him. "So, what's up with you and Phoebe?"

Max bristled. "Why do you instantly think something's wrong?"

"I didn't," Luke said. "But I guess I hit a nerve anyway."

Max set his mug down on the corner of Luke's desk and his boss immediately slipped a coaster under it. "She doesn't want me to go to England with her anymore."

"Did she say why?"

"Some crap about not wanting me to have to deal with her family."

"And you think she's wrong about that?"

"I *think* I'd like to be there to protect her from those idiots, but she's gotten some crazy idea in her head that she has to protect me from them."

Luke sat back; his gaze interested. "Why? What's so important about you being there in the flesh?"

Max weighed his options. "Phoebe says they don't believe I exist."

"Like you're a figment of Phoebe's imagination?"

"Something like that." Max tried to think of how to share why that mattered without giving too much away.

"They want to meet you and Phoebe thinks it's a bad idea."

"That's right.

"And she says it's because she doesn't want you to get hurt, but you don't think that's true."

"Yeah." Max looked everywhere but at Luke and blurted out the unthinkable. "Maybe she doesn't think I'm good enough."

"Have you mentioned that to her?"

"*Hell*, no."

There was a long enough pause that Max ended up glancing at Luke who was looking unbearably sympathetic.

"Can I ask why?"

"Because I don't want her thinking I'm making it all about me when she has a million other problems with that bunch of dickheads to worry about."

Luke nodded like it all made perfect sense.

"And why I'm asking you for advice when I practically had to lock you in a room to sort out the most basic stuff with the woman who's loved you forever, I don't know," Max said.

"Other people's problems are far easier to solve than your own."

"That's what I said to Phoebe."

"How did that go?"

"She told me she knew her family best and that I should butt out."

"Okay, so here's how I see it." Luke leaned back in his chair. "You have two options. One, you accept that Phoebe thinks she's protecting you and let it go, or two, you ask her if she thinks you're not good enough to be seen as her partner at her sister's wedding."

"What if she says yes?"

"To which part?" Luke's brow furrowed.

Max forced the words out. "That I'm not good enough."

"Then you'll know." Luke met his gaze head on. "But I've seen the way she looks at you, bro. She's not going to do that."

"I wish I had your confidence." Max took a sip of his coffee. "You don't know the half of it."

"I know you're married to a woman you barely know, and you're trying to make things work, and that's good enough for me." Luke took a drink of his own coffee. "I'd like you to be happy, Max."

"Not sure I trust that feeling," Max muttered. "It's not something I'm used to."

Luke grinned. "Poor little Max can't deal with someone who actually likes him and wants to be with him."

"Not sure about that. I mean, how can I ask someone who lives in a castle to come stay here?"

"Hey, that's my family ranch you're talking about," Luke protested.

"You know what I mean."

"I guess that's something else you're going to have to talk to Phoebe about." Luke held his gaze. "One thing I've learned is that if you really want something, you have to get over yourself and ask the honest questions."

"Took you long enough," Max grumbled. "And you needed several assists."

"Exactly, so benefit from my experience and don't screw this up." Luke pointed at him. "And if Phoebe says she's happy to stick around, feel free to build yourself a house next to Noah's."

"Not sure I want to be that close to him," Max said. "I have to see his face all day at work as it is."

"Then build a ten-foot fence so you don't have to look at him," Luke said. "Come on, Max. It's not like you to be negative."

Max nodded. "Thanks for the offer. It means a lot." He paused. "I haven't had a home since I left my parents place."

"You mean since they kicked you out."

"They weren't bad people, Luke. I made their lives hell."

Luke folded his arms. "Doesn't matter."

"They didn't kick me out and they did me a favor by sending me to military school." Max held Luke's skeptical gaze. "They could've washed their hands of me and let the juvenile court system take over, but they took responsibility, paid my fees, and that helped me get back on track."

"If they were so wonderful, why aren't you in contact with them now?"

Max shrugged. "Because they did their job, and they don't need me screwing up their lives again. Can we get back to where we were talking about our feelings?" He made a face. "I can't believe I just said that."

"Sure." For a moment Luke looked uncertain. "I wanted to ask your opinion on something."

"Okay, shoot." Max sat back; his mug cradled in one hand. "Want some more relationship advice because man, you suck at that."

"Maybe," Luke said. "I want to propose to Bernie."

"Well, that's a shocker."

Luke opened his desk drawer and took out a small velvet box. "Mom said she'd be thrilled if I wanted to give Bernie this family ring."

He passed it over to Max, who whistled when he opened the box.

"Nice! Two diamonds and a sapphire set in gold. Bernie will love it."

"I hope so."

"So, what's the problem?"

"Bernie's very down to earth so I was thinking, should I just give her the ring next time I see her and not make a big deal out of it?"

Max stared at his boss and slowly shook his head.

"What?" Luke demanded.

"Did you see the way Jen and Bernie were cooing over Phoebe's ring? Bernie would *totally* want you to make a big deal out of getting engaged. Even Noah managed to take Jen out for a nice meal and get down on one knee."

A crease appeared between Luke's brows. "Should I do it at the wedding?"

"Hell, no!" Max sat up straight. "Number one, that's Jen and Noah's big day, and number two, it makes you look cheap."

"*Cheap?*" Luke looked offended.

"Like you're too tight to pay for your own celebration and you're hijacking someone else's."

"Oh, right. I see that, now." Luke nodded. "I'll take her out to dinner after the wedding and do the whole getting down on one knee thing. I've never asked someone to marry me before."

"Trust me, that's the easy part."

"You would know—although, all Bernie and I have to decide is whether she's okay coming to live here or if she wants me to build her a separate house."

"Half on her dad's land and half on yours?"

"That would be cool." Luke grinned.

"You could live next door to Noah," Max suggested and started to get up. "I hear there's a plot available."

"Funny." Luke hesitated. "Do you think Bernie would prefer a surprise party?"

Max groaned and sat back down. "It's gonna be a long night."

Chapter 12

Phoebe gazed out of the window as Jen drove Noah's big truck toward the outskirts of Reno. Sally sat in the passenger seat, and they'd picked up Lucy from the hotel and Bernie and Penny from the café. The truck had seven seats so was ideal for the journey. It also meant Noah couldn't suddenly decide to head out by himself without alerting the others who were expecting him to join them for "dinner" with their military friend.

Luke had even taken Jen's truck keys, so Noah didn't have access to them. He said that if Noah asked, he'd say Jen must've accidentally taken them with her. Phoebe was quietly amused with the extent of the military planning involved to get Noah to his own bachelor party. And she needed something to cheer her up when her own life had suddenly become more complicated.

Should she have explained her reasoning to Max more carefully? That she didn't want him used as a weapon by her family to exert pressure on her to conform and it was safer for him to remain behind?

But she hadn't been at her best after the tense conversation with George, and Max hadn't stuck around after she'd told him he couldn't come to England with her.

He'd been nice as pie since—almost as if nothing had happened, and maybe he was over it, and she was the only one still obsessing because they didn't owe each other a thing. She had to remind herself of that constantly and that she might have imagined that jolt of hurt she'd seen in his blue eyes.

Pen, Bernie's cousin, nudged her in the ribs. "Hi! Have we met?"

"I think so." Phoebe smiled at her blond companion. "You work with Bernie at the café, right?"

"Yes!" Pen said. "I do! I remember you now." She smiled encouragingly at Phoebe. "Well, I remember your face. But I'm not sure I know your name."

"It's Phoebe."

"Oh, that's lovely! And you're not American."

"I'm British."

"Then why are you here?" Phoebe looked genuinely confused. "Did you get lost?"

Bernie caught Phoebe's eye over Pen's head. "We already went over this, Pen. Phoebe is married to Max who works with Luke up at the ranch."

Pen's mouth formed a perfect *O*. "Max is married? Why didn't we get an invite to the wedding, or was it just me, and no one told me about it?"

"It's okay." Phoebe reassured her. "We were married in Reno four years ago."

Pen's brow crinkled. "You've been at the ranch for four years and this is the first time we've been out together? Did Max have you locked in a dungeon or something?"

Bernie reached over to pat Phoebe's knee. "I'm

sorry about my cousin. She takes everything very literally and loves to ask a million annoying questions."

"It's fine," Phoebe reassured Bernie and turned to
Pen. "I haven't been here all the time. I only just arrived. I had to deal with some family issues in England."

Pen nodded. "I'm glad you made it out here in
time for Jen's wedding. I absolutely adore her."

"Me too," Phoebe said. "I was thrilled to be included in her bachelorette party."

"It's going to be lots of fun," Pen agreed. She sat
back, smiled sweetly, and put her earbuds in. "It's
time for my meditation session. Speak to you in an
hour."

Phoebe turned her attention to the endless forest
passing by her window and allowed her eyes to gently
close. She hadn't been sleeping well and had woken
up the previous night to find Max wasn't there. They
hadn't made love again, either. She'd heard all the
jokes about him never being able to sleep at night
but hadn't experienced it herself until then. Was he
stressed about having to share a bed with her now?
Should she offer to move out?

She cursed her innate British politeness, which
made it difficult for her to ask directly for what she
needed. Perhaps a relaxing time at the spa would
help her work out how to approach Max and make
sure he understood exactly why she didn't think it
was a good idea to bring him to meet her family. He
certainly didn't deserve to be questioned or bullied
by George or her grandmother.

She opened her eyes. No one deserved to be
treated like that.

Including her.

* * *

Max glanced at his phone and looked over at Noah who was settled at the kitchen table with his laptop and was muttering to himself.

"Do you want more coffee?"

"Sure, thanks," Noah said. "Have you heard from Phoebe?"

"Why would I?" Max asked as he refilled Noah's cup and set it at his elbow.

"Because she's your wife?" Noah looked up.

"She's a grown woman who can take care of herself, and as she's currently with every female we know, I think she's in good hands."

"Jen texted me to say they'd arrived."

"So, we know they're all where they should be—unless someone got left behind at a gas station—and I think we'd have heard about that." Max patted Noah's shoulder. "Lighten up, dude."

"I've done a security assessment of the spa and checked out the owners, and it all looks okay, but you never know."

"I'd back our women against a bunch of terrorists any day," Max said as he placed his mug in the dishwasher. "What time is Luke thinking of heading out this evening?"

"As to that." Noah cleared his throat. "I'm not one hundred percent certain I should go out. What if Jen needs something?"

"Then she'll call or send you a text," Max said firmly. "You know she'd be mad at you for babying her and she wanted you to go out."

"But what about Sky?"

"Bernie's sister Mary is coming over with her mom to babysit." Max stared at Noah. "Come on, man. You already know all this stuff." He lowered his voice. "You have to come. What if Luke freaks the hell out and we need to get him back to the ranch? I can't handle him on my own. We both know he only listens to you."

Noah frowned. "Maybe Luke shouldn't be going either."

"Luke is trying to get over his fears and the least we could do is be supportive," Max said. "He needs us, Noah, whether he realizes it or not."

Noah turned back to his laptop. "Fine, I'll come. Luke said to be ready at eighteen hundred hours."

"Great. That gives me plenty of time to get the barn in order."

Max went outside, passing Luke who was coming in and gave him a thumbs up.

"Noah's good to go. He thinks he's doing it to support you, so don't act too confident."

"It's okay, I'm still genuinely terrified."

"We're only going down the road. You'll barely be off Nilsen land." Max kept moving. He was on a mission to make sure everything he'd planned worked out. "I'll check in with Olly and Fred, and make sure we're still on for seven."

"Great, now all we have to do is stop Noah from bolting, make sure I don't have a panic attack, and hope Fred is still as good a guy as we remember," Luke said.

Max raised his arm and snapped his fingers. "Piece of cake."

Phoebe laid on her bed and stared out of the window, the gentle sound of running water hardly disturbing the tranquility of the spa complex. She was due down for dinner, and then there might be swimming, which she always enjoyed, or a hot tub to try for the first time. She glanced at her phone, but there was nothing from Max. Should she send him a message? Make believe that everything was fine, and that if they both pretended hard enough, they could go back to where they'd been before she'd let him down?

She turned around so that the view was behind her head and snapped a photo to send with her text.

The spa is beautiful. Hope your plans are going well. X

He replied almost instantly.

All good here. Have a great and relaxing time. Cell reception might get bad after 7 so don't worry if you can't get hold of me.

Phoebe stared at the message for at least a minute. What had she expected? That he'd say he was missing her after four hours apart? She really needed to be honest with herself about what she wanted from him. With a groan, she sat back against the pillows. She wanted him to take her seriously. She wanted something he hadn't agreed to and insisted he didn't have the capacity to give.

Her cell buzzed again, and she picked it up.

p.s. You look hot.

She smiled foolishly at the screen, rolled onto her side, and got up. She had ten minutes to get some clothes on and present herself at the bride-to-be's dinner. For whatever reason, she suspected Bernie had organized a few extra surprises, and she couldn't wait to see what they might be.

It was far warmer than the ranch, so she wore a

maxi dress with long floaty sleeves that Jen had described as boho when Phoebe tried it on in the department store. She slipped her feet into silver
sandals and wished she'd had time before the meal
for the manicure and pedicure that were on her spa
to-do list. Not that she looked bad. She and Jen had
spent the previous evening painting their nails, de-
fuzzing, and plucking anything that dared to grow
where it wasn't wanted. It was the most fun that
didn't involve Max that Phoebe had had in ages.

Jen was easy to like, a great and sympathetic lis-
tener, and wise beyond her years. She'd regaled
Phoebe with stories of the mythical Dave whose ran-
dom appearances at the ranch to see his son always
caused drama. Her theories as to why she'd been
foolish enough to hook up with Dave in the first
place were equally hilarious and Phoebe had cried
with laughter.

In return, she'd told Jen about some of the more
eccentric members of her family including her
Great-uncle Cuthbert who insisted, despite not being
the slightest bit Scottish, in parading around in a kilt
playing the bagpipes at dawn and dusk, scaring all
the wildlife, drowning out the birdsong, and annoying the occupants of the house. She'd even shared
the video she'd secretly taken, which made Jen howl
almost as much as the bagpipes. Noah had even
popped his head into the room to make sure they
were both okay.

After deciding to be her father's main caregiver,
Phoebe had lost touch with most of her eventing and
college friends and only had her family around her.
It was nice to have a friend again even if Phoebe

couldn't confide everything to her because of her loyalty to Max. She sensed that Jen knew things were complicated because she deliberately steered clear of the more controversial questions like, "are you coming back here to live," or "how on earth did you and Max get together in the first place".

Phoebe checked her reflection in the mirror, found her handbag, making sure she had her key card at least three times, and left the room. When she came out of the elevator, she saw her group gathered by the entrance to the dining room. Bernie, who was wearing red, beckoned her over with a big smile.

"There you are, Phoebe. I hear Max has taken to calling himself Mr. CSR. Is that true?"

"Why would he do that?" Pen asked. She was wearing a short pink dress with ruffles and what appeared to be fairy wings on the back.

"It's their initials," Bernie explained to her cousin. "Creighton-Smith-Romero."

Jen grinned. She wore a tiara and a sash that read 'Bride to Be' over a fitted blue dress. "CSR sounds like a crime show." She looked at Phoebe. "That dress looks great on you."

"I really like it." Phoebe did a twirl. "It even has pockets."

"Did you hear from Max?" Jen asked as they were escorted into their private dining room.

"He said everything was going according to plan and not to worry if I didn't hear anything after seven because the cell phone reception might be a bit dodgy in the woods." Phoebe took her seat at the table between Bernie and Lucy.

"That sounds ominous," Lucy said. "What exactly are they going to do to Noah?"

"Oh, they're going to blow his mind." Jen grinned. "I just wish I could see his face right now."

Noah's frown deepened as Max slowed his truck and stopped at the gate.

"I thought we were going to a restaurant?"

"We are." Max got out, tapped in the code Oliver had given him and the gate swung open.

"Here?" Noah looked around the pristine wood-land.

"It's a bit farther in," Max said as he started driving again.

Beside him, Noah shifted restlessly in his seat. Max considered setting the child locks on all the doors.

"You doing okay back there, Luke?" Max called out.

"I'm good so far." Luke patted Noah's shoulder. "Hang in there, big guy."

"Aren't we supposed to be meeting Fred?"

"He'll be there." Max came around the bend of the curving loggers track and pointed at some lights in the distance. "He's waiting for us."

Max parked the truck alongside the others and went around to open Noah's door.

He was met with a blast of suspicion and a death glare.

"You know I don't like surprises, Max."

"Nothing to surprise you with." Max shrugged. "Just a group of old friends meeting for dinner."

For a second, Noah looked like he wasn't going to get out of the truck and Max braced himself for an argument. Luke came to stand beside him, looking as calm as a mill pond. He sniffed the air.

"Something smells good. I'm starving."

"Fine," Noah growled at them both. "I'll come, but don't think I'm going to forget about this."

"Like you forget about anything," Max murmured. "You've got a memory like a steel trap."

Noah didn't hear him as he was stalking purposefully toward the tentlike structure in the center of the glade. Fairy lights had been strung around the edge of the canvas and the lower hanging branches of the redwoods making it look magical. The smell of barbecue drifted out from the rear of the tent along with a hint of hops. Max had asked the caterers to keep everything low-key because Noah had never met a steak or a burger he hadn't instantly devoured.

A woman stepped out from the entrance of the tent and smiled at Noah.

"Welcome!"

Noah halted and looked down at her. "Hi."

"You're Noah, aren't you?" She smiled sweetly and offered him her hand. She had long, gray hair and wore yoga pants and a silky tunic top. "I'm Jane."

"Nice to meet you,"

Whatever Max might say about Noah, he did have excellent, if intimidating, manners.

Jane kept hold of Noah's hand and led him inside.

"Your friend is here. Once you have all been reintroduced, help yourself to some drinks, and then we can begin."

Before Noah had a chance to ask any more questions, she disappeared into the rear of the space, which Max thought was super smart of her.

Two sides of the tent were open to the forest, on

the left was an area with circular seating and on the
right a table already set for dinner. A man rose from
one of the couches and came toward Noah.

"Noah the Arkie! Awesome!" He enfolded Noah
in a hug and slapped him hard on the back. "Same
miserable bastard as ever."

Max came forward and was hugged as well. "Max,
you old devil. Still chasing the ladies?"

"I'm a respectable married man, now," Max said.

"No!" Fred grinned at him. "Me too! How about
you, Luke?"

"Just about to get engaged." Luke shook Fred's
hand.

"That means all three of you are settling down."
Fred shook his head. "I can't believe it."

"You're not the only one," Max said. "I never
thought any woman would look at these two knuckle-
heads and think they were worth marrying."

Noah and Luke both looked at him and he raised
his eyebrows. "What? I guess the truth hurts."

Fred gestured at the trees as he helped himself to
a beer. "I love this venue. How did you find it, Max?"

"Olly put me on to it," Max said. "He's employed
by the forestry commission to save our trees or something useful like that."

"Then he's doing a great job." Fred looked up.
"This place is amazing."

"This was Olly's idea?" Noah turned to Max. "You
didn't mention that."

"Why would I?" Max opened his eyes wide.

"Because you suggested Fred was the one setting
the agenda."

Luke touched Noah's arm. "Does it really matter,
Noah? We're in a beautiful place, and we're about to

have a nice evening reminiscing with an old friend. How about you just relax and enjoy yourself."

"Yeah, chill out, bro," Max added.

For a moment, Noah looked like it really *did* matter and then let out a breath.

"Fine."

Jane reappeared and clapped her hands. "We're ready for you outside."

Fred and Luke walked either side of Noah with Max bringing up the rear just in case Noah changed his mind and decided to bolt.

There was a firepit in the center of the clearing with large cushions around it that Olly was busy straightening up. He was a slight, dark-haired man who had briefly dated Bernie before Luke had gotten his head screwed on straight.

"Welcome!" He gestured at the cushions. "Please take your seats so we can begin."

"Begin what?" Noah murmured as Luke maneuvered him toward the firepit and "helped" him sit down.

"Your stag night," Max said.

"What the hell is that?" Noah demanded.

"You said you didn't want a bachelor party, so we're giving you the British version."

"I don't want either of them."

"Too late. You're already here." Max smiled sweetly at his scowling friend. "Now, sit down and enjoy it."

Phoebe gazed up at the stars, her neck comfortably supported by the back of the hot tub she was sharing with her newfound friends. She'd had three glasses of wine with her dinner and some kind of spe-

cially designed cocktail, which she'd had to try because it was made for Jen, and she was feeling pleas-
antly buzzed.

"This is heavenly," Jen said from beside her. The
bride-to-be still had her crown and sash on over her
swimsuit. "I mean, I love being a mother and a midwife, but sometimes it's really nice to just have some
me-time."

Everyone nodded. Bernie had bundled her red
hair on top of her head and her pale, freckled skin
was already flushed, which she said was normal for
her. Pen had her eyes closed and was basically float-
ing, while Lucy looked like she was doing math problems in her head.

"I wonder whether Noah's worked out that he is
having a bachelor party yet?" Jen said.

"I should think so." Bernie consulted her phone,
which sat on the side. "It's gone eleven and I haven't
heard of any murders being committed."

"Noah's not that bad," Jen protested.

"He is slightly intimidating," Phoebe said. "But I
always remind myself that looks can be deceiving."

"Truth." Bernie nodded. "Actions speak louder
than words."

"Although he is also very loud," Jen acknowledged
with a chuckle.

"So, I've heard," Phoebe murmured. "Especially at
night."

It went quiet and she opened her eyes to see that
everyone was looking at her.

"What did I say?"

"You said Noah was loud." Bernie grinned. "Is that
true, Jen? Is Noah a shouter?"

Phoebe sat up so abruptly that she created a wake.
"Oh! I didn't mean *that*, I—"

"He is loud." Jen was laughing. "But we do try and keep it down to be considerate of others." She winked. "I can't wait until we move into our own place where he can roar like the beast he is."

Bernie looked at Phoebe who was blushing up a storm. "Is Max?"

"Is Max what?"

"Loud."

"He's . . ." Phoebe considered what to say. "Just lovely."

"Which doesn't answer the question because let's be honest here, girls, we've all thought that Max would be great in the sack because he's so hot," Bernie said.

"Not all hot guys are good in bed," Lucy said. "In fact, they can be the worst because they are so busy admiring themselves that they forget we're also there."

"Like Dave," Jen said.

"Dave . . ." Everyone groaned and nodded.

"Back to Max," Bernie said. "How would you rate him, Phoebe?"

"Ten." Phoebe said instantly. "He's amazing."

"I'm glad to hear it," Jen said and turned to Bernie. "How about Luke?"

"Also, a ten." Bernie said. "That man is thorough!"

Pen giggled and they all joined in. Jen checked the time.

"I want to be up early for my massage, so I think I should turn in. Thanks everyone for making this such a special occasion." She hesitated. "It's always been hard for me to make friends that stick around, and this feels different to me—more permanent."

"Damn right!" Bernie held up her glass. "Friends forever, okay? All of us."

Phoebe politely raised her glass even as she knew they couldn't really mean her and then caught Jen looking at her.

"I'm trying to persuade Phoebe to get Max to build a house next to ours so we can be neighbors."

"That would be awesome." Bernie climbed out of the tub and offered Jen her hand. "Unless Phoebe's planning on taking Max to England to live in that castle of hers."

"It's not my castle." Phoebe got out and wrapped a towel around herself. "Thank goodness."

Jen waved goodbye and set off toward the main house, her crown slightly askew leaving the others to clean up. The air felt cool after the heat of the hot tub and Phoebe shivered.

"I'd love to live in a castle," Pen said. "If you do go back and live there, Phoebe, can I visit?"

Bernie rolled her eyes. "We're all going to be visiting her, friends forever, right?"

"But what would Max do?" Pen asked. "I don't think they have cowboys in England."

"They have farmers, which are the same as ranchers, right?" Bernie checked with Phoebe.

"Yes. My family have an interest in several."

"Well, that's okay, then. Max can run one of those while Phoebe swans around the castle looking glamorous and mysterious."

"I could do that," Phoebe said as she put on her sandals and toweling robe and followed behind Bernie.

The hotel was still alive with guests who were dining and enjoying the bar facilities, but Phoebe was looking forward to her bed. She said goodnight and was hugged by Lucy and Pen who were sharing one room and went with Bernie to their adjoining rooms.

Just as she was about to say goodnight, Bernie touched her arm.

"I'm sorry if we embarrassed you earlier."

"I don't think you did," Phoebe said cautiously.

"With all the questions about Max." Bernie made a face. "You fit in so well that I forget you're not really used to the way we talk to each other."

"I wasn't offended," Phoebe rushed to reassure Bernie. "I thought it was sweet you included me so completely."

She only realized how much she meant it when she said it out loud. She couldn't remember the last time she'd felt so relaxed with a group of women who'd made her feel like she belonged.

"Max really is a great guy once you get to know him," Bernie said earnestly and then rolled her eyes. "Like I'm telling you that. The woman who's married to him."

"But I hardly know him at all," Phoebe blurted out. "And it's driving me crazy."

Bernie blinked at her. "Okay. How much have you had to drink, my friend, because—"

"I've spent less than a month with him in our entire lives," Phoebe said. "But everything I said about him was true."

Bernie held her gaze and slowly nodded. "Then that's okay, isn't it?"

"No, it isn't really because what am I going to do with him?" Phoebe asked. "He won't want to live in England, and he hasn't asked me to live with him here."

Bernie held out her hand. "Give me your card key."

"What are we—"

The next minute she was being ushered into her room and Bernie was closing the door behind them.

"I think you need someone to talk to that isn't Max, so sit yourself down and tell me everything."

Chapter 13

Jane waited until everyone occupied a cushion and faced the groom-to-be with a smile.

"Welcome, Noah. Thank you for allowing me to participate in the celebration for your upcoming marriage."

Max tensed, but Noah didn't say a word.

"Deciding to spend this evening with the loving community of your friends in a state of mindfulness is incredibly affirming and will set the stage for the health and well-being of your marriage."

Noah raised an eyebrow and slowly turned to glare at Max, who tried to look innocent.

"Let's start by closing our eyes and focusing on our breathing. Just follow my lead."

To Max's astonishment all the guys immediately did what Jane suggested. He tried it, too, and started to relax for the first time since Phoebe had decided he wasn't good enough to go to England with her.

Jane talked them through a few exercises and Max let himself fall into the calmness of her voice. The pine-scented air smelled good and behind his eyes the silence blossomed into a million fragments, making him aware of the slight breeze rustling the branches, the call of a bird, and the squirrels scrabbling for purchase on the rough, redwood bark. He pressed the pads of his fingers into the moss and pine needles scattered over the forest floor releasing the rich smell of earth.

It was good to be alive.

Especially after what the four of them had gone through in the military.

"You may open your eyes," Jane said. "Please come forward and choose one of the singing bowls my assistant has placed in front of me. Noah, you should go first."

Noah rose to his feet and came around the fire pit to where a variety of metal bowls sat on a bamboo mat.

"What are they made of?" Noah asked as he hunkered down to examine the bowls more closely.

"Seven different metals," Jane said. "Lead, tin, iron, copper, mercury, silver, and gold. Pick the one that speaks to you."

Max waited to see if Noah would have a million more questions, but he simply nodded, and spent a few minutes touching every bowl before settling on one of the larger ones.

Luke followed, then Fred, and finally Max.

He was surprised his hand was reaching toward one bowl before he'd even thought about it.

"That one really spoke to you." Jane nodded. "That's good."

"Do you know why?" Max asked.

"I suspect that will be revealed when you use it."

She waited until Olly chose his bowl and then she sat down cross-legged on her cushion.

"I'm going to show you how to use your singing bowl and then when you are ready, we can go around the circle, and you can all have a try."

Noah raised his hand and inwardly Max sighed. It had all been going so well . . . "What's the purpose of this exactly?"

Jane smiled at Noah. "That's a valid question. You strike me as the kind of man who needs evidence to accept that something has value. Perhaps if you allow me to demonstrate you will understand the benefits in real time?"

"Go ahead," Noah said. "I'll report back."

Jane held the bowl in one hand and the striker in the other and gently struck the rim of the bowl. A surprisingly loud and resonant sound echoed around the clearing and settled somewhere in Max's chest. Before the peal had completely diminished, Jane swirled her striker around the rim of the bowl maintaining the pulsing resonance of the single note.

"I want you all to focus on the sound while breathing in through your nose and out through your mouth. Try not to think of anything else but the tone and let it calm your mind."

Max was slightly unnerved by how easily he was falling under the bowl's spell. It was almost magical. All he'd wanted was to find a way to calm Noah down before his wedding. He hadn't expected to be affected as well. He took a sneak peek around the circle and found everyone looking similarly dazed, which made him feel better.

"Would any of you like to try with your own bowl?" Jane asked.

Everyone put up their hands.

"Excellent. Then let's start with Noah."

Bernie looked expectantly at Phoebe. "You can trust me. After all the help Max gave me and Luke, I owe him big time."

"I don't want to sound rude." Phoebe sat on the bed and kicked off her sandals. "But I feel as though it would be disloyal to Max if I shared our current issues with anyone."

"Max has the biggest mouth on the planet," Bernie said. "If he hasn't already told Luke what's going on, I'd be amazed. Hold on." She got out her phone. "Shall I ask Luke?"

"No!" Phoebe said hastily.

"Okay, bad move." Bernie nodded and joined Phoebe on the bed, crossing her legs in front of her. "Let's keep this between us. Now, what's the problem? If you don't mind me saying, you and Max look great together. I've never seen him so happy, but I can understand that where you choose to live might be an issue."

Phoebe wasn't sure if it was the wine or if Bernie had the most sympathetic and trustworthy face ever, but she couldn't seem to stop herself from responding.

"Max hasn't met any of my family, yet. They are demanding I bring him to my sister's wedding because they don't believe he exists."

"Okay, wow." Bernie's eyebrows shot up "That's way more complicated than I thought. I guess my question would be—why haven't they met him already, and why are they kicking up a fuss about it now?"

"It doesn't matter because I just told them I'm not bringing him."

Bernie held up a finger. "I think you jumped a couple of steps there, Phoebe. Could you back up a little and explain?"

"I could," Phoebe said. "But I'm not sure that I want to."

Bernie looked at her and Phoebe's resistance crumbled.

"The short version is that my family want me to parade Max like some kind of prize bull in front of them to see if they approve of him and I'm not willing to expose him to that."

"I don't think Max would mind. He always steps up to the plate when someone he cares about needs support."

"I'm sure he does, but I don't expect him to do it for me, and my family shouldn't be expecting it at all. I had a terrible argument with my brother George about the whole mess." Phoebe sighed. "But I think I hurt Max's feelings when I said he shouldn't come with me because he thinks it's about *him* and it really isn't."

Bernie looked deep in thought.

"What is it?" Phoebe asked.

"I'm still trying to get my head around the idea that someone *could* hurt Max's feelings." Bernie shrugged. "He always strikes me as the kind of guy who sometimes does things without thinking."

"He's not shallow," Phoebe jumped to Max's defense. "He might joke around, but it doesn't really mean anything by it."

"Maybe he's like that with you, Phoebe, but I've seen him be very sharp with Luke and Noah."

"It's okay, he keeps telling me he's not a good person. And now I've given him the perfect excuse to believe that's true because I've stopped him from coming to England."

"Have you told him all this?"

"I haven't had the chance. He's behaving like nothing is wrong, and I don't know how to bring the subject up."

"Is it possible he's okay with it?" Bernie asked.

"I've been wondering that myself." Phoebe looked down at her linked fingers.

"You know what I'm going to say, don't you?"

Phoebe rolled her eyes. "That the only way to find out is to talk to him."

"Then that's what you're going to do." Bernie reached out and placed her hand on top of Phoebe's restless fingers. "Because you deserve to know, and, more importantly, I can't wait to find out how it all goes."

When he stood up, Noah had the slightly dazed look of a man who'd drunk too much beer and Max stepped over to him.

"You, okay?"

"I'm good." Noah gave his head a little shake. "I feel . . . weird. Like all relaxed."

"That was the idea." Max turned him toward the interior of the tent. "Now, let's eat."

So far, the bachelor party had gone well. Noah hadn't thrown a hissy fit, Luke seemed relaxed, and despite settling down, Fred hadn't changed at all, which considering what he'd gotten up to in the Marines was hard to believe.

They filed past the two barbecues where they could fix their own plate full of beef, corn, chicken, and baked potatoes with all the trimmings. Noah piled his plate high and took his seat at the head of the table to the cheers of his friends.

Max produced a glitter-covered paper crown and passed it to Noah.

"Sky made it, so you'd better put it on."

Noah's thumb ran over the squiggles Sky had drawn on the cardboard and he smiled.

"It's awesome. Make sure you get a picture for Jen."

Max took several and then settled down to eat, Fred on one side and Olly opposite him. There was beer for those who wanted it, and soda and water for the drivers, and abstainers.

Fred was busy texting when Max came back from getting his second plate of food.

"I was just checking in with my beautiful wife, Moira," Fred said. "Want to see a picture?"

He showed Max at least ten, including his two young children and then chuckled and shook his head.

"Sometimes I can't believe how damn lucky I've been. I left the service thinking I'd never find anyone who understood what I'd been through unless they were as screwed up as I was." He grimaced. "I dated a few who were me in female form and it never worked."

Max winced. "I know how that goes."

"And then I met Moira when I took my nephew to the library and suddenly everything changed." He paused. "For the first time in my life, I wanted to be the man she thought I was."

Max nodded. He totally understood that desire.

"So, I set about convincing her that I was right for her. It took a while, but eventually I wore her down." He grinned. "She's just amazing."

"She must be if she tamed you," Max agreed.

"You might say the same about your lady," Fred said. "Because when you told me you'd been married for four years I was surprised."

Two seconds later, Max found himself whipping out his phone and showing Fred a couple of pictures of Phoebe.

"No kids yet?"

"Nah, not ready for that. We're still deciding where we're going to live. Phoebe's British."

"I can't see you fitting in too well in the UK, Max. You're too loud."

Max shrugged. "I guess I'll leave that up to Phoebe to decide. I just want her to be happy."

Fred raised his beer bottle. "Happy wife, happy life."

Max clinked his bottle against Fred's. "Amen to that."

Jane came to stand beside Noah.

"There's still plenty of food and dessert if you're hungry. Coffee and tea will be provided, and you can help yourselves." She smiled at Max who winked back at her. "And when you've finished that, three different experiences await you. We have a tarot card reader if you wish to explore your future, a reflexologist for your feet, and a henna tattoo artist."

Once Jane finished speaking and Noah went to get more food, Luke looked over at Max.

"You did good, bro."

"Like you doubted me?"

"All the way." Luke grinned at him. "Can we do the same thing for my bachelor party?"

"You'll have to ask Olly. It was his idea."

Olly looked up from his ice-cream sundae. "You and Bernie are getting married?"

"If she'll have me," Luke said.

"Congratulations, and if you want your party here, I'm sure we could arrange that." Olly grinned. "I really like the way it's turned out." He looked over at Max. "Thanks for all the input. You made my vision a reality."

Max shrugged. "I just thought of all the things Noah would run a mile from and picked them."

"Ha!" Luke pointed his finger at Max. "You're a genius."

"I know. I'm totally surprised he's still here."

"You drove him here."

"True, but if he'd really hated it, he would've jumped me, taken the truck keys, and left us behind in the dust."

"Yeah." Luke nodded. "Are you going to try the tarot cards?"

"Maybe later."

Luke looked over toward the seating area where a woman was laying out her cards. "I'm going to get in there before Noah comes back." He stood up and walked past Max. "You should go next. If anyone needs to find out what the future holds, it has to be you."

Even though Max smiled, he wasn't sure he agreed because he couldn't see a way forward, and the last thing he needed was for someone to confirm that he was right. But one thing was clear, Phoebe would be leaving after the wedding to go to England without him, and whether she came back, was still up in the air.

He had to stop dancing around the subject and have an adult conversation with her about it. All the progress he'd made in being a better person meant nothing if he couldn't face up to the most important conversation of his life so far.

Fred went off to see the reflexologist. When Noah returned, he took the vacated chair next to Max and set his plate down with a decisive thump. He still wore the crown Sky had made and had glitter in his beard, which Max wasn't going to mention. He looked way more approachable than Max had ever seen him.

"I just wanted to say thank you for all of this."

Max nodded warily. "You're welcome."

"I didn't want a fuss and I only agreed to the dinner because Jen made me, but I'm having a great time."

"That's good."

Noah smiled. "I know we don't always see eye to eye, but I'm always here for you, Max. You just have to ask."

"Right back at you."

Noah leaned in and hugged him, leaving Max speechless. "Thanks again."

Noah stood and glanced over at the tarot card reader who was chatting away to Luke as if they were old friends.

"I guess I'll try the henna stuff first. Jen will love that."

Max watched him go, still dumbfounded by the bear hug. Noah had never been a demonstrative person and Max could count on his fingers the times they'd hugged. A sense of satisfaction filled him. He'd done something good for his friend and there was no better feeling than that.

Perhaps he should try it more often.

After Bernie departed, Phoebe had a shower and got ready for bed. She was already regretting the wine and made sure to drink lots of water to counteract the headache she could already feel creeping up her neck. She got into bed and checked she'd set the alarm on her phone. She had a full day of pampering to get through before they drove back to the ranch tomorrow evening and she intended to enjoy every minute of it.

She noticed she had a couple of new messages including one from Max. She couldn't help but smile at the selfie of him and the other men gathered around the table in the middle of the forest.

Success! Noah didn't murder me.

Phoebe checked the time and wondered if the guys were still at the party or heading home. Suddenly, wanting even the slightest connection with Max, she texted back.

Well done!

His reply came through immediately. **Wish you were here with me right now.**

Phoebe held her breath. Was that the first time Max had indicated he missed her?

I think you'd prefer this big bed at the spa.

True, probably less bugs.

Phoebe paused, wondering what to say next when he sent a follow-up.

And you'd be in the bed with me, obvs.

Phoebe smiled as she replied. **It feels very big with just me in it**.

I bet. And now I'm thinking about that and missing you even more.

Really? Phoebe went still.

100%. We should talk about that when you get back.

Yes, we really should.

Good night sweetheart.

Night Max x

Chapter 14

Of course, saying that they'd talk about what was going on between them was easier than finding the time to do it because the wedding was approaching fast. Phoebe was busy with her flowers and helping Sally with a million little details. She'd even driven Max's truck and braved the journey into town to pick up a bunch of stuff from the post office when Sally had to attend the clinic.

Noah spent most of his time out on the ranch, which meant he took Max and Luke with him for long, hard, arduous days. The only person who didn't seem affected by all the fuss was Jen, but she'd worked through many disaster scenarios on her medical ship and insisted it took a lot to get her flustered.

Phoebe, having run countless events at her family home, was almost as calm as Jen and actively enjoyed using her skill set to make things move swiftly along. Jen found her at the kitchen table on the evening before the wedding with a cup of tea next to her elbow, going through her notebook.

"Everything okay?" Jen refreshed her tea for her and sat down. "Anything I can do to help?"

"I can't think of anything." Phoebe looked up from her list checking. "I'm just making sure that all is in order for tomorrow."

"I can't believe we made it this far without Noah taking over," Jen said. "If it hadn't been for you calming him down and constantly reassuring him everything was on track, I don't know what he would've done." She smiled at Phoebe. "You're really good at this."

"I've had lots of practice," Phoebe said. "My family home is rather large and has high maintenance costs. The only way to keep it going is to rent out parts of it for various reasons. We've had film crews, advertisers, weddings, conferences, book festivals . . . you name it, we've hosted it."

"That's amazing." Jen sipped her tea. "We could do with someone like that out here."

"I did wonder about that," Phoebe said. "But I'm still not sure . . ." It was her friend's wedding day tomorrow. The last thing she wanted was to make everything about her.

"Hasn't Max asked you what your plans are?"

"We haven't really discussed it."

Jen frowned at her. "If you're waiting for Max to broach the subject, you'll have to wait a very long time."

"This is his home. Surely, he gets to decide whether he wants me to stay or not?"

"I'm not sure Max knows how to ask for anything for himself," Jen said thoughtfully. "I don't think he's ever felt safe enough."

A pang of sympathy shot through Phoebe.

"I didn't see a lot of my family when I was growing up. I get the same vibe from Max sometimes—that he can't quite believe anyone really wants him around," Jen smiled. "Obviously, I'm getting better at that, but it took Noah a lot of persuading to get me to start believing I was loved and wanted."

"So, you think I should reach out to Max?" Phoebe asked.

Jen held her gaze. "Only if you truly want to stay here with him."

"Once the wedding is over, I'll talk to him."

"Promise?"

Phoebe nodded.

"And even if I am on my honeymoon in Hawaii, I still expect to be kept informed of any progress. I want you both to be as happy as I am." Jen stood up. "I'm heading over to the snowmobile barn to check that everything is in order for Noah's family and then I'm going to put Sky to bed."

Phoebe consulted her notes. "I'll check in with Lucy at the B&B to see if the other guests have arrived, and make sure the cabins are ready for Maria and the two guys from Noah's former unit."

After Jen had gone, Phoebe stayed at the table, thinking through what Jen had said about Max. Phoebe had always sensed there was a distance within him— wrapped within a laughing, funny, barrier to stop anyone really getting to know him. Could she make him understand that she was with him for good?

And when had she decided that? Had she been in love with him all along? How was she going to reconcile her fierce desire to get her rightful inheritance in England with the wonderful complications of falling in love with a California cowboy?

"Feebs?"

She jumped as if she'd been shot as the object of her desire came in from the mudroom.

"You okay?" He stopped and stared at her.

"You . . . scared me."

"Sorry." He grinned at her. "I do that to a lot of people. How's the wedding planning going?"

"Great!" Phoebe said brightly, her voice sounded weird even to her. "All in hand."

"I'm picking Maria up from the bus station downtown at five." Max went into the kitchen, washed his hands, and looked in the refrigerator. "I offered to drive to Reno, but she said she'd be fine on the bus."

"It will be nice to see her again," Phoebe spoke to his wrangler-clad arse as he reached farther into the back of the refrigerator. "She was very kind to me."

Max emerged with a huge block of cheese and a jar of Sally's pickles in his hands. "Do you want a snack, Feebs? I'm going to be late for dinner after I pick up Maria and get her settled in the cabin."

"No, thank you. I must get on."

Max looked at her. "You don't look like you're going anywhere right now, and you sound kind of dazed. Are you sure you're, okay?"

"I'm absolutely fine."

"It's never good when a woman says they're fine." Max got some bread out of the pantry and started fixing himself a sandwich. "But I don't think this one is on me seeing as you haven't set eyes on me all day."

Phoebe shot to her feet. "I really do have to go. There's still a lot to do."

Max put down the knife and came across to her, his expression full of concern. He placed his hand on her shoulder. "You're shaking."

She found a smile somewhere. "It's just adrenaline

because I'm so busy. I'll feel much better once I tick all the boxes on my to-do list."

"When's the last time you ate?" Max asked.

"I'm . . . not sure."

"Then let me make you a sandwich." Max strode back into the kitchen. "Hell, have mine."

Phoebe grabbed half the sandwich off the plate, took a large bite, and turned on her heel.

"Thanks so much." A bit of pickle shot out of her mouth as she hurried through to the mudroom and put on her wellies. "I'll see you later."

"Phoebe . . ."

She ran.

Max checked the time, got out of his truck, and watched the bus come around the corner at the end of the street. It was a warm evening and sunlight glinted off the windows and heat rose in shimmering waves from the metal. The bus slowed to a stop in front of him and the doors opened with a loud flourish, releasing a waft of stale air and the first couple of passengers. Maria was the last to get off. She waved at Max and tipped the driver when he extracted her case from the luggage bay beneath the coach.

"Max!"

He made sure her bag was on the sidewalk and then bent to give her a hug. She was petite like their mother, her skin a shade darker than his because his father was second-generation American and half-white.

She hugged him hard and patted his face. "It's so lovely to see you!"

He appreciated her making the effort to speak to him in English. He barely spoke any Spanish, even though he could understand it pretty well, but it was Maria's preferred language.

"You ready to go or do you need anything in town?" Max asked as he took control of her wheeled case, which was surprisingly heavy.

"I think I packed enough for a month's stay," Maria made a face. "I couldn't decide what to bring."

"Always good to have plenty of choices," Max was just glad he'd parked the truck close.

"And I brought food. I wasn't sure if that was included with the cabin."

"It's all included. You'll be eating with us in the main house," Max reassured her as he unlocked his truck and manhandled the suitcase into the back. "Why don't you hop up in here and I'll take you back to the ranch."

He gave her a boost up into the seat, which made her laugh, and she settled in beside him.

"Is it far?"

"Fifteen minutes max at this time of year. When it's snowing? Maybe not at all." He turned on the A/C, eased out of the parking space, and onto the county road. "We were completely cut off last winter."

Maria shuddered. "I don't think I could live in such a cold place."

"I kind of like the variety," Max said. "You never know whether you'll be shoveling snow or putting a fire out."

Maria turned her attention to the scenery and Max focused on getting out of town and onto the quieter road up into the forest.

"How is Phoebe?"

"She's good." Max paused to look both ways before crossing the logging track. "She's been riding the range like a real cowboy."

Maria laughed. "I can't imagine. She seemed to be such a lady."

"She is, but she rides better than me."

"I cannot believe it. Your father made sure you were a very good rider."

Max remembered his father's voice in his ear, holding him tight and close, telling him everything would be okay as he settled him on the back of his horse. He'd liked it even more when his dad had gotten up behind him and ridden around the field. There hadn't been a safer place in his world . . .

Maria was pointing at the distant mountains. "I see snow."

"Yeah, it usually disappears by the end of June, but sometimes it doesn't go at all." He shook off the memories and concentrated on his driving. "The weather's set to be fine tomorrow for the wedding, not too hot, or too cold."

"That's great," Maria said. "I can't wait to meet your friends, Max."

"They're looking forward to meeting you." Max hesitated. "I got a lot of crap for not mentioning you earlier, so don't be surprised if they go on about it."

"You didn't tell them you had a big sister?" She turned to look at him, her expression so like their mom's that he almost did a double take.

"I didn't tell them I had any family at all," Max admitted. "I guess I thought once I told them about the one person I love and who looked out for me, they'd want to know about the rest of them."

She went quiet for a while and looked out of the window again.

"They still exist, Max."

"I get that." He cleared his throat. "Can we talk about something else? How's work?"

"The same as ever. Casinos will always need accountants, so I doubt I'll ever be out of a job."

"Smart woman," Max commented as he slowed the truck and indicated that he was about to turn left.

He reached over his head to activate the gate clicker and barely had to pause to get the truck through.

"It's bumpier down here," he warned Maria. "You might want to hang onto something."

He eased the truck down the driveway, past the snowmobile barn where a minivan was now parked and up toward the main ranch house. The cabins were to the right of the house, so he parked near them and got out to help Maria descend the step.

"First one on the left," he called out to her as he struggled with her suitcase. "Door's open."

"*Gracias*," Maria headed up the path and he followed behind.

"Oh my . . ." She stopped just inside the door. "It's lovely!"

Luke had converted the old bunkhouse into three separate cabins with a bedroom, a bathroom, and an open plan kitchen and living space. The floors were wood, the walls a creamy white and the furniture simple and modern. Someone, probably Phoebe, had placed a vase of fresh flowers on the small kitchen table along with a basket full of provisions.

Maria set her backpack on the couch and went into the kitchen. She picked up the card and read out the words.

"Welcome, Maria! We are all so glad that you could come to the wedding!"

She pressed the card to her chest, her eyes shining, then turned to Max. "Is there a refrigerator?"

Max studied the row of cabinets. "I'm sure there is. Why, what's up?"

"Because I have food to put in there." She directed him to lay her case on its back on her bed so that she could open it. "And I don't want it to spoil."

When a beaming Maria came into the kitchen with Max, Phoebe rushed over to give her a hug.

"It's lovely to see you again!"

Maria patted her cheek. "You look very well, *querida*. Max tells me Luke's been putting you to work."

"Yeah, free labor's awesome." Max grinned at Phoebe.

"I think I should be paying Luke, actually, I've had so much fun," Phoebe said. "How was your trip?"

"It all went very smoothly," Maria said. "Max was there to pick me up at the bus stop, so I didn't have to worry about a thing."

Sally and Luke came over to be introduced and Phoebe stepped back to let Max make the introductions. Noah and Jen had taken Sky to the new house and were having a barbecue with Noah's family who had arrived from San Diego earlier. The two guys who would be occupying the other cabins were due in the morning of the wedding and would only need them for the night.

Phoebe had spent most of the day double-checking everything and was beginning to believe the wedding would be a resounding success. She planned to get up at four to finish the flower arrangements, which needed to be as fresh as she could make them. She had forgotten to eat since Max's half-sandwich and the sight of Sally putting a huge lasagna on the table made her stomach grumble.

"You hungry, Feebs?" Max asked.

"Starving." She smiled at him. "I've been rushing around like a blue-arsed fly."

"That's a descriptive phrase," Sally said. "I'll have to try and remember it."

Phoebe blushed. "I'm sorry."

"What for? No one here knows you were saying ass." Max cut into the lasagna.

"They do now," Luke murmured. "Thanks for the clarification."

He turned to Phoebe. "Did Bernie mention what time she's arriving tomorrow when you saw her?"

"Six, I believe. She said she had a lot to do to get her temporary kitchen ready."

"I've set her up under an awning to the back of the house so she can have access to the main kitchen, as well," Luke said. "And there's a whole nother structure for the sit-down buffet, which is already up."

"Noah's mom and stepdad have arrived at the B&B and his sisters are here at the snowmobile barn," Sally added. "I spoke to them earlier."

"I saw the minivan when I came down the drive," Max said. "Are they partying with Noah and Jen?"

"I think that was the idea," Luke said. He glanced over at the empty space at the head of the table. "It's weird not having Sky here."

"Better get used to it," Sally said. "He'll be moving out in a couple of weeks. I'm going to miss seeing his little face."

"He's only going to be a few hundred yards down the road," Luke reminded her. "I'm sure Jen won't mind if you pop round."

Phoebe ate two platefuls of the lasagna and helped clear up afterward while Max took Maria on a stroll around the ranch. When they returned, Phoebe was just making herself a cup of tea and offered one to Maria who shook her head.

"*Gracias*, Phoebe, but I think I am ready for bed. It has been a long day." She looked up at Max. "I am so happy for you, *hermano*. Your life here is beautiful. You are truly blessed."

Max's gaze fastened on Phoebe. "Yeah, I guess I am."

"Would you walk me back to my cabin, please, Phoebe?" Maria asked. "I'm sure Max has lots to do having spent so much time with me."

"I suspect he'd much rather be with you than mucking out the stables," Phoebe said as she followed Maria to the door of the cabin through the balmy night air. "He was so pleased you were able to come."

"I am very glad that I did." Maria went into the cabin and shut the door behind Phoebe. "It makes me feel much better about what I have done."

She turned to face Phoebe, her hands clasped together at her waist. "Has Max told you about his family?"

With a feeling of unease, Phoebe sat on the couch. "He mentioned he has no contact with anyone but you."

"He was a very bad boy. Our parents were at their wits end."

"So I understand."

Maria sat opposite her. "He got in trouble with the

police and ended up in court. The best solution seemed to send him away to military school to avoid the possibility of prison, and that's what they did, but it was very hard for them."

"Forgive me, Maria, if they were truly conflicted, why didn't they resume contact with Max after he straightened himself out and enlisted?"

"I believe they tried, but Max wanted nothing to do with them."

Phoebe didn't contest that, even though Max had implied something very different.

"From what they told me, Max refused to apologize for his behavior, or even meet them on their terms," Maria continued. "I told my mother he would not respond well to what he would see as an ultimatum, but she refused to change her mind about how to deal with him."

"And I assume that means they didn't speak at all."

Maria nodded. "Max and our mama are both very stubborn. Over the years, I passed on basic information about Max just so they knew he was alive. They were very grateful to me for doing that, but recently my mother has been asking for more."

"More information about Max?" Phoebe asked. "Have you told him that?"

"Of course not. That is why I am talking to you."

"I don't quite follow."

"I told them Max was married!" Maria threw her hands in the air. "I thought that might be enough to stop Mama from bothering me, but she was thrilled."

"You really need to talk to Max about this, Maria. I can't—"

"She wants to talk to you." Maria looked pleadingly at Phoebe. "I have told her how wonderful you are and what an excellent influence you have been on Max."

Phoebe shot to her feet. "I can't do that without Max knowing all about it, Maria, so talk to him, and he can let me know what he wants me to do."

Maria sighed, "As you wish, *querida*. I hoped to keep it amongst us women. I will tell Mama that I need to speak to Max first."

"I think that would be for the best," Phoebe assured her and went toward the door. She paused before leaving. "Do you think there is any particular reason why your parents are suddenly interested in getting to know Max? Has anything changed in their lives?"

Maria smiled at her. "I think they are just getting older, and I suspect Mama has some regrets about how she dealt with Max when he was just a teenager." She winked. "And maybe she is thinking about her future grandchildren."

For a fleeting second, Phoebe remembered her nanny admonishing her about lying, and how the lies mounted up until they buried you, and bitterly regretted her impulsive decision to involve Max in her schemes to inherit her rightful property.

"Then perhaps the person she should be reaching out to is the one she hurt," Phoebe said. "Goodnight, Maria. We'll be serving breakfast in the main house from seven until nine tomorrow morning."

"Goodnight, Phoebe. Thank you for listening to me."

Phoebe was halfway back to the house when she stopped, gulped in some much-needed air, and changed direction. She made her way down to the barn and leaned against the fence staring into the darkness over the horse pasture. If she went back in and Max asked about Maria, she was afraid he'd read her face too easily, and start asking some awkward questions she really didn't want to answer.

At some level, she understood why Maria had come to her. It was a tradition in her own family for her and Eugenie to share secrets and support each other against their brothers. But she couldn't do that to Max.

"Phoebe."

She turned her head to see Luke coming out of the barn. He joined her at the railing, one booted foot on the first railing and his chin resting on his crossed arms as he stared at the horizon.

"You look stressed."

"I'm fine, Luke." Phoebe continued to look out at nothing. "I just needed a moment."

"You've been amazing. I'm not sure we would've pulled this off if you hadn't been there to corral all the pieces together."

"You would've managed just fine without me."

"Yeah, if we'd let Noah take over." Luke paused for a beat. "Bernie was saying we could do with a good wedding planner around here and that she'd be your first customer."

"That's very sweet of her."

"She's right on both counts, though. We need it and you're good at it."

"A match made in heaven." Phoebe tried to laugh it off.

"Just making sure you know there's a place and a way to make your living out here even if you ditched Max."

Unaccustomed tears choked Phoebe's throat. "Thank you, Luke. That means a lot to me."

Luke nodded and continued to look out over the pasture. "One thing I've learned about relationships recently, Phoebe, is that you have to try and be honest with the other person even if it might be a painful conversation."

Phoebe considered what to say. "But what if the information you've just been given isn't yours to share?"

He glanced over at her. "That's very specific."

"I don't want to be put in the middle of a . . . family issue."

"Then don't be. Step out of the firing line and tell them to sort it out themselves."

"That's what I'm trying to do." She sighed. "But now I know stuff I didn't want to know, and I don't have the right kind of face to *hide* that I know it."

Luke reached out and patted her shoulder. "You sound just like Bernie."

"What does she do in these situations?" Phoebe asked.

"Blurts it all out, usually." Luke grinned.

"I can't do that." Phoebe shuddered. "I'm already in trouble for laying down the law with my own family."

"So, I've heard. Max doesn't have a high opinion of how they've treated you."

"Max is . . ." Phoebe paused. "Wonderful."

"He's something all right." Luke smiled. "I just want him to be happy."

"So do I."

"Then we're on the same page." He straightened up and gave her a friendly nod. "I'd better turn in. It's going to be a busy day tomorrow."

Phoebe turned to face him. "Thank you for making me feel so at home, Luke."

"That was easy, Phoebe." He smiled. "You just fit right in."

He walked back up to the house, leaving her in the shadowed light coming from the barn and the vast expanse of the redwood forest at her back. It was the first time in her life anyone had told her she wasn't the odd one out, the one who wouldn't conform, or do what was expected, and it was surprisingly moving.

Could she do it? Could she leave her home and come and live on the ranch with Max and his newfound family? The very idea seemed preposterous, especially as she was currently engaged in a fight to release property from the estate and was about to take her family to court over it.

And Max hadn't asked her to stay or even whether she planned on coming back after her trip to England . . .

She checked the time and started back toward the house. After the wedding, she'd have to stop being such a coward and have what would probably be a difficult conversation with Max. He'd been nothing but generous by agreeing to marry her and supporting her through the lies that had now engulfed his own family. He deserved her honesty for that alone.

She stopped walking. The thought of not being with him made her heart clench, but he'd never tried to make her fall in love with him. That was on her.

The house was quiet, the scent of coffee and Bernie's cinnamon rolls lingering in the kitchen. Phoebe drank some milk, used the bathroom, and tiptoed into Max's bedroom. She knew he was there because he was gently snoring, which often happened when he slept on his back. She didn't bother with her nightie, just stripped, and got into bed.

Max immediately rolled over and cuddled in, one hand around her waist, his chin in the hollow of her neck.

"Feebs . . ." he murmured. "I missed you."

She bit down hard on her lip. She'd miss him so much. Why had she refused to take him to England? What if he'd liked it enough to want to stay there with her? She tried to picture him with her family and failed miserably. They wouldn't understand him, or even try to, and they'd treat him accordingly.

He moved closer, his hand drifting downward to cup her between the legs and she immediately wanted him. It had been like that from the day they'd met and there was nothing she could do about it. He flexed his fingers, and she arched her back, her body already anticipating his next touch as his cock hardened against her bottom.

He shifted slightly behind her, bringing his right arm underneath her, pulling her hip wide and her body higher into the shelter of his torso. Phoebe leaned her head back and let him play her like a violin, his fingers parting and entering her, his thumb insistent and then rough on her clit.

"Okay like this?" He sounded half-aroused, half-asleep and very turned on, and she didn't want him to ever stop touching her.

"Yes. Don't stop."

He slid his cock into her, making her gasp at the unfamiliar angle and the new sensations he was arousing in her. He rocked his hips anchoring her firmly against his working body and she caught his rhythm and went with it. One of his hands closed around her breast and his fingers squeezed her nipple in time to his thrusts making her come so hard she saw stars.

He growled and bit her neck, which set her off again. He thrust harder and she forgot words and just hung on and wallowed in sensation as he pushed her through two more climaxes before he finally joined her with a guttural roar that left them both shaking. It took her a long while to breathe normally and longer to open her eyes because she simply didn't want the feelings to end.

His gentle snore made her smile. Even though she knew she was a coward, she was glad she could put off talking to him and simply enjoy being with him for one more precious night . . .

Chapter 15

When his alarm went off, Max woke from a fantastic dream of making love with Phoebe and reluctantly opened his eyes. Phoebe's side of the bed was empty. He frowned. Had she come to bed at all? His gaze fell on a damp spot on the sheet, and he went still. She'd definitely been there.

"Shit," Max muttered and got out of bed. He ran to the bathroom, which was empty and smelled of Phoebe's shampoo. His quick shower gave him more evidence that he hadn't used a condom and he cursed himself for his stupidity. All his primal instincts were shouting how good it had been and how many times he'd made Phoebe come while his modern-day feelings were way more complicated.

He got dressed fast and hurried into the kitchen. From out the back he heard voices and Anton, Bernie's patisserie expert, came in carrying about twenty stacked containers.

"Hey, Max. Where's the refrigerator? Bernie said to stick these in there."

"It's here." Max showed him the right door, grabbed some coffee, and swallowed it down way too hot. "Sorry I can't hang around. I've got to get on with my chores."

"No problem," Anton said. "We're just getting set up ourselves." He glanced around the kitchen. "I think I can work with this space."

As he ran down to the barn, Max tried to remember where everyone was supposed to be. Jen had stayed at the new house to prep for the wedding, Phoebe was doing the flowers and he and Luke were in charge of the regular barn duties. Of course, the first person he saw when he went in was Noah.

"You're late."

"Why are you even here?" Max asked. "Don't you have a wedding to go to or something?"

"I can multitask," Noah said. "All I have to do is shower, put on my new shirt, and I'm good to go." He paused. "And if I sit around thinking about everything that could go wrong, I'll drive myself crazy."

Max nodded. "Understandable. What do you want me to do?"

"Just the usual. Luke's working his way down the right side so why don't you take the left?"

By the time he was ready for breakfast, he still hadn't seen Phoebe. He hoped she was up at the house so that he could have a quiet word. Unfortunately, the kitchen was full of guests having breakfast and Bernie's café staff borrowing things and taking up space. Maria was also there but she was busy chatting with Sky and Sally. She didn't seem inclined to come over to him, which was just fine.

"Anyone seen Phoebe?" he asked as loudly as he could.

"She was out attaching flowers and vines to the wedding gazebo about half an hour ago," Sally said. "I saw her when I was out with the dogs."

"Thanks, I'll take a look."

Max grabbed a breakfast burrito from the tray and one of Bernie's cinnamon rolls and ate them both in record time. He made some tea in a disposable cup from Bernie's stash, topped it with milk and snuck two more rolls into his pocket. His stomach wasn't impressed as he went out through the back door, past Bernie's temporary kitchen, and into the garden area at the rear of the house. He'd forgotten how diffcrent it now looked—what with the dance floor laid out on the left and the wedding tent and gazebo to the right.

He spotted Phoebe up a ladder and went toward her. She had her hands raised above her head and was threading ivy or something clingy through the slats.

"Hey, what's hanging?"

She jumped and he reached out to steady thc ladder and grabbed her ankle.

"Sorry. I'm always scaring you."

"It's fine. I was quite safe." She climbed down, her face flushed, and busied herself looking in her basket of supplies. "What can I do for you?"

Max looked at her averted face and let out a breath.

"Are you mad at me?"

That got her attention.

"No! Why would you think that?"

"Because I—" He made a gesture toward his groin and then at hers. "Didn't—"

She put her hand on his arm. "Max, I was fully awake, you were half-asleep, and I was okay with it."

"We should've discussed it first."

She slowly raised her chin. "Hang on, are you cross because I took advantage of *you*?"

Max frowned "That's not what I'm saying, Feebs, and you damn well know it."

"Well, that's what it sounds like." Her brown eyes were shooting sparks. "I apologize. I was in the wrong and I promise I will never do it again. Now, if you will excuse me, I need to finish this."

She stomped up the ladder and started working, leaving him staring up at her like a fool.

"For the record, I am not mad at you. I do not blame you, and I just wanted to make sure you were okay about what happened," Max said. "I wasn't even sure whether I'd dreamed the whole thing, until—"

"Fine!" He'd never heard Phoebe raise her voice before. "You were asleep, the fault was mine because I'm a bloody fool, now will you please go away before I forget myself, and drop something heavy on your head?"

He looked up at her. "This is stupid."

She ignored him and he sighed.

"Feebs, I don't want to fight with you. Can we start this whole conversation again?"

He waited another couple of seconds, but she wasn't coming down the ladder, or getting off her high horse any time soon. He set the cup of tea and the cinnamon rolls on the top of her workbasket.

"When you want to talk, just come and find me, okay?"

He turned away, running the conversation through his head, trying to work out when it had gone so spectacularly off the rails. He was still thinking about it when he arrived back at the house to find Luke looking for him.

"You up for moving some chairs and hay bales?" Luke asked. "Mom wants us to set up the wedding tent and the dining area."

"Sure." He went with Luke to where the rented chairs were stacked against the side wall. "Hey, have you ever felt like Bernie was just looking for something to be mad about with you, and that whatever you said to defend yourself or explain just made it worse?"

"Oh, yeah. I've been there, bro." Luke picked up three chairs in each hand.

"I just had the weirdest conversation with Phoebe." Max took the same number of chairs and followed Luke into the dining area. "It was like she was determined to pick a fight with me."

Luke set the chairs where Sally had marked the planked floor around the tables.

"Obviously, Phoebe's not Bernie, but I usually find it's because they don't want to get into an argument with you about something else."

"That makes no sense."

"It does to them," Luke said. "And usually, the thing they don't want to talk about is the important thing."

"Jeez . . ." Max groaned. "So how do you get them to talk about that?"

Luke shrugged. "You don't."

"I've got to put up with Phoebe being mad at me for something I don't know that I've done, and she won't tell me, because we're fighting about something stupid?"

"That about covers it." Luke grabbed more chairs. "Let her work it out herself and when she's ready she'll talk about it."

Max studied Luke who appeared to be avoiding his gaze. "Do you know something I don't?"

"Like what?" Luke had never been a great liar. He was way too nice.

"Something Bernie told you that Phoebe told her maybe?"

Luke's eyebrows rose. "Even if that were true, I still wouldn't tell you."

"So, you do know something," Max pounced. "How about some solidarity here, boss? Help a guy out."

"Nah." Luke grinned at him. "It's way more fun watching you suffer. Kind of payback on a grand scale."

Max might have banged the chairs around when he put them out, but Luke appeared oblivious. When they'd finished and were about to move on to the gazebo, Max spoke again.

"Can I summarize here, boss? Phoebe's mad at me, but not for the thing I think she's mad about," Max said. "And according to you, I just have to wait until she wants to tell me what's really going on."

Luke winked at him. "Got it in one."

Max gave him the finger.

Phoebe hurriedly finished the last flowers in the gazebo as Luke and Max approached with the chairs. She felt a bit guilty about getting cross with Max. She'd lost her nerve when he'd come up behind her and all her carefully thought-out speeches about asking him what their future together might look like had flown out of her head and she'd panicked and picked a fight.

And now she didn't know how to fix it.

And she was genuinely hurt that what she'd believed was amazing lovemaking had barely registered to Max who'd only noticed something was off in the morning, It was a good reminder that what might be earth-shatteringly new to her was old news to Max. Thank goodness she hadn't blurted out that she loved him—although whether he would've been awake enough to hear her was another matter.

She picked up her ladder and basket and went back to the greenhouse where she'd stored the last of the flowers. There were two women she hadn't met admiring the blooms who looked up when she came in. Their smiles looked vaguely familiar.

"Hi! You must be Phoebe. We're Noah's sisters. We've come to help."

"How lovely," Phoebe said. "I could do with some help. There are half a dozen table decorations to put together, and I haven't even started them."

Two hours later, all the flowers were in place and Jen's bouquet had been tenderly carried over to the new house where she was getting ready. Phoebe went into the house and straight to the kitchen which was full of people she didn't know. Bernie came through the back door, took one look at her, and pointed at a chair.

"Sit. When did you last eat?"

"I'm not sure," Phoebe said. "I'm not terribly—"

A large glass of cold milk, two doughnuts and a cinnamon roll were put in front of her.

"Eat. I'll get someone to make you a mug of tea."

Bernie in full boss mode was something to see as she directed her staff in a thousand tasks. Phoebe halfheartedly nibbled the bun and immediately set about tearing it apart and devouring it. A mug of tea made just how she liked it appeared at her elbow and she drank it down like the addict she was.

"That's better," Bernie said. "You started work about the same time I did, and it's almost eleven now."

"I'm just about done," Phoebe mumbled through a mouthful of roll. "This is delicious."

"You wait until you see what we've done for the wedding buffet. It will knock your socks off." Bernie held up her hand and someone put another mug of tea in it, which she handed to Phoebe.

"Why don't you go and get ready?" Bernie suggested. "Sally said to use her bathroom so the boys can have the other one."

"I still have to go through my checklist and make sure everything has been done," Phoebe said. "I'm not sure if the sound system has been tested yet."

"Noah's dealing with that." Bernie grinned. "We had to give him something to do before he went mad. But Luke's keeping an eye on him and will get him to the altar on time."

"Luke strikes me as a remarkably efficient man." Phoebe finished the second mug of tea and finally felt human again.

Bernie looked over Phoebe's shoulder and rattled off about ten different orders which were instantly obeyed by her staff.

"I'm keeping you from your work and you need time to get changed, too." Phoebe started to get up.

"Nah, I've got plenty of time," Bernie said. "The secret to being the boss is employing incredibly talented staff who make you look good."

"You got that right, boss," Anton said as he walked past them.

Bernie grinned at him and then looked back at Phoebe. "Check your list and then go off and get changed, okay?"

"Yes, boss." Phoebe smiled back. "I'll do that."

After another quick tour of the wedding venues where there was no sign of Max, Phoebe went back into the house and into the bedroom. Her new dress was hanging on the back of the door. It was a classic tea dress made with chiffon over satin and had puffed sleeves and skirt that reminded her of her grandmother's rose garden. Despite knowing that any hat that wasn't a cowboy hat probably wasn't essential at this particular wedding, she'd bought a floppy straw hat and intended to tie the sash from the dress around the crown.

She gathered up her clothing and makeup bag and skedaddled down the hall into Sally's bedroom suite where she discovered her host stuck halfway into her dress.

"Thank goodness you're here!" Sally said, her voice muffled by the linen. "I didn't undo enough buttons!"

Phoebe rushed over to help, and Sally soon emerged looking rather pink, but still laughing. "I thought I'd have to stagger into the kitchen and get one of Bernie's staff to release me."

"Then I'm glad I turned up just in time!" Phoebe couldn't help smiling. "That color looks amazing on you."

Sally shrugged as she smoothed out the creases in the mirror. "Oh, this old thing. It's one of my favorites from the '80s when I used to attend a lot of medical conferences and had to look smart. I decided to recycle my wardrobe about ten years ago and rarely bother to buy anything new."

Phoebe set her things out on the bed.

"Why don't you go and use the shower, Phoebe?" Sally suggested. "I've finished in there, and we might as well keep things moving along so that it's all freed up for Bernie."

"Phoebe?"

Max knocked before he went into his own bedroom, but he might not have bothered because she wasn't there. Her dress was also missing as was her cute hat and makeup bag.

"Where'd you go?" Max muttered. "It's like you're avoiding me or something."

He didn't have time to worry about that right now. Luke had asked him to make sure Fred and their other two Marine buddies were in their positions under the wedding gazebo before the ceremony started. He also had to make sure Bernie hadn't forgotten to get dressed, and to remind her, if necessary, because Luke had his hands full with Noah who was fretting.

And a fretting Noah was never good news.

Max got changed and shot off a quick text to Luke to reassure him that everything was going to plan. He had no idea if that was true, but he sensed the best man and groom needed the encouragement. He grabbed his best white Stetson and headed out, almost knocking Phoebe down as he came through the door.

"Sorry!' He grabbed her forearms to steady her. "You okay?"

From the way she was wincing, he guessed the answer was no.

"I'm fine." She took a tentative step forward. "Good thing you didn't have your boots on."

"Shame you didn't wear yours." He gently released her arm. "You look amazing."

"Thank you." She finally met his gaze. "So do you."

"Feebs . . . can we talk after this? Like *really* talk?" Max asked quietly.

She nodded. "I think that would be a very good idea."

"Thank you." He leaned in and kissed her nose. "I'll see you at the ceremony."

Max rushed off, collected Fred and the Marines, and got them settled in their seats. The sun had come out and it was warming up, which was a bonus. He took a moment to glance around the assembled congregation and almost everyone was in place. There was no sign of Luke or Noah. He suspected his former boss would be keeping Noah out of the way until the last possible second to stop him from losing his shit about everything that might go wrong.

The scent of lilacs wafted around him, and Max looked up at the pergola. Phoebe had done a brilliant job on the flowers, transforming a utilitarian space into a thing of beauty. He'd have to remember to tell her when they finally got a chance to talk. The fact that she'd agreed to a discussion was making him feel so much better about everything. His gaze fixed on an empty space on the groom's side, and he frowned. Where was Maria?

He excused himself from the guys and headed over toward the cabins. Maria's window was open, and she was talking away in Spanish, presumably to someone on her phone. Max knocked on the door and waited for the conversation to end. When she

didn't emerge, he knocked again and cautiously
tried the door, which was locked.

"The weddings gonna start in ten minutes, Maria.
You okay in there?" Max asked.

The door opened and Maria came out, her face
flushed, her gaze anywhere but at him. "I'm sorry. I
had to take that call."

"It's fine," Max said easily. "I'll escort you to your
seat."

She fussed around with the shawl draped over her
elbows, which had caught on the handle of her
purse. Max tried to help untangle the fringe, but she
told him to stop.

"I think you're making it worse. I'll fix it when I sit
down."

"As long as you can deal with it. Are you sure you
don't need scissors?"

"Goodness, no! That would ruin it. All it requires
is a little patience."

"Not one of my strengths," Max admitted.

Maria patted his arm. "You're so like your mother."

"So, you keep telling me." Max escorted her to her
seat, which was right next to Bernie's family and introduced her to everyone. "You'll be in great company, here."

"We'll take care of her, Max," Bernie's sister Mary
said. "And I can practice my Spanish!"

Max was still smiling as he strode down the aisle
and met Luke and Noah coming the other way.
They'd decided on blue shirts for the wedding and a
casual western style because they all felt most comfortable in cowboy hats and boots. Noah was frowning, which wasn't a surprise at all. He checked his
watch and scowled at Max.

"The guests should have been in their seats by now. Where's Bernie and the rest of her crew?"

"Bernie's on her way." Max used his most soothing voice. "Lucy was delayed at the B&B by some unexpected guests, but she'll be here any moment, so we're all good."

"Where's Phoebe?" Noah asked.

"Probably helping Bernie." Luke patted his arm. "Let's go say hi to your mom and take our positions at the front, okay?"

Luke rolled his eyes at Max as he persuaded Noah to move off and murmured. "Talk about groomzillas."

Max went to the back of the structure to keep an eye out for the latecomers and await the arrival of the bride and the rest of Noah's family. Bernie rushed past and blew him a kiss as she went to sit with her family. There was no sign of Phoebe and for the first time Max began to worry.

The bridal truck adorned with white ribbons arrived and Max went to open the door. Noah's sister Bailey, the oldest, got out and grinned at him.

"Max! Phoebe's awesome!"

"She is." He kissed her lightly on the cheek. "How's Jen holding up?"

"Calm as a US hospital ship in the middle of a hurricane." Bailey winked. "How's Noah?"

"Guess."

As he was talking to Bailey, Jen was exiting the vehicle assisted by the twins who wore identical blue dresses.

"Jen said she didn't need any bridesmaids, but the twins decided they were doing it for her anyway."

Bailey said. "Luckily, Phoebe had enough flowers to make them matching bouquets."

She turned back to Jen who wore a simple white wedding dress with a single flounce. She looked her usual composed self, but her eyes were bright with emotion.

"You look beautiful, Jen," Bailey said. "I'm going to sit down before I cry and ruin my makeup before the ceremony even starts."

"Thanks for everything, Bailey," Jen said, her voice shaking just a little. "I couldn't have done it without you."

Bailey blew her a kiss and Max swallowed hard.

Sally tapped him on the shoulder, and he almost jumped.

"I'm going to walk Sky up the aisle in front of Jen. He's going to throw some flower petals. It was the only way we could persuade him to behave."

"Sounds good." Max nodded. The wedding procession was getting longer by the minute, "Any idea where Phoebe is?"

"She's just getting Jen's flower crown. She wanted it to be as fresh as possible," Sally said,

He turned and saw Phoebe coming carefully down the steps, her hands full, and had to stop himself from going to her.

"Here it is, Jen." She hadn't yet noticed him, her attention on the crown. "I had to make sure it was free of moisture."

"I have pins," Jen said.

"Excellent." Phoebe was tall enough that she didn't need help to secure the crown on Jen's head. "You look amazing."

Jen briefly touched her cheek. "Thank you for everything."

Max cleared his throat as Phoebe stepped back and put her hat on. "You're seated next to me in the front row on the left. I'll join you in a minute."

She nodded and slipped away up the side aisle while Max assembled his little procession.

"Sally and Sky go first, followed by the twins, and then, Jen." One of the twins rolled their eyes, but he wasn't sure which one. "Jen, this is on you. When you're ready?"

Jen took a deep breath and looked down the aisle where Noah was pacing like a caged lion. "If I don't get there soon, he'll come and find me."

Max walked over and proffered his arm. "I know you don't need anyone to walk you down the aisle, but I'd be honored if you'd let me."

She met his gaze. "I can't think of anything I'd like better. Thank you, Max."

Chapter 16

Phoebe wasn't consciously avoiding Max, but it was a long time before she saw him for more than a few moments. The wedding was beautiful. Noah had ended up holding Sky as he and Jen made their vows, which was perfect, and Phoebe had tried very hard not to cry. Max had held her hand during the whole ceremony and only released it when he'd rushed off to make sure the photographer had arrived.

The buffet was as amazing as Bernie promised. Endless food had emerged from the small kitchen without pause as the day went on and the menu changed into the nibbles for the evening party. Half the town had been invited for the dance and Phoebe barely recognized anyone anymore. Noah, Jen, and Sky had left for the airport half an hour previously, but the party was still in full swing.

As the music changed to a slower pace, she felt a touch on her shoulder, and she turned to find Max smiling down at her. His blue shirt made his eyes look like sapphires and her gaze was drawn to his luscious mouth.

"Care for a dance Mrs. CSR?"

"Yes, please." She went into his arms. "My feet are killing me."

He glanced down at her fancy sandals. "You should've worn your boots."

"I'm planning on taking them off and putting my slippers on very soon," Phoebe confided. "But I'm scared that if I sit down, I might never get up again."

"It's been a long day." His fingers stroked the back of her neck, making her sigh and press close to him. "But I think it's been a good one."

"Noah and Jen look so happy," Phoebe agreed. "I can't imagine—" She trailed off and buried her face in his shoulder.

"How could anyone look at Noah like that?" Max asked. "I agree. It's a miracle."

Phoebe didn't contradict him, and they continued to dance in silence. She'd been thinking more about how amazing it would be to have someone love her like that, but that was a conversation Max had never wanted to have with her.

"The whole Noah and Jen thing actually gives me hope," Max said. "That there really is someone for everyone out there."

"I suppose you just have to get lucky." Phoebe smiled up at him.

"Yeah." He held her gaze. "Maybe you do." He took a quick breath. "About that—"

"Max?"

He broke off and looked behind him. "Hey, Lucy, what's up?"

Lucy grinned at him. "So glad we had that room cancellation, and we could fit them in!" She pointed toward the dining area. "I sat them down with Maria, if you want to go and say hi."

Max went very still. "Who's them?"

"Your parents. They said it would be a surprise!"

Lucy waved and walked away, leaving Phoebe and Max stationary on the dance floor. Phoebe glanced up at Max who had no expression on his face at all.

"Oh, my goodness."

He took her hand. "I guess we'd better go and say hello."

He strode off and Phoebe almost had to run to keep up with him. Maria saw them first and jumped to her feet, clapping her hands.

"Max! Isn't this wonderful?"

Phoebe stared at the man and woman who had slowly risen to their feet. Max had his mother's beauty and his father's height.

"Hey." Max smiled as if he bumped into his parents every day.

"We were traveling through Nevada, and we decided to stop at Maria's only to find she was here with you," Max's father said, his tone pleasant. "She suggested we pop by to say hi." He paused. "You look well, son."

"Thanks."

Max's grip on Phoebe's hand became almost painful.

Maria stepped into the awkward silence. "This is Phoebe, Max's wife. I told you she was pretty, Mama."

Phoebe automatically stuck out her hand. "It's nice to meet you both. I hear you're staying at the B&B in town."

"Yes, it's very pleasant," Max's mother said, her gaze fixed longingly on her son. "Won't you sit down, so that we can catch up, Max?"

"Catch up?" Max's tone was pleasant, but Phoebe wasn't fooled. "That would be awesome, but I'm kind of busy right now." He glanced over his shoulder. "I've got a wedding to steer through to the end."

"Surely—"

Phoebe spoke up. "Max really does have a lot to do." She looked at Maria. "Perhaps you can organize something at a more convenient time?"

Maria looked like she was going to cry. "I thought—"

Phoebe took Max's hand and nodded to his parents. "It was lovely to meet you. Enjoy the party and be careful on your way back to town, these roads can be dangerous at night."

She squeezed hard and led Max away until they cleared the fairy lights and were past the far side of the barn beside the pasture. She let go of his hand and he walked away from her, his back turned, his hands fisted at his side. She waited for what felt like hours and then risked speaking.

"I had no idea Maria intended to do that. I mean, she *said*—"

"She said what?" He swung around and it was like looking at a stranger. "You knew about this?"

"I knew she'd recently been in contact with your parents, but—"

A muscle flicked in his jaw. "And you didn't think I'd like to know about that?"

The cold fury in his voice finally raised her ire.

"If you let me finish a sentence, I might be able to explain."

"Explain what? That you and my sister thought it would be a great idea to ambush me with my estranged parents at my best friend's wedding? I specifically remember asking you not to meddle."

"I'll repeat. I didn't know Maria was planning on doing this," Phoebe said, trying hard to keep her cool. "And it might just have been one of those things. If your parents really did just pop in on her and she was here, she probably thought it would be fine to get you all together."

"Are you listening to yourself?" Max demanded. "Could you possibly believe that's true?"

"Why not? Coincidences do happen."

"You're defending my parents, now?"

"No!" Phoebe scowled at him. "I'm simply trying to look at all the logical explanations as to why they turned up here!"

"Are you feeling guilty about it, Feebs? Is this why you got mad at me this morning over nothing?" He glared at her. "Because it sure sounds like it. Maybe you encouraged Maria to think it would be a good idea."

She raised her chin. "I did no such thing. In fact, I told her she should talk to you and not involve me at all."

"Which you also failed to mention."

Phoebe opened and closed her mouth, her fingernails digging into her palms to stop herself from crying. It was like facing her grandmother and being treated like a dishonest child. She took an unsteady breath, then another, and tried to think. All she had to do was tell Max the truth and then he *had* to believe her. She met his gaze and took all the anger out of her voice.

"Maria said your mother wanted to talk to me, and I refused. I suggested she talk to you and leave me out of it. That's it. I'm sorry I didn't tell you. I thought I was doing the right thing."

"The right thing for you or for me? I asked you not to get all invested in 'happy ever afters' with my parents."

Phoebe pressed her lips together.

"No more excuses, Feebs? At least I know why you've been avoiding me all day."

Stung by his lack of trust, she retaliated. "You're not being fair. How *could* I tell you?"

"Why not?" His smile wasn't meant to make her feel better. "You tell me everything else."

She looked down at her feet, noticing the blood on her third toe where a blister had formed and took a deep breath. Flinging that at her when it had taken her so much to confide in him hurt far more than she'd anticipated. She didn't have the words to deal with the anger and hurt radiating off him.

"Okay." She nodded and walked past him, her gaze on the lights surrounding the house.

"Phoebe . . ."

She didn't look back. She couldn't or else the fragile shell of the composure drummed into her from an early age would crack and she'd be laid bare as the pitiful naïve fool that she was.

"I didn't mean it, I—"

She ran and didn't stop until she reached Sally's bedroom where she took off her blasted shoes and cried as if her heart were broken.

Max closed his eyes, but he could still see Phoebe's stricken face. But, hell, she deserved his anger, didn't she? Of everyone who surrounded him, he'd thought she'd be the one to defend him and tell him the truth.

"Max?" Maria's trembling voice came from behind him. "Oh, Max, I'm so sorry. I acted on impulse. When Mama called and said she was in Reno, I just thought it would be great if they could join us here."

Max remembered the phone call he'd heard when

he'd gone to escort Maria to the wedding. If that had been his mom, it was possible Phoebe hadn't known anything about Maria's sudden change of plans.

"Did you tell Phoebe they were coming?" Max asked.

"No, because after we talked, I promised her I would not involve her in our family issues." Maria tentatively touched his arm. "If you wish to be angry with anyone, it should be me. Mama and Papa are also confused and that is my fault." Her mouth quivered. "I handled everything very badly. I just want you all to love each other again."

Max looked heavenward as he patted her shoulder while she cried. In his arms.

"Did they think I wanted to see them?" Max finally asked.

"Yes," Maria nodded. "As I said, they are very upset."

"Are they still here?"

"They were a moment ago, but Mama was thinking about leaving."

Max headed back up to the party, Maria by his side, and made his way to where his parents sat like two statues, staring at the guests still enjoying themselves. He took a seat opposite them.

"Look, I guess we all came into this with different expectations, and I apologize for my part in that." He made himself meet his father's apprehensive gaze. "I didn't know you were coming. To say it was something of a shock is an understatement."

"That was my fault," Maria said.

"But now that you are here, I do have something I want to say." Max took a deep breath and his parents visibly braced themselves. "Thank you."

"What?" His father sounded shocked.

"For helping to set me straight," Max said simply.

"You hated us," his mama said. "You said you never wanted to see us ever again."

"I was fourteen, of course I said that. You didn't have to take it so literally." Max shrugged. "I don't hate you now. I wish you nothing but the best."

His mother started crying and his father put his arm around her.

Max stood up. "You did the right thing. I understand how hard it was, and I respect you for that."

"Respect?" His father repeated.

"Yeah, that's all I've got." Max nodded. "Now, why don't you both enjoy the party or Maria can show you around." He paused. "I really have to do some stuff. I wasn't lying about that."

He walked away and ended up in the kitchen where Bernie was helping her staff clear up. He went down the hallway and paused outside his bedroom. The door was ajar, but Phoebe wasn't there. But why would she be? She was probably out dancing and wishing him dead. He paused, one hand on the door, and silently cursed.

She wouldn't be out there enjoying herself. He suddenly remembered how she'd stepped in to defend him from his parents, taken his hand, and led him away to safety. And how had he repaid her? By directing all his anger at his parents and Maria onto the person who least deserved it. He'd basically called her a fool to her face, and he wasn't sure how he was ever going to make that up to her.

"Max?" Luke came down the hallway. "We're winding things down in the next half hour. Can you help with the guest side of things while I focus on clearing up?"

"Whatever you need," Max said automatically. "I'll make sure everyone gets home safely."

"I appreciate it." Luke paused. "It was a great wedding. We should do it again sometime."

Max pretended to groan. "Just consider it a dress rehearsal for your own and we can hand it over to Noah to micromanage the whole thing."

"I think I'd prefer Phoebe doing it. Bernie and I are trying to convince her to set up as a wedding planner. She'd be amazing."

"She would." Max followed Luke out. "Have you seen her around? I lost track of her about half an hour ago."

"No, but if I do see her, I'll tell her you're looking for her," Luke said.

"Nah, she's got enough to do without worrying about me."

"Truth." Luke was already heading out the kitchen door. "Text me if anything goes wrong. Bernie's staying over tonight, but the rest of her team is going home. I'll help them load up when all the guests have gone."

An hour later, Max waved a final farewell to a trio of inebriated volunteer firefighters and their thankfully sober driver and shut the gate behind them. The fairy lights still twinkled, but the wind had picked up and it was getting too cold to hang outside. He walked around the whole site, making sure there were no unconscious bodies in the bushes and helped clear a few tables when the staff was struggling to keep up against the stiff breeze.

There was no sign of Phoebe, and he was beginning to worry. Had she left? He hadn't checked the bedroom closet or the suitcase she'd slid under the bed. It wouldn't be hard for her to have gotten a lift into town after the party. The thought scared the heck out of him. He needed to make it up to her. Somehow explain himself.

By the time he got back to the house, the kitchen was back to its original state, and Sally and Bernie sat at the table in their dressing gowns drinking hot chocolate and discussing the events of the day.

"Hey, Max." Sally waved at him. "Come and join our self-congratulatory party."

Bernie toasted him with her mug. "You were great, by the way."

"Thanks, but I think I'm headed straight to bed."

"Lucy said something about having unexpected guests at her B&B," Sally said.

"Yeah, my parents turned up."

"Are you okay?" Sally asked, her expression concerned. "Were you expecting them?"

Max looked at her. "No, and no, and I don't want to talk about it right now if that's okay."

"Understandable." Sally nodded. "But you know where I am if you do."

"I appreciate that." Max hesitated. "Have either of you seen Phoebe?"

"She was asleep on my bed when I came in, so I've left her there." Sally smiled. "I'll sleep in Noah's old room tonight."

"Awesome." A weight lifted from Max's heart. "I'll catch up with her in the morning. Goodnight, Sally, and Bernie the food was amazing."

He took a quick shower and went into his bedroom, which seemed quiet without Phoebe chatting

away to him. He sat on the side of the bed and
shoved his hands through his hair. He felt like his
world had come off its rails and he didn't know how
to process any of it. He remembered his mother
telling him that a good night's sleep always made
things better and hoped she was right because today
had been an unmitigated disaster.

Chapter 17

Phoebe woke up and immediately panicked when she didn't recognize her surroundings. It took her a minute of floundering around to grab her phone and realize she was in Sally's bed and that it was late. Her clothes sat in a heap on the floor and someone, probably Sally, had put a blanket over her while she slept. She hadn't intended to stay, but after a bout of crying, exhaustion had set in, and she'd closed her eyes to blot out the horrors of the day and didn't remember a thing after that.

Phoebe rolled onto her back and stared up at the ceiling. She had to get up and face Max, and she wasn't sure she could do it. If he was still angry, he might be eager to avoid her as well. There were millions of small tasks left over from the wedding that would keep her away from the barn where Max primarily worked.

Even though it hurt, Max had reminded her of something important. Their marriage wasn't real and all her silly imaginings of falling in love were just that—silly. She'd projected her pathetic need to be loved onto him, and she had to stop. She pressed a hand to her cheek as she recalled all her stupid attempts to engage his interest. He was too kind to try and stop her, so she had to regroup, strengthen her armor, and go back to being what he'd agreed on— his temporary wife.

Phoebe got up, aware of a headache descending and wished she hadn't drunk any champagne. She used Sally's bathroom, gathered up her discarded clothes and other items and went back into Max's bedroom. The bed was made, and she guessed he'd been gone for several hours. She was fairly confident she wouldn't be disturbed as she put on her jeans and one of his old T-shirts he'd given her.

She went into the kitchen where a pot of coffee fragranced the air and made herself some tea and a bowl of porridge in the microwave. There was no sign of anyone, but her cell buzzed with a text from Sally, and she checked her phone.

Had to go into work today—will see you at 6. Can you start dinner for everyone? Ingredients for beef casserole are in the refrigerator chopped and ready to go.

Phoebe texted her reply. **Will do. I'll put it in the oven about 5.** And received a thumbs-up in return.

Ten minutes later, she put her wellies on and went out to the wedding pergola where she needed to take down the flowers before the structure could be removed. Most of them had wilted or been torn apart by the wind, but there was still a lot to do, and it would keep her busy while she ran through three thousand scenarios about how to deal with Max when she encountered him.

Part of her wished she hadn't fallen asleep and that she'd packed her bags and run away, but Max deserved better. She was worried about how he felt at seeing his parents after all those years and if he wanted to talk about it. She set the ladder against the first corner post, took off her boots and climbed up.

Not that he'd want to talk to her about anything, but . . . She reached over her head and began the laborious task of untangling the stems, vines and holding wires. She had a pair of wire cutters and scissors in her pocket which made the task a little easier.

She was so engrossed in her work that she didn't hear someone approach until Max cleared his throat directly beneath her.

"Hey, Phoebe."

She looked down, her heart thumping and offered a tentative smile. "Hi."

He had shadows under his eyes and hadn't yet bothered to shave. She wondered if he'd slept at all.

"Any chance you'd come down the ladder and talk to me?"

"Yes, if you give me ten minutes to finish this tricky bit," Phoebe said.

"How about while you're doing that I go and make you some tea and bring it out to you?" Max offered.

"That would be great."

Phoebe clipped away with some speed as she tried to line up her defenses then descended the ladder. There were still a few rented tables and chairs waiting to be collected so Phoebe opened a couple of chairs and sat down to wait for Max. He came back with two mugs, his head down as he carefully navigated the uneven ground.

"Here you go."

"Thanks." Phoebe took a grateful sip. "It's starting to warm up quite considerably."

She sternly reminded herself not to gush, not to

overload him with her feelings and emotions, and just to be his friend.

For once Max seemed at a loss for words so for a while, they both sipped in silence before he eventually spoke.

"I shouldn't have gotten mad at you last night, Phoebe."

"It's quite all right."

"No, it isn't." He met her gaze. "I'm sorry."

"You were under a considerable amount of stress and sometimes it's easier to get cross with a friend than with those who truly hurt you. No one likes to be ambushed, Max. You have my complete sympathy for that."

"Maria said she did it on impulse."

"Not that it is any of my business," Phoebe said carefully, "but I assume she just wants you all to get along and tried to make that happen."

His smile was wry. "Yeah, that about sums it up. She was very upset."

"Poor Maria."

Phoebe sipped her tea and Max shifted around in his chair. She was dying to ask him a million questions as to what had happened after she'd left, but remembered she had no right to know what went on in his family.

"She didn't stay the night here. She left with my parents."

She nodded and silence stretched between them.

"Are you feeling okay?" Max asked.

"I have a small headache after imbibing too much champagne, and my feet hurt but, other than that, I'm fine. Thanks for asking." She offered him a bright smile. "Considering how busy I was yesterday, I'd call that a success."

He sat back and regarded her from beneath the brim of his Stetson. "I meant the other kind of feelings. The ones I trampled all over last night."

"You were rightfully upset, Max." She shrugged. "It happens and you've apologized. I don't know what else you want me to say."

"So, we're good?"

"Absolutely." She smiled again. "After all, what are friends for?"

At the dinner table, which looked weird without Sky, Jen and Noah, Luke was complaining about the rental company that hadn't turned up to pick up their tents and other structures.

"Max and I spent all afternoon dismantling those suckers to make it easy for them, and they didn't even bother to call to tell me they wouldn't make it until five."

"That's very annoying," Phoebe said. "Would you like me to call them tomorrow, Luke? I'm sure you've got a lot to do without having to worry about them."

Phoebe was quieter than usual, and Max couldn't work out if it was because she was tired or if there was something else going on. He'd tried to convince himself that they were okay after their earlier discussion, but something was off, and he couldn't put his finger on it.

"If you've got time that would be great," Luke said. "I'm not sure I'll be using them for my wedding."

"I'm not sure you'll have a lot of choice if you hold the wedding here," Sally said. "There aren't that many companies willing to come out this far. That's why they also think it's okay to mess you around, but if they try to charge you extra that's on them." She pointed at Luke. "And while we're on the subject, when are you planning on proposing to Bernie?"

"Soon." Luke gave his mom a long-suffering look. "You'll be the first to know." He winked at Phoebe. "Aren't you glad you escaped all this madness by just marrying this guy? You even had to supply your own engagement ring."

"That's on me," Max said. "I should've done something about that straight away."

"It's not important," Phoebe said quickly. "Max did get me a wedding ring. I'm the one who didn't reciprocate."

"Max wouldn't have worn it anyway," Luke pointed out.

"Because at the time I didn't want you guys to get on my back about it when we had more important things to worry about," Max said to Luke but kept his gaze on Phoebe. "And I was keeping my promise to Feebs."

"Why did you choose to keep it a secret, Phoebe?" Sally asked. "Max won't say."

"Because I knew my family wouldn't approve, and there were some legal matters attached to my marriage that I needed to sort out before it became common knowledge. Max was kind enough to accommodate my wishes, which was very good of him."

"I can't imagine Max being all considerate like that," Luke mused. "I must have missed something."

"Maybe it's a tribute to the power of love," Sally said. "Phoebe makes Max want to be a better person."

Phoebe laughed and shook her head. "It's nothing to do with me. He's always been a good person."

Sally reached out and gave Phoebe a high-five. "I agree."

Luke rolled his eyes. "Max has always been great at getting all the women on his side."

"You jealous, bro?" Max asked. "I can't help my God-given gifts."

"Can we stop talking about him before his head gets so big, he can't get out the door?" Luke complained. "He's insufferable as it is."

"We could talk about how my parents turned up last night," Max said.

Luke looked at his mom. "You told me not to mention that and now here's Max just laying it out there."

"It's Max's story to tell," Sally said. "I assume Maria invited them?"

"Apparently they dropped by her place in Reno, found she was out of town, and Maria invited them to join her here and see me."

"Did she mention that to you?" Sally asked.

"Nope. I only found out when Lucy said they were staying at her place."

Luke whistled. "That's . . . not great."

"Tell me about it." Max made a face. "I'm not sure what Maria was expecting, but I didn't handle it well."

"I'm not sure I would've done any better," Sally consoled him.

"Maria was gutted and after I calmed her down, I did go back and talk to them." Max paused. "They believed I wanted to see them and were equally upset."

"Hardly equally," Luke muttered. "What did you say?"

"I thanked them," Max said simply. "For doing what they thought was right even though it must have hurt them to do it."

"That's . . . mighty forgiving of you, Max." Sally cleared her throat.

"It needed to be said," Max insisted. "I also told them I respected their decision."

"And then you fell into each other's arms and made up?" Luke asked.

"No, I left it at that." Max smiled. "I'm not a saint, Luke. I still have a few grudges left in me."

Phoebe leaned across the table and took his hand, her eyes shining. "I'm so glad, Max. I hope it brings you some peace."

"And closure," Sally said from her end of the table. "Do you think they'll try and keep in touch?"

"I don't know." Max sat back. "And to be honest, I'm not sure how I'd feel if they did."

"Why did Maria reach out to them in the first place?" Luke asked.

"She's always told them what I've been up to." Max shrugged. "I guess she mentioned I was married, and Mama got all excited about the prospect of grandchildren."

His gaze moved to Phoebe who was looking down at her clasped hands. He wanted her to look at him, but she wasn't giving anything away, and it bugged him.

"Not everyone wants a family, Max," Sally said. "You don't owe anyone grandchildren."

"You've been bugging me about that for years!" Luke protested. "You have a whole closet jammed full of baby essentials up until the age of five."

"That's different." Sally smiled at him. "I was just hoping you'd work out that Bernie was the woman for you and get on with it years ago." She looked at Max. "I'm proud of the way you handled your parents."

"Thanks."

"I agree," Luke said. "I would've bet on you losing your temper and ordering them off the ranch."

Phoebe's gaze flicked over him, and Max tried to hold eye contact. "Phoebe helped me not to do that. She was great."

"I just stood next to you, Max," Phoebe said. "Everything else was all you." She rose to her feet and started collecting the plates. "Does anyone want pudding?"

"We have pudding?" Luke asked. "What kind?"

"Pie, I think. Bernie left us some in the refrigerator." Phoebe went to check. "Yes, peach and apple. It's a shame we don't have any custard."

"Pie isn't pudding," Luke said.

Phoebe frowned. "I suppose it isn't. We call all desserts pudding in England."

"Which is weird."

"Especially since all puddings aren't desserts."

Luke patted her seat. "How about you sit down and explain that to me while Max does all the work?"

"If you wish." Phoebe took a seat. "Shall I start with the savory puddings and work from there?"

A week later, Max still wasn't sure what was going on with Phoebe. She listened to him talk, answered all his questions, and laughed at his jokes, but something had changed, and he didn't know how to get it back. She was still the same loving person, but she wasn't *his* Phoebe, and the more he tried to talk to her about it, the more frustrating it became because she agreed with whatever he said, apologized when necessary, and didn't offer the slightest criticism.

Max paused as he removed the last plates from the dishwasher. Was that it? Was she too scared to disagree with him because she'd seen what he was like when he lost his temper? Even the thought of that made him feel bad. He shut the door and went to get more coffee. He'd already been out and done his chores and was about to start cooking breakfast. Phoebe hadn't come down to the barn to help since the night of the wedding and he missed her.

Jeez . . . Max wanted to kick something. He was the one who broke things, not the fixer. He'd never cared enough about anybody or anything to go back, pick up the pieces, and make things work.

"Oh!" Phoebe came in and halted in the doorway. "Hi! I thought you'd be out working. I was just thinking of getting breakfast started."

"I finished early," Max said. "And I had the same idea."

"Then we can do it together." Phoebe smiled at him. "Just remember not to cook too much because Noah isn't here to finish everything off."

"Copy that." Max stepped to the refrigerator and got out the eggs, bacon, butter, and maple syrup. "Pancakes okay for you, Feebs? I'll do the bacon."

She went into the pantry to get the flour and some oil and mixed up a big batch of batter in Sally's stand mixer. She poured it into a jug and set it on the counter.

"I'll just let it sit for a minute."

Max glanced at the large griddle, which hadn't quite gotten to the right temperature yet. "Plenty of time. I'll text Luke to make sure he knows we're cooking."

Phoebe washed her hands, her back to him. "I need to start planning my trip back to England for Eugenie's wedding."

Max didn't have anything he wanted to say about that.

"Is there a cab company around here that could take me to Reno to catch my plane?"

He frowned. "I'll take you."

"You're shorthanded right now with Noah being away. I don't want to leave Luke all by himself."

"Screw Luke. I'm taking you."

Her sigh was faint, but he heard it. "Okay, thanks, Max. I appreciate it."

He tested the griddle and slapped a dozen pieces of bacon down one side, which immediately spat and sizzled.

For some reason he couldn't seem to let it go. "How could you think I wouldn't want to drive you to the airport?"

"I said it was fine, Max."

She brought over the jug of batter and started dropping perfect little circles on the free side of the griddle. Max handed her a spatula to flip them.

"I know we've had our issues recently, but while you're here, you're still my wife and my responsibility."

Her face assumed the pleasant mask he'd come to dread, and she focused all her attention on the pancakes.

"You can disagree with me, Feebs. I'm not going to bite."

She laughed as if he were making a joke. "I am quite a competent person you know. I managed to get all the way to Reno by myself."

"Are you really going to take your family to court?" Max asked.

"Yes." She looked up at him, her brown gaze fierce. "I don't see any alternative."

"Then let me come with you." Max hadn't meant to say that. He'd never begged for anything since his parents had handed him over to the school and never come back. "We can face those idiots together."

"That's very sweet, but you've done a lot more than you signed up for when I made you marry me. I can't expect you to do that for me."

"You didn't make me marry you."

Her eyebrows rose. "I was the one who suggested it."

"That's not what I meant." Max realized his temper was igniting and it probably showed on his face. He needed to get control.

She reached out and touched his arm, her expression so sincere that it almost hurt him to look at her. "You've been absolutely wonderful to me, Max, but at some point, I have to stand on my own two feet. Can you understand that?"

"That's still a choice, Feebs." Man, and he thought his mama was stubborn. "You don't have to do it alone."

Her expression softened. "I know, and I love that you'd do that for me." She went to kiss him and then backed off. "Oops! My pancakes are going to burn if I don't take them off. Let me get a plate."

He went to grab her wrist, but she was already on the move, leaving him staring at the bacon as if he didn't know what it was. She was obviously totally at peace with walking away from him, and wasn't mad about their fight, so why wasn't he cool with it? He'd always preferred his relationships to be conflict-free.

She took a couple of large plates out of the cupboard and brought them over with a smile.

"Here you go. I'll start on the next batch right away."

Phoebe's smile disappeared as soon as she flung herself onto the bed and she counted to ten. It was exhausting pretending everything was fine. She truly wanted Max to be happy and had forgiven him for getting cross with her. Being close to him, still having feelings for him, and knowing she'd been a fool were a hard set of emotions to constantly juggle.

Max came into the bedroom and shut the door behind him.

"Feebs, can we talk this out?"

She blinked at him. "I thought we already had."

He leaned back against the door and regarded her. "You say that, but something's off."

Phoebe scrambled to sit up and braced herself for another difficult conversation.

"Are you afraid I'll get mad at you again?"

"No one likes being shouted at, Max, but as I've already explained, I understand why you were angry, and—"

He held up his hand. "I get that. It's not what I'm asking."

Phoebe crossed her arms over her chest. "I don't know what you want me to say."

"I want you to be . . . you. To feel free to say what the hell you want to me." He held her gaze. "You're holding back, and I don't want you to feel like that around me."

Phoebe looked down at her feet. "I'm doing my best, Max."

"That's . . ." He looked heavenward. "Not. It."

She pressed her lips together.

"I've got a temper. Sometimes I get mad, but I'm working on it—I really am."

She nodded.

"Phoebe." He came and crouched by the bed, his voice gentle. "What can I do to make things right?"

It took everything she had not to fling herself into his arms, tell him how she really felt, and let herself be comforted. Instead, she gave him what she hoped was a reassuring smile.

"We're fine, Max—really. I'm just exhausted from all the wedding preparations and worrying about what awaits me at home."

She risked a glance at him and immediately regretted it because he looked so sincere.

"Are you sure you're not still mad at me for wanting to come to England with you?"

She frowned. "I'm not cross about that at all."

He looked steadily at her. "It's okay to say I wouldn't make the grade with your folks. I'd be embarrassed to take me anywhere, but—"

She belatedly remembered what Jen had suggested to her about Max's childhood and reached out to cup his chin. "Max, that isn't it at *all!* On the contrary, they don't deserve to meet you." She gathered all her resources and hoped he could see the sincerity in her gaze. "There's just been a lot going on and I'm worn out."

She leaned in to kiss him and rose to her feet. "I have a load of washing to do before I leave, and I want to get it outside to dry while it's still warm."

Max stood up as well, his gaze troubled. "Whatever it is, Feebs, and whenever you're ready, I'll listen, okay?"

Her phone rang and she paused to check the number before answering it.

"Hello?"

"Phoebe? It's Lucy. I have someone here who says he's your brother."

Specks of black floated past Phoebe's eyes and she took a deep breath. "I beg your pardon?"

"He says he's the Earl of Westhaven! Does that ring any bells?" Lucy sounded thrilled. "Do you want me to give him directions up to the ranch or will you come down?"

"I'll come down," Phoebe said faintly. "Thank you."

She ended the call and stared at Max. "My brother . . ."

"Has agreed to your terms?"

"Not quite." Phoebe swallowed hard. "He's at the B&B."

Max grabbed his jacket. "Then I guess we should go and see what he wants."

Chapter 18

By the time they reached the hotel, Phoebe still hadn't worked out what she intended to say to her brother. She knew she should have gone alone, but Max had simply swept her along with him, and secretly, she was glad. He hadn't said much, just got her into his truck, had a quick word with Luke, and started driving.

"You holding up okay, Feebs?" He glanced over at her as he parked the truck opposite the hotel.

"I'm not sure." She took a deep breath. "I have no idea why he's here."

He came around to open her door, reached inside, put his hands on her waist and set her gently on the sidewalk.

"We'll know soon enough." He paused, his expression intent. "I'm coming with you."

She nodded, then took his hand, and they crossed the road together and went into the tall, white Queen Anne-style building.

Lucy was waiting for them at the reception desk. "Hi! I've never had a lord come to stay here before,

Phoebe! I had no idea he was connected to you until he explained."

Max looked down at her. "Your brother's a *lord?*"

Inwardly, Phoebe sighed. "He's the Earl of Westhaven. Creighton-Smith is our family name."

"Which means that Phoebe here, is actually *Lady* Phoebe. I looked it up," Lucy said, her eyes wide.

"It's not something I use in everyday life," Phoebe said. "It's simply for legal documents."

Both Max and Lucy were staring at her as if she'd grown another head and she made a face. "And this is why I don't mention it because people get freaked out and think they have to curtsey or something."

"Should I have curtsied to your brother?" Lucy gasped. "I didn't think—"

"No, he's not royalty, you're fine."

"Does that make Max a *lord?*" Lucy asked.

"No, it's not that kind of title," Phoebe explained. "I have it through my father who was the previous earl."

Lucy frowned and picked up her phone. "I'll have to google that."

"Can you take us to George, please?" Phoebe asked.

"Yes, of course! He's having tea in the drawing room." Lucy went ahead of them. "I'll bring a fresh pot and some coffee for Max."

Phoebe spotted George immediately and made her way through the room to the far corner where he sat reading the local newspaper. He looked up as she approached and rose to his feet, his expression not exactly welcoming. He was slightly shorter than her, which she knew bugged him, and had the same brown eyes and wavy hair he kept ruthlessly short.

"Phoebe."

"George, what an unexpected surprise." She gestured to Max. "Max, may I present my brother the Earl of Westhaven."

Max reached out and firmly shook George's hand. "It's good to finally meet you."

George sat down. "I'd agree, especially since we'd begun to believe you were a figment of Phoebe's rather adolescent imagination."

"Oh, I'm real all right." Max smiled and took the seat beside Phoebe. The contrast between him and George was remarkable.

Lucy arrived with the refreshments and thankfully didn't linger. George looked around the room.

"This place is nicer than I expected to find out in the sticks."

"Lucy is very proud of it," Phoebe said. "I'm surprised she had any vacancies at this time of year."

"My secretary sweet-talked her into finding me a room." George smirked.

"I still don't understand why you are here." Phoebe narrowed her eyes at him. "Has someone died?"

"Not to my knowledge." George raised an eyebrow. "I simply decided that if you were determined to be difficult, I should come and sort things out face-to-face." His gaze flicked toward Max. "And meet your 'husband'."

"I intended to return for Eugenie's wedding next week," Phoebe said. "There was no need to come all this way."

"I wanted to see what the attraction was." He looked Max up and down in a way that made Phoebe stiffen. "You're not normally this difficult to deal with."

Her hand fisted into a ball and Max set his own over it.

"I think what your brother is trying to say is that he thought I might be telling you what to do, Feebs, and that he came out here to make sure you weren't being held against your will." Max offered George an easy smile. "That's it, right? I suppose I can admire a man who's looking out for his sister's welfare, but I sure as hell ain't doing any of that."

Phoebe raised her chin. "I can assure you that I am perfectly free to make my own decisions, George, and that my disagreements with you have simply escalated because of your unwillingness to follow the letter of the law."

A flicker of annoyance ran over her brother's face, and he turned to Max. "Well, it was nice to finally meet you, but I think all further discussions should be between me and my sister."

Max looked at Phoebe. "It's your call, boss."

"I think I would appreciate a word with George in private, Max, but it won't take long." She smiled at him and stood up. "Will you wait for me?"

"Always, sweet pea." He picked up his coffee cup and took a sip. "I'll be right here if you need me."

Phoebe followed George up to his room and closed the door behind them.

"What in God's name were you thinking marrying a fool like that?" George asked. "He's obviously dumb as a post. And that fake cowboy act?" He shook his head. "I suppose you did find him in Reno, a city full of fakes."

"Have you quite finished, George?" Phoebe asked. "Max is a decorated Marine and a real cowboy who works full time on a ranch."

George strode over to look out of the window. "This is ridiculous. He's obviously got some kind of hold over you. Does he know how wealthy our family is?"

Phoebe was so tired of having to constantly defend herself.

"I am not here to discuss Max. I want my inheritance and if you aren't willing to follow the dictates of father's will then I will take you to court."

"Did Max tell you to do that?"

"Don't be absurd."

"I've had him investigated, Phoebe. He's a criminal. I'm not lying." George turned around. "He was in trouble with the police from the age of twelve and ended up in juvenile detention."

"And then he went to a military school with his parents' approval, graduated at eighteen, and went straight into the Marines where he served with distinction. There is nothing dishonorable about that," Phoebe snapped. "In fact, he's to be commended for turning his life around."

"You knew and you still married him?" George shook his head. "It's worse than I thought."

"I *married* him because he's a good man."

George's laugh wasn't kind. "Don't be ridiculous. You married him because you wanted your inheritance, and you decided it was the only way to force my hand."

"I wouldn't have had to 'force your hand' if you'd abided by the terms of our grandfather's will and father's amendment in his."

"A will that was conveniently changed when you were father's primary caregiver." George held her gaze. "How do you think the court will view that? A dying man coerced into making decisions by a greedy woman."

"How *dare* you."

George took an involuntary step back as she stuck her finger in his face. She was so angry she was shaking.

"I didn't ask him to change anything. I'm not one of the witnesses to his new will. I wasn't even aware that it existed until the solicitor read it out after the funeral. I'm happy to swear on a bible in a court of law that is the truth, and I know everyone who was involved in producing that document will stand with me."

"Except me and your grandmother."

"That's up to you," Phoebe said. "Maybe you should make up your mind as to whether I'm too stupid to understand that Max is manipulating me, or a conniving bitch who forced her own father to change his will in her favor." She glared at him. "Which is it, George?"

He tutted, which set her teeth on edge. "This is your problem, Phoebe. You get everything out of proportion and lay on the dramatics. It's not appealing in the slightest. A hysterical woman will never win in a court of law."

"Bloody watch me!" Phoebe turned to the door. "We're done. I'll see you at Eugenie's wedding."

She stormed down the stairs and into the entrance hall and was out on the street before she remembered she'd left Max behind. She stood staring at the door into Bernie's café breathing hard, her whole body shaking.

The door opened. "Are you coming in?" Bernie

asked, and then did a double take. "Are you okay, Phoebe?"

"She's good." A firm touch on her shoulder made her gulp in more air. "You want something sweet to eat, Feebs?" Max asked. "I'm sure Bernie's got something nice in there. We can get it to go if you'd rather."

Phoebe wouldn't go into details about what had happened between her and her brother, but Max already wanted to get up close and personal with George and teach him some manners. He'd never seen Phoebe so distraught. She'd eaten two doughnuts on the way back to the ranch and then gone to bed with a headache. He hoped she'd open up to him at some point, but things being the way they currently were between them, he wasn't one hundred percent certain that would happen.

Should he push the issue? He already knew George had taken an instant dislike to him; the man had barely bothered to conceal his hostility. He was pretty sure George thought he had some hold over Phoebe, which would be almost laughable if the situation wasn't so serious. Phoebe had him helpless in the palm of her hand and she didn't even know it.

For the first time in his life, Max wished Noah was around. He had a way of seeing through the bullshit that Max would appreciate right now. He left the barn and went to find Luke in the ranch office.

"Hey, have you got a moment?" Max asked as he stuck his head around the door.

"Totally." Luke looked up from his laptop. "I hear you were in town."

"I suppose Bernie's already told you what happened." Max sat down in front of the desk.

"She said Phoebe was very upset."

"Did she mention Phoebe's brother turned up at the B&B?"

"Yup, she got that from Lucy. He's a duke or something, right?"

"An earl," Max said gloomily. "I have no idea what that means, but I guess he has a crown or two stashed away in that castle of his somewhere."

"Is Phoebe okay?"

"She's gone to bed with a headache."

"So, no, then." Luke frowned. "Any idea what's going on?"

"From our short conversation, I guess the earl's decided I'm a bad influence on his little sister and that if I'd just go away, she'd go back to doing what she's told."

"Okay, that's slightly understandable if he's an over-protective brother," Luke said cautiously. "But he's definitely underestimating his sister."

"He treated me like the hired help, and he wasn't respectful to Phoebe," Max said. "I'm beginning to understand why she didn't want me to go to England with her."

"So where did you leave it?" Luke asked.

"George asked to speak to her alone and Phoebe agreed." Max paused. "Ten minutes later she went steaming past me in the entrance hall and ended up across the street staring at Bernie's place as if she wanted to burn it to the ground. Whatever her dick of a brother said made her equal parts mad and upset, and I'm not okay with any of that."

Luke looked at him. "You know what I'm going to say, don't you?"

"Yeah, let her come to me and tell me if she wants me to know about it." Max frowned. "But that doesn't feel right this time. I feel like I should be asking her."

"Why?"

"Because she's hurting, and I want to make things better for her."

Luke's grin was annoying.

"What?"

"You're totally gone over her, aren't you?"

"I'd feel the same about anyone I care about," Max insisted.

"Sure, you keep telling yourself that my friend," Luke said. "And in the meantime, maybe work up the nerve to ask her to come back after she goes to England?"

Max stood up. "I don't know why I ask you anything. You always say the same old bullshit."

"You just hate it because I'm always right."

Max was still fake laughing when he closed the door behind him and went into the kitchen to start fixing dinner. Half an hour into his prep, Phoebe came in and reached for the electric kettle.

Max intercepted her. "Sit down. I'll get it for you."

"I'm not ill, Max." Phoebe sat at the table. Her shirt was crumpled, half her hair was sticking out at a weird angle, and her eyes were red as if she'd been crying.

He set the tea that was made just how she liked it in front of her. "Do you want anything to eat, or can you wait until dinner? I'm making pork with an apple and cider sauce."

"It sounds lovely." Phoebe managed a smile.

"Tastes even better. It's a Nilsen family favorite." Max was determined not to bombard her with questions and turned back to his chopping board.

She sipped her tea as he finished measuring out the sauce ingredients. "Thank you for being with me today."

He shrugged like it was no big deal. "You're welcome."

"George thinks you're manipulating me for my money."

He did turn around at that. "George is an asshole."

"True." she acknowledged. "We've never gotten along and now things are the worst they've ever been." She met his gaze. "I told him you were one of the best men I'd ever met."

Max went still.

"You had a difficult start, and you made the best of it, and that's something to be incredibly proud of." She half-smiled. "George thought I didn't know about your past."

"He looked me up?" Max asked.

"I'm sorry," Phoebe winced. "It was inexcusable."

"It's all good. I bet Noah does the same thing for every one of his sister's boyfriends."

Max stirred the sauce, added extra apple slices, and poured it over the pork. He checked the oven had reached the right temperature and slid the roasting pan onto the middle shelf.

"If it wasn't for Eugenie, I wouldn't go to the wedding." Phoebe wrapped her hands around her mug. "But she'll kill me if I don't support her through this."

"Can't have that." Max started cleaning up. "And I suspect George will behave himself in company."

"He can be very charming when he wants to be."

"I'm sure. He sounds even posher than you do."

"He went to a very exclusive public school, called Eton," Phoebe said. "That's how they all sound."

Her phone buzzed and she flicked the screen. "Dammit."

"What's up?" Max strolled over, wiping his hands on the towel. "Don't tell me your granny's arrived?"

"No, it's George. He's apologizing profusely and blaming the jet lag. He wants to see us again." She groaned and buried her face in her hands. "He's not going to go away, is he?"

Max sat opposite her and held his tongue until she looked up again, her eyes clear.

"I have an idea."

"Yeah?" Max raised an eyebrow. "Let's hear it then."

"We invite him here."

"To the ranch?"

"He seems to think you're not a real cowboy. We'll see if he has any energy left to argue with either of us by the end of your regular working day."

Max clinked his mug against hers. He couldn't wait to see the earl on his home ground, "Feebs, you're an evil genius and I love it."

She finished her tea and sat with him at the table while he peeled potatoes and snapped beans. He turned aside her offers to help and just enjoyed being with her. He didn't like seeing her under siege, but he was beginning to understand how resilient she was.

She texted her brother and received an enthusiastic yes even when she mentioned he needed to be at the ranch by seven in the morning.

"So, what's the plan, Feebs? I take him out and lose him somewhere in the forest?"

She chuckled and he'd never been happier to make someone laugh in his life.

"I think that might cause an international incident." She paused. "The thing is, Max, I don't want to fight with him."

Max nodded. "I get that."

"But sometimes you do have to take a stand. Like you did with your parents."

"Hell, don't use me as a role model," Max said. "I'm the screwup here."

She took his hand, her gaze clear. "Actually, you're not. You've drawn well-defined boundaries as to what's okay with you about your parents, and that's something I'm dismally bad at."

"I guess you've got to work out what you're willing to lose," Max said slowly.

"That's true." Phoebe met his gaze. "Should I give into family pressure and restore peace while sacrificing my own needs, or should I make them accept that times have changed and ignore the grumbling?"

"Whatever you choose I'm on your side, Feebs."

Her smile was a delight and all for him.

"Thank you, Max. You really are the best."

Chapter 19

To Max's surprise George turned up at the ranch before seven and spent a long time chatting amiably to Luke about the horses, the barn, and the state of ranching in California while helping with the chores. He'd come dressed in jeans and a fleece with a weird green waxed jacket in case it rained. Luke offered him boots and a hat to complete the cowboy look and they were on their way.

Phoebe had decided to stay at the ranch and meet them at lunch, which suited Max fine because he was more than ready for a quiet word with George if he got out of line. Like his sister, George was an excellent rider and Max had no worries that he wouldn't cope with the pace. They were headed to the far northern boundary of the ranch where they'd had reports of broken fences and escapees near the county road, which was never good news.

Part of the route was on an old logging path through the redwood forest, which none of the retired Marines liked navigating because the visibility was so poor. Max did like the dappled shade and the horses certainly appreciated it. Luke called for a halt in a clearing by the creek and everyone dismounted and made sure their mounts had access to water.

George came straight up to Max with two cups of coffee.

"Peace offering?"

"Sure." Max took the cup.

"I was not at my best yesterday and I apologize for how I must have sounded." George met Max's gaze; his eyes the same color as Phoebe's. "I obviously misinterpreted the situation."

"You mean, I'm not a gold digger?" Max asked.

"As I said, I was rather jet-lagged, and my temper was short. Phoebe and I have always had a somewhat volatile relationship, but it was bad form on our parts to exhibit such behavior in a public place and in front of you."

Man, George liked the big words and the sound of his own posh voice.

"It's all good," Max said. "We're family, right?"

"I suppose we are—if only temporarily."

"What makes you think that?" Max knew he was walking into something, but if he didn't take the bait, he'd never know what George was after.

George looked around the clearing. "With all due respect, Max, can you really see Phoebe living here?"

"Right here?" Max said. "Nah, it's a bit remote. We're planning on building closer to the main house. I'll show you when we get back."

"I meant in the US. Her family roots go back to the Norman conquest."

"We all have roots. Sometimes they benefit from a transplant and some grafting."

"That is certainly true. We've had some right nutters in our family when cousins married," George laughed heartily. "But as Phoebe's brother, I just can't imagine her being happy here."

"And, as her husband, I'm going to disagree with you there, buddy. But that's up to Phoebe. I'm not going to make her live anywhere she doesn't want to."

"That's good to know," George said.

"And, hey, I could come over, right? I bet you've got some cows that need herding on one of those farms Phoebe says you have."

George smiled. "I can't quite see you on a dairy farm the size of a sixpence, but I'm impressed you'd be willing to try considering my sister tricked you into marrying her."

"She didn't fool me for a minute," Max said.

"That's very generous of you, Max, but she did put you in a remarkably difficult situation. I can only apologize."

"There's no need."

George didn't look convinced. "One would've thought that if Phoebe wánted you to become a farmer, she would've mentioned it years ago and insisted you came over."

"I was busy here," Max said. "And Phoebe was looking after her father."

"I suppose so." George held out his hand. "May I take your cup? I think we're about to 'move out' as you might say."

Phoebe looked out of the window for the umpteenth time and finally caught a glimpse of some movement down by the barn. Max had texted her that they were on their way back ages ago and she and Sally had prepared lunch together. Eventually, two cowboys appeared walking closely together, and chatting. Phoebe only recognized George when he took off his borrowed hat. Luke went on through to the kitchen, leaving them alone in the mudroom.

"Phoebe." George looked at her. "I am deeply sorry for my behavior. I'd really like to try again. This situation benefits no one."

He looked contrite but she wasn't sure she believed him.

"What did you do with Max?" she asked.

"He'll be here in a moment. He kindly offered to deal with my horse so that I could have a moment to speak to you alone." He paused. "He's a nice man, Phoebe. I'm not sure why you dragged him into all this."

Phoebe went still. "What exactly is that supposed to mean?"

"He seems to think you'll come and live here."

The outside door opened, and Max came in. His gaze met Phoebe's over George's head.

"Everything okay?"

"I was just telling Phoebe that she needs to be honest with you, Max."

"She is."

George looked at Phoebe. "Have you told him what you're trying to get from the estate?"

"I'm not sure that's relevant to—" Phoebe started to speak, but her brother talked over her.

"Phoebe needs to stay married."

"Okay." Max didn't seem upset. "So, we stay married."

"I bet she didn't tell you why that's important."

George cleared his throat. "Originally Phoebe thought all she needed to do to break the entail on the property willed to her by our grandfather was to get married. When that didn't quite do the trick, she regrouped, and somehow managed to convince *you* to stay married to her, and our father to add a codicil to *his* will that allowed what she wanted to happen."

"You think I planned this all out like a master strategist, George?" Phoebe asked. "That I used Max and then my dying father to get what I wanted?"

George shrugged. "I'm sorry, but that's what it looks like to me, Phoebe. Please feel free to offer me an alternative version."

Max put his arm around Phoebe, directing George's attention back to him.

"Phoebe devoted three years of her life to taking care of your father, right?"

George nodded.

"Meaning the rest of you could just get on with your lives without worrying because you knew he was in good hands." Max looked at George. "Did it ever occur to you that your father changed his will because he was grateful for what Phoebe gave up for him, and he wanted to set her free?"

Silence fell and Phoebe only realized she was crying when a tear slid down her cheek.

George frowned. "That's all very well, but—"

Max interrupted him. "How could you look at Phoebe and see anything but good intentions there? She gave up everything for your family and this is how you repay her by making shit up?"

"Max . . ." Phoebe stepped between him and her brother.

"I'm just sorry she used you, Max." George still hadn't finished.

"She didn't," Max said simply. "Now, do you two want to eat lunch like civilized people. It's never good to argue on an empty stomach."

Max ate something, smiled at the right time, and laughed when Luke made one of his so-called jokes, but his mind was busy rerunning the earlier conversation with George and Phoebe. He had so many questions it was hard to focus and only Phoebe could answer them. Eventually, he met her apprehensive gaze across the table.

"Can I borrow you for a few minutes, Feebs?"

"Yes, of course." She stood up and smiled at her brother. "I won't be long."

She followed Max into the bedroom and waited until he closed the door.

"Thank you for sticking up for me, Max. I can't tell you how much it meant to me."

"You're welcome." He leaned back against the door. "I want you to know I'll always support you in public against your brother and family, but I'd like an explanation as to what he said."

Phoebe sank down on the side of the bed. "What exactly would you like to know?"

He shrugged. "The truth? All of it? Because I think I deserve it before you leave."

"George made it sound as if I planned everything. I didn't." She gulped in a breath. "I told you the truth when we met that I needed to be married to receive my inheritance. When I returned to England, I was told that wasn't good enough. At the time, I didn't have the ability to do anything about it because I was too busy looking after my father and I didn't know your whereabouts. I had *no* idea my father changed his will until after he died or that he'd added that clause to further negate the original instructions from Grandfather's will to release the property to me. They are two totally separate events that George tried to merge into one to make me look bad."

He studied her for what felt like forever. "I wish I'd heard all that from you upfront rather than from George."

"I didn't want to drag you into a fight that wasn't yours."

"That's kind of a lame excuse, Feebs. If I were a suspicious man, I might wonder at your timing."

She blinked at him. "What do you mean?"

"You came to find me after your father died."

"Yes." She frowned.

"You told me there were still legal issues because our original marriage hadn't fixed everything."

"That's correct."

"But if your father's will had already cleared the way for you to receive your inheritance, why did you come all this way to find me? You could have divorced me by mail."

"I told you. Because my brother was still refusing to release the property. He said he didn't believe I had *ever* been married and that he and the family solicitors needed proof."

"So, you came to take me back to England to show your family you were married so that you could inherit your property."

"Yes." Phoebe paused. "What's wrong?"

"Then why all this? Why not tell it to me straight?" He gestured at the bed. "Why get all tangled up with me when you knew you were going to leave?"

"I couldn't help myself," Phoebe said simply. "It just happened."

"That's not an answer, Feebs."

"Then why did you let me? If you haven't trusted me this entire time, why did you encourage me?"

"This isn't about me."

"Fine. I wanted to see you again." Phoebe took a deep breath. "And, as soon as I saw you, I wanted you. Is that honest enough? And I'm not blaming you. I was the one who got carried away."

"Carried away?"

She stood up. "Now, who's asking questions?"

"I'm just trying to understand things here. You came to sort out your legal issues and stayed because you . . . wanted *me*?"

"Yes." Her half smile almost broke his heart. "And it's okay. I know that wasn't what you signed up for."

Max tried to think straight. "This is getting way too complicated."

"You started it."

"Just . . . hold up a second." He met her gaze. "I want to get this right."

"It's ridiculously simple, Max." Phoebe walked toward him, and he tensed. "I came here to persuade you to come back to England with me for what you might consider purely mercenary reasons, but I got distracted, because you . . ." She just looked at him. "Are so gorgeous, I couldn't keep my hands off you."

He went to speak, and she held up a finger. "Can I finish before I lose my nerve and you tell me to get out? I forgot we had a marriage of convenience and I wanted more—*so* much more, but that wasn't fair of me, Max, because that's not what you agreed to, and I understand that."

She squared her shoulders. "I'm going to talk to

George. He now knows you exist and there shouldn't be any reason why he can't agree to follow the dictates of our father's will."

She paused to go up on tiptoe and kiss Max's mouth.

"Thank you for everything."

"Phoebe, you can't walk out right now after saying all that."

She stroked his cheek. "It's okay, I know you don't want what I want, and—"

His arm snaked around her hips, pulling her against him and he kissed her with a rough possessiveness that left her gasping. When he eventually raised his head, his breathing was as harsh as hers.

"First thing to get straight is that I don't mind you wanting more, Feebs. I . . . kind of feel the same."

"You do?" She gazed into his eyes. "You want me?"

"All the damn time."

"Oh," she sighed. "That's the nicest thing anyone has ever said to me."

"I'm not nice. I want you naked, on your back, and screaming my name when I make love with you every night," Max said. "You drive me nuts, but somehow I like it."

Phoebe still hesitated. "Does that mean you'd consider staying married and letting me come back here to live?"

"If that's what you want."

"Oh, Max." She hugged him hard. "I think I'd like that very much." She kissed him again and gently eased out of his arms. "I need to talk to George and I'm sure we can sort everything out."

Max reluctantly moved out of her way and opened

the door. "Don't let him talk you out of anything, Feebs."

She blew him a kiss, her eyes shining. "I won't."

She went off in search of George who was sitting in the family room with the newspaper and a mug of tea looking remarkably at home.

"Phoebe." He looked up. "Have you explained yourself to Max?"

She sat beside him and smiled. "I think so."

"Then you can accompany me home when I leave tonight."

"I'm not due to leave for another two days, George. There's no rush." She paused. "I intend to come back here after the wedding."

She and Max still had a lot to talk about, but he cared for her—he'd said he wanted more just like she did.

"From your expression, I assume Max has forgiven you for deceiving him."

"I didn't deceive him." Phoebe met George's skeptical gaze. "He understands what really happened and didn't believe your conflated conspiracy theories."

Her brother's expression darkened, and Phoebe hastily remembered that she needed to be nice to him.

"But none of that matters now, does it?" she said brightly. "You've met Max, you know he exists, and there can be no more delays in giving me my inheritance."

George looked at her for a long moment. "I suppose you're right."

"Thank you." She reached for his hand. "Now we can enjoy Eugenie's wedding without any of this hanging over us."

After dinner, Max found himself walking beside George down to Noah's new house. The earl was due to leave for the airport soon but was interested in seeing how Luke was expanding the accommodation on the ranch. Sally and Phoebe had gone ahead to water the indoor plants and make sure everything was okay in the house. Max wasn't sure how he felt right now. Phoebe had suggested she would come back, and it was such a big deal that his stupid heart couldn't take it all in.

She wanted him.

Him.

The screwup, the loudmouth, the man she'd asked to marry her in a bar in Reno, risking everything on her first impression of him. He still wasn't sure he was good enough, but he'd been offered the chance to try and be that man. Something inside him yearned to step up and prove her right and everyone else wrong.

"I asked Phoebe to come back with me tonight," George said, breaking into Max's thoughts.

"She's booked for Saturday, right?" Max asked.

"I can easily alter her ticket."

"Why?"

George shrugged. "Because I think she needs to be home where she belongs."

"As to that—"

George stopped in his tracks, his expression sympathetic. "I don't know what she said to you, Max, but I don't understand why you insist on believing she'll return to you."

"Maybe because she told me she would?"

"The whole reason we've been fighting has been over property. Property that has belonged to the estate for generations and that Phoebe wants to own outright and use for her own purposes."

"Okay."

"If she didn't intend to live on that property, why would she have put up such a fight to keep it?"

"Because its rightfully hers?"

"It's more than that, Max, and you know it." George let out a breath. "It's important to her to honor our father's wishes and the plans they made together. She intends to run a riding stable and three-day event training for disadvantaged and disabled kids at her new place."

That news didn't surprise Max. It was just the sort of thing he could see Phoebe doing. It also made sense of her determination to get what she was owed, not for personal gain, but to benefit others.

"Whatever you or I think, Phoebe has a right to make her own decisions," Max said. "You've met me, there isn't any reason why you can't let her have what she deserves."

"There are plenty of ways I can block this legally."

"Why would you do that to your sister?" Max frowned.

"Because I want her to stay in England."

"It's not your call," Max spoke slowly, but he had a sense that George wasn't really listening to him.

"I could tie her and her barrister up in court for years. She'd run out of money a long time before I did, and then she'd have nothing, and the property would revert to me anyway." He paused and looked right at Max. "Or you and I could come to a gentleman's agreement."

Max knew he should've seen the counter offensive coming but he was still blindsided.

"To do what, exactly?"

"I'll let her have her property without any further legal action if she stays in England."

"That's a big ask."

"I'm not asking you to get a divorce, Max, and if you chose to come and live in England with Phoebe, I won't say a word because you're obviously a decent chap. I just don't want you encouraging her to come back here straight after the wedding. I want you to give her time to enjoy her win and plan her new future safely at home with me and her family." George paused. "It's not that much of an ask, is it?"

Max hated the fact that he couldn't immediately tell George to go screw himself because logically what he was saying wasn't unreasonable at all. Max wanted Phoebe to choose to be with him free and clear. It was obvious from what George was saying that she had big plans and dreams on the other side of the Atlantic. The question was—why would she be willing to give it all up for a joker and a loser like him?

"I'll think about what you've said." Max started walking again, his thoughts in turmoil.

Whatever George implied, Max knew he'd never be good enough for the earl's family and when Phoebe finally worked that out, she'd be quick to initiate a divorce. He felt stupid, like the whole world was laughing at him for daring to dream he could have a happy ending when that's not how it went for people like him. Phoebe deserved better and he was the only man who could set her free to find her true happiness.

"Hey."

Phoebe looked up from her sketch of the garden to see Max coming toward her with his usual easy smile. He'd spent half his time at dinner staring at her, which had made her feel deliciously warm. She couldn't wait until George left and she could take Max to bed. She'd been honest, she'd taken hold of her future and asked for what she wanted, and it felt glorious.

"We'll need to go back soon. It's getting dark," Max said as he came to stand alongside her.

"And George has to leave. Do you know he even suggested I come with him?" Phoebe chuckled. "He's remarkably bossy."

"As to that—have you thought about going?" Max said in a deliberately casual voice. "You'd have someone to travel with, which is always nice."

There was something about his tone that made her study his face.

"I planned to go on Saturday."

"Why wait? The sooner you get there, the quicker you can get into your new place."

"I am looking forward to seeing the dower house and the vast stable yard attached to it. I have such plans . . ." She paused, aware that he must have been talking to George. "But they can wait."

"Nah." Max took her hand. "You should go and celebrate your victory."

"You're trying to get rid of me now?" She tried to

make a joke of it. "Is this because you think I'll be back sooner."

He hesitated. "There's no rush to come back, Feebs. Take your time."

She pulled out of his grasp and walked away, her back to him. She'd done it again hadn't she? Pushed too hard, asked for too much, and scared him away. She stared at the bleak snow-covered mountain caps and took an unsteady breath as anger churned in her stomach along with hurt. She was a bloody fool. He hadn't said he loved her; he'd said he wanted to keep having sex with her.

"Phoebe . . ."

She slowly turned around. "Fine, Max. I'll go."

He shoved a hand through his hair. "That's not what I want—"

"I know what you want—me in your bed screaming." She found a smile somewhere. "How about this? I'll pop over occasionally and we can screw each other's brains out."

He winced and she raised her chin.

"Isn't that what you like about me, Max? That I'm in lust with you? That I'd do anything you want in your bed—although, I am grateful for all the experiences you've given me."

"That's not fair." He took a step toward her. "You mean much more than that to me."

"So much that you're too scared to accept what I'm offering on a bloody plate and would rather send me home with my brother."

He set his jaw and looked past her.

"Nothing to say to that? Then I guess I was right." Tears crowded Phoebe's throat, but anger still won out. "I love you, Max Romero. I'm sorry you're too much of a coward to say it back."

She brushed past him, went around the side of the house, and found George loitering on the driveway.

"Ah! Phoebe, I was looking for you. I have to leave soon. Are you sure you won't change your mind and come with me?"

"What did you say to Max?"

"Nothing that he didn't already know, Phoebe." His voice softened. "I'm sorry, love."

Phoebe glared at him. "Give me ten minutes to gather the essentials and I'll meet you in the car."

Max let out his breath and stayed where he was until he heard footsteps behind him. He half-turned, hoping Phoebe had come back to tell him what a fool he was, and that she'd decided to stay anyway, and found Luke instead.

"Hey."

Luke wasn't smiling. "I was in the kitchen with the windows open and I overheard you and Phoebe talking."

"Great," Max muttered. "Just fricking great."

"Can I ask you something?"

"Shoot."

"Why did you push her away like that?" Luke demanded. "What the hell were you thinking?"

Max didn't even have the energy to explain. "If that's what you thought, it's a shame you didn't intervene and make everything right."

"How could I when I don't understand what's going on? She loves you; you love her—" Luke paused. "You did tell her that? After everything I went through not doing it right with Bernie, you screwed up?'

"Can you stop talking? You're giving me a headache," Max groused as he walked through the side gate onto the unfinished driveway.

"Max, get up to the house, tell that woman you love her, and that you want to spend the rest of your life with her."

"You don't get to order me around anymore."

"I'm still your boss."

"Then goddam fire me."

Luke just looked at him. "We're not doing that again, okay? If there's something wrong, we can talk it out and fix it."

"We absolutely, one hundred percent, cannot fricking do that," Max snapped. "Just because your little fairy tale worked out doesn't mean mine will."

"Why not? You love each other." Luke pointed up the road. "Go and tell her. Make it right."

Max gave Luke the finger and marched off up the road with no real idea what he intended to do next. If he tried to tell Phoebe that he loved her, she might want to stay, and then her dick of a brother would stop her getting her rightful inheritance. But shouldn't he tell her that? Give *her* the choice rather than deciding for himself and making her doubt everything between them? But he didn't want her to be estranged from her family like he was from his, and he still wanted her to be committed to being with him.

Maybe he needed to try a bit of that honesty Phoebe was so good at.

It was quiet inside the house as Max went through to his bedroom. Ten seconds was long enough for him to realize she'd erased herself from his life. Max sank down on the bed and put his head in his hands. She'd gone and the only person he had to blame was himself.

Sally knocked softly on his door and looked in.

"I'm so sorry, Max. Phoebe said she had to leave with her brother and was packed and gone in ten minutes."

Max slowly looked up and Sally came toward him. "Oh, my poor boy."

She sat next to him and drew him into a hug. He wanted to cry, but he didn't because he'd learned long ago that it never made any difference.

Chapter 20

Three months later.

"I still don't understand why the hell we're doing this," Max grumbled as he helped Noah set the window frame in straight. "I don't want my own house."

"Maybe because Luke's getting married at Christmas and he doesn't want to see your naked ass in his bathroom every morning?" Noah adjusted the angle of the sill, checked it was level and banged a couple of nails and a wedge in to keep it where he wanted it. "You can rattle around here all by your lonesome."

Noah's tan had faded from his honeymoon in Hawaii, but he occasionally smiled and looked almost happy, which was just plain weird. He'd also taken to annoying Max, which wasn't new, and hanging out with him, which was.

"Why are you always here?" Max demanded. "Doesn't Jen need you at home? Or is she sick of you already."

"She's totally in love with me. She understands why I'm doing this."

"Well, I wish someone would explain it to me." Max held the frame steady as Noah leveled the top edge. "I don't need babysitting and I'm not a flight risk."

Noah looked at him. "That's an improvement. Last time things didn't go your way, you disappeared on us."

"I'm not going anywhere."

"Hey, I appreciate any signs of maturity coming from you, bro." Noah anchored the window and carefully stepped back. "Now, if only there was something we could do about your pigheadedness."

"That's a big word for you. Have you been talking to Luke?"

Noah's grin was infuriating. "We talk about you all the time."

Max was aware everyone was treating him like an invalid, and he hated it. Noah wouldn't even be goaded into a fight and Max would love to kick someone's ass.

"I'm fine." Max stepped back over the unfinished floor to look at the window. "Shall we get the other one?"

"Might as well and then you can come over to my place and have dinner. Jen's expecting you."

Eventually, after extracting a promise from Max that he'd be over when he'd cleaned up, Noah headed out. Max made sure all his tools were back where they should be and swept the floor where they'd been working. He glanced out of the newly fitted windows that faced the view at the back of the ranch house he'd grudgingly helped design. The sun was setting, and the forest was ablaze with color.

They'd been lucky so far with no outbreaks of fire near them, which, after the terrible winter, was a relief. Cattle died just as easily during drought as in the winter storms and they couldn't take another financial blow.

Max took a tour of his new home, which had three bedrooms plus the master and en suite, a small study, and a large kitchen/family room in the center with spectacular views.

He'd put in a lot of work—not particularly because he wanted to live alone in a house meant for a family, but because it kept him from thinking too hard, or running, He'd heard sporadically from Maria, but nothing from his parents, which suited him just fine. Phoebe hadn't contacted him since she'd let him know she'd arrived safely back in England, but that was hardly surprising. He'd sent her away—held the door open and almost pushed her through it with a cheery wave. No wonder she was pissed with him.

He was pissed with himself.

He took one last look at the sunset and picked up his toolbox. Once the windows were in, the house would be insulated from the outside, and they could install drywall, finish the plumbing and electrical, and get the wood flooring in. Max smiled to himself. That would keep him busy until Christmas. After that? He couldn't allow himself to think that far ahead.

Phoebe wiped the sweat off her brow and contemplated the wall she'd just finished painting white. It was the last of the interior walls of the stables and outhouses attached to the Georgian dower house she'd finally pried out of George's hands. The home itself had been rented out for years but was in remarkably good condition. It was a large square box with four windows on each side of the central door, two stories and attics above that. Wisteria and roses grew along the front, and it was surrounded by a stone wall.

She'd coveted it for years and when her father told her that it was *her* dower house, she'd immediately started making plans as to what she'd do with it. Those adolescent plans had included marrying either royalty or an Olympic show jumper, neither of which had come true, but she still loved the house.

She stashed her paint pots and washed the brushes, aware that she'd be stiff in the morning and that there was no one to offer her emu oil or a massage. She let herself in through the stone-flagged kitchen and made herself a cup of tea. The room was always warm courtesy of the Aga installed where the old range had sat.

She suspected the antiquated heating system would struggle to keep up in the winter. George had offered her the services of the team of estate handymen who maintained his land and properties, and she'd accepted his olive branch with gratitude. He was a surprisingly frequent visitor along with her grandmother and occasionally Eugenie. If Phoebe had been of a suspicious nature she might wonder if they were checking up on her. Did they think she'd fly back to the US?

The kettle whistled, interrupting her thoughts and she made herself some tea. After sending her a thumbs-up acknowledging her text about her safe arrival, Max hadn't contacted her once. To be fair, she hadn't reached out to him either because part of her was still cross. He could have fought for her—asked her to stay, begged her to change her mind, but he'd literally pushed her into leaving with a smile and a wink.

Phoebe groaned. She was tired of running her last few conversations with him through her head and micro interpreting them. Had he really meant he felt the same about her as she did about him, or had he just been joking? Maybe the whole thing had been a giant laugh for him all along.

Her head said yes, but her heart and her gut said no. She'd *reached* him and his reactions to her had been genuine. She knew it in her soul. But his faith in her had been rattled by Maria's clumsy intervention in his life, and then George had turned up spewing nonsense . . .

She missed him so badly.

Her cell buzzed and she took it out of her pocket, noticing a smear of paint on the back.

Hi, how are things? Finished your painting yet?

Eugenie was working in London, but she still made time to contact Phoebe every day.

Just about done with the stables. Hot carpenter is coming tomorrow to look at the woodwork.

Ooh, I love a man who's good with his hands. Is he married?

I'm married, Eugenie.

Then you'd better set about getting that divorce, then. Love you x.

Phoebe's smile died as she finished sending her sister a happy face. Was history repeating itself? Was she going to have to chase Max down again to obtain the divorce he obviously wanted?

Dammit. She set her phone on the table with more force than was probably necessary or good for it.

She didn't want another man. She'd given her heart

to her husband. If *he* wanted a divorce, maybe it was time for him to get off his arse and come and get her.

She scrolled through her contacts and stopped at J.

Hi, Jen! I know it's early where you are, but I'd love to talk to you.

She'd barely finished typing when her phone rang.

"Hey!" Jen said. "Thank goodness you've called. We've got to do something about Max. Any ideas?"

"It's looking good," Noah said as he took a glug of water from his flask.

Luke had just gone back to the ranch to check on dinner and Max and Noah were admiring the new floor that had just gone in. They'd hired some professional help and acted as labor because they weren't about to damage the reclaimed redwood they'd painstakingly gathered from the forest floor.

"You pleased with it?" Noah looked over at Max. "You haven't said much."

"It's awesome." Max contemplated the kitchen. "I'm just working out how I want to finish the kitchen cabinets to tone in with the floor."

"You could go full on redwood," Noah suggested.

"Too dark," Max said. "But something with warm tones to complement the floor."

"You need a woman."

Max raised an eyebrow. "What's that got to do with what we're talking about?"

"You need someone to knock ideas around with, and give you their opinion."

"Fine, I'll get Bernie and Jen to help."

"They're not who you should be asking." Noah screwed the lid on his flask.

"Sally, then?"

"Don't be an ass." Noah faced him. "You have a wife."

"Who lives in England."

"You could still call her."

"Why?" Max demanded. "To make her mad at me all over again? To make her think I want her back when she's already made her decision?" He turned toward the door. "I'm sick of all these insinuations, Noah. If you've got something to say, then say it, or get off my case."

"The thing with you, Max, is that you're really good at handing shit out and terrible at taking it."

"Tell me something I don't know."

Noah strolled toward him. "Okay, here's a direct question for you. If you've decided your marriage is over, then why haven't you divorced Phoebe?"

"Maybe because she's the one who left?"

"You practically laid out a red carpet to make her leave the country!" Noah said. "And last time you were an inconsiderate bastard, she chased *you* down, so why should she have to do it again?"

Max unbuckled his tool belt. "You know this is none of your business, right?"

"Hell, like you weren't the first person sticking his nose into my and Luke's love lives."

"Because you both needed help!"

"And you don't?" Noah raised an eyebrow. "You're miserable as shit without Phoebe and you do nothing to fix the situation."

"I did what I thought was best." Max set his jaw.

"For whom, Max? From how I see it, you asked her to marry you as a joke, got stuck in a commitment you didn't want, and then when you realized she was a real person with feelings, you panicked and got rid of her as fast as you could."

Max pressed his lips together and tried to get past Noah who was now blocking the exit.

"Which just proves you don't know shit." Max walked right up to Noah. "Excuse me."

"Tell me where I'm wrong then, genius?" Noah didn't move an inch. "Gonna run away again because it's too hard to admit what you did?"

Max slowly raised his head to meet Noah's gaze.

"Don't do this, okay?"

"Do what? Ask the guy who's supposed to be one of my best friends why he made a good woman marry him just for kicks?"

"I didn't goddam ask her to marry me!" The words were out of his mouth before he could stop them and somehow, he couldn't shut up. "And I let her go because it was the best thing for her."

Noah looked at him and Max sighed.

"She needed to be married to get her inheritance."

"Okay."

"And she needed to go back to the UK with her brother."

"Why?" Noah frowned. "You might as well spit it out, Max. You're not going anywhere until I understand what's going on."

"You're going to physically stop me?"

"Sure." Noah shrugged. "But I hope it won't come to that because Jen told me to try and be nice."

Max gauged the size of his opponent. If Noah really meant it, he didn't stand a chance. He sighed.

"There were . . . legal complications about Phoebe's inheritance. First off, they didn't believe I existed, and then when I finally met George, he shuffled the deck and made me an offer."

"Let me guess," Noah said. "He paid you off?"

Max scowled. "Hell, Noah, do I look like the kind of guy who'd do that?"

"Maybe." Noah considered him.

"Thanks for nothing."

"Then if he didn't offer you money, what did he offer? Let me guess." Noah's eyes narrowed. "Something for Phoebe's benefit?"

"Yeah." Max nodded. "What she wanted free and clear if she didn't come back to the ranch after the wedding."

Noah stared at him and said nothing for so long that Max got irritated.

"You out of smart remarks? Can I go now?"

"You did it for love," Noah said slowly. "You let her go so that she could get what she wanted without any strings attached, which makes you—"

"One of the strings," Max said firmly. "And I'm going to tell you something, bro, being noble ain't all it's cracked up to be."

Noah reached out and gripped Max's shoulder hard. "Still proud of you for doing it, though."

"Get off me." Max finally managed to push past Noah, who was looking way too sympathetic for Max's liking. "Now, if you wouldn't mind erasing this entire embarrassing conversation from your Neanderthal brain, I'd be delighted."

"Not happening, Max." Noah called after him and Max held up the obligatory finger.

He knew that by the time he sat down for dinner, everyone at the table would have been informed of the current pitiful state of his love life. He contemplated going to the next town over and finding a bar. But at some point, he'd still have to come home—to the house he was building and coming to love.

And, hell, if anyone at the ranch could offer him a way out of the Phoebe problem that didn't involve him jumping on a plane and throwing himself at her feet, he was all ears. Because, house or no house, living without her was killing him.

He set off back to the main house, the heat of the day radiating from the ground beneath his boots. There was a dryness in the air like a caught breath waiting to fan the flames of a single spark. He hated that sense of waiting for the worst, but it was inescapable at this time of year. He hated waiting, period, but for the first time in his life he didn't have a plan to get out.

He wanted Phoebe here and she needed to be in England to fulfill her dreams. He paused to look back over the sprawling ranch. It wasn't his land, yet it felt like the first home he'd ever had. But he knew how quickly things could change, how whole villages ended up in flames, families shattered, lives upended. Could he give it up? And even if he was willing, would Phoebe still want him?

Phoebe's phone lit up with a text and she turned over and grabbed her cell from the nightstand.

It was from Jen.

Ask your brother what he did to make sure you came back to England with him.

Phoebe frowned as she typed. **What??**

Noah and Max had a chat and I guess a lot of what we thought was wrong.

Phoebe struggled to sit up. She'd forgotten to shut the curtains and a full moon was shining through the wavy, old glass window.

Max and Noah chat now?

I think Noah pushed a few of Max's buttons to get some real answers. I decided not to ask for details.

Okay, I'll talk to George. He's due to come over tomorrow to review my progress as I'm still connected to his estate.

I'll be interested to hear what he says. X

Jen signed off and Phoebe remembered to plug the charger into her phone before she put it away. She lay back against her mountain of pillows and contemplated the dark outline of the oak tree outside her bedroom window. There was very little breeze, and the humidity was high, making her hair curl, which meant she'd looked like a mess in the morning. She'd left the room just as her Great-aunt Margaret had decorated it and felt like the heroine of a Gothic novel in her four-poster bed and three randomly ticking clocks.

What could George have possibly done to make Max want to get rid of her?

A thousand and one scenarios immediately filled her head. Phoebe sighed and got out of bed. She'd make herself some hot chocolate and write a list. It was the only way she'd ever get back to sleep again.

Max finished his dinner and looked up. "Will you all stop staring at me? It's like being in a horror movie."

"We're just concerned for your welfare, Max," Sally said.

"Then assuming Noah's blabbed everything, what do you think I should do?"

Luke looked around the table. "Did you all hear that? It sounded like Max was asking for our help."

"I think that's a good thing." Jen smiled warmly at him. She'd just returned from putting Sky to bed in his old room. "I'm proud of you."

"The problem as I see it," Luke said, "is that you think Phoebe won't move over here because she's finally gotten what she wanted over there."

"Correct." Max nodded. "And I helped her get that."

"Which was very romantic of you, Max," Jen said.

"I just wanted her to have what was hers and not fall out with her family over it." Max shrugged. "It's no big deal."

Everyone looked at him. "What?"

"It *is* a big deal," Sally said. "But I think we all understand why you made the choices you did now."

Max snorted. "Noah thought I'd taken a bribe."

"I didn't bro. I just wanted you to get mad enough to tell me the truth." Noah smirked. "It's called the Max attack."

"You've got a valid passport?" Luke asked.

"Yeah, I checked when I thought I was going to England for the wedding." Max hesitated. "I keep thinking I should just get on a plane and go talk to her—lay it all out there and give her the choice—but that's stupid, right?"

"Not necessarily," Luke said slowly. "I guess she might appreciate you chasing her down for a change."

Max sat back. "I thought you'd all tell me I was crazy to even think about it."

Sally smiled at him. "I think you need to decide

what's important to you, Max. Where you live doesn't matter if you're with someone you love."

It was on the tip of Max's tongue to ask how anyone knew he loved Phoebe, but even he wasn't stupid enough to try that when they'd had to live with his miserable face for months.

"This ranch will always be your home," Sally continued. "You'll have a place in our hearts and in our houses."

Luke and Noah nodded. For a horrible second, Max seriously wondered if he was about to cry like a baby.

"Hey, she might come back with me—although, she'd have to put up with Noah as a next-door neighbor."

"And me," Jen piped up.

"She'd like that part," Max agreed. He rose to his feet. "I guess I'll go pack. Do you think I should let her know I'm coming or keep it a surprise?"

"Why don't you let me deal with that?" Jen offered. "I'll give her a heads-up when you're getting close."

Max was halfway through the door when he stopped and turned around.

"*Shit.* I don't know where she lives."

Jen was the first to start laughing and everyone joined in—including Sky from the bedroom.

"I've already sent you a text with all those details."

Noah looked up from his phone. "And I've booked you on a flight leaving tonight. So, get going."

Max paused. "Thank you, guys. I really mean it."

Luke waved him off. "Just be happy, Max. That's all we want for you."

"I'll do my best," Max promised. "So, expect me back in three days."

He rushed into his bedroom, packed his old military backpack, made sure he had his passport, and ID, and went back into the kitchen. Noah was waiting for him, keys in hand.

"I'll drop you at the airport."

"You sure?"

Noah smiled. "I need to make certain you've really gone. Luke and I have a bet."

Chapter 21

"It's all going remarkably well, Phoebe." George offered her a fond smile. "I'm impressed. When do you think you'll open your doors?"

"There's a long way to go before we reach that point. I'll need staff, horses, ponies, suppliers . . ."

Phoebe poured him a cup of tea from the pot and offered him the milk and sugar lumps, which he used lavishly. He'd been remarkably pleasant since he'd gotten his own way.

"I can help with the equine side of things. Speak to Watkins, my new head groom. I'm sure he'll be delighted to get rid of a few nags and save me a few pennies."

"What happened to Benson?" Phoebe asked.

"He retired. He's happily ensconced on a brand-new cottage on the estate and enjoying every minute of it."

"I'll have to pop in and say hello. That man was a saint." Phoebe knew that she might be prevaricating, but she was desperately trying to think how to phrase her question without it sounding like an accusation.

"Heard from Max at all?" George asked, his tone nonchalant.

"It's interesting that you asked that," Phoebe said, glad he'd brought up the subject she'd been dreading.

"Why?" George's amiable expression disappeared. "What has he done now?"

"What would you think he's done that would get you into such a flap?" Phoebe asked. "You look quite guilty." She paused. "It's almost as if you might have interfered with my marriage."

George set his cup down, his cheeks flushed. "Now, come on, Phoebe. A man must protect his family."

"Max *is* family."

"I suppose the blighter told you what I said to him." He sighed. "He didn't argue with me at the time because I'm fairly certain he knew I was right, and that he was doing what was best for you."

"I don't think you and Max should be deciding what's best for me, do you?"

"You're missing the point, Phoebe. Max understood what I offered him all too well and decided he didn't want you facing unnecessary litigation. Did he mention that I offered no objections to him coming to live in England if he agreed to do as I asked? I bet he forgot that part because he has no intention of joining you, which proves my point."

Phoebe finally joined all the dots. "You promised not to take me to court over the wills if Max agreed I should come back to live in England."

George snorted. "Apparently, he did forget my concession."

"You had no right to interfere at all, George." Phoebe held his defensive gaze.

"I couldn't see you being happy on a cattle ranch in the middle of nowhere." He hesitated. "And self-ishly, perhaps, I wanted you here."

"So that I could look after our grandmother? You've already dropped several large hints as to my suitability for that position."

"We all have a duty to our family," George countered. "I had no choice about inheriting the title and neither will my son."

"I've always done my duty, and you can hardly complain when you inherited three estates, vast lands, and the income to maintain everything to your par-ticularly high standards," Phoebe pointed out. "We're *all* responsible for our grandmother."

"Eugenie, Arthur, and I have professional careers. You . . ." he made a gesture at the drawing room. "Live off your income and are free to indulge your-self in whatever takes your fancy."

"I'm trying to do some good in the world with that income." Phoebe tried not to let her irritation show. "I expect to be extremely busy over the next few years."

"Too busy for your own grandmother?" George asked.

Phoebe sat back. "As I said, I am more than willing to share that responsibility with you and my siblings. I am not doing it all by myself."

George set his cup on the tray and rose to his feet "I can see you are going to be as difficult about this as everything else."

"Yes, I think I am." Phoebe looked up at him. "Are you going to renege on your promise to Max and take me to court to get this house back?"

George looked at her for a long moment and sighed "No, of course not."

"Thank you." She blew him a kiss. "Now about that heir you were talking about. Shouldn't you be thinking about finding a girlfriend first?"

"Don't you start." George turned to the door and Phoebe got up and followed him out.

"You're an earl with a sizeable bank account, you're reasonably good looking, and you're not too weird." She patted his shoulder. "I'm sure there's *someone* out there desperate enough to put up with you."

He gave her a long-suffering look as he kissed her cheek.

"Good day, Phoebe. Don't forget to talk to Watkins."

He drove off in his battered Land Rover and Phoebe went back inside. For the first time in her life, she felt like she'd won a battle and paused to savor the moment. George might be a pompous pain in the arse, but he was still her brother, and, in his heart, he loved her as much as she loved him.

She almost wasn't surprised when an hour later her grandmother arrived and settled herself in the drawing room with her three beagles. The dowager countess always had George's back and Phoebe was fairly certain her brother had run straight home and told her everything.

"Good afternoon, Phoebe."

"Good afternoon, Grandmother. How lovely to see you." Phoebe smiled. "Would you care for some tea?"

"No thank you." She gestured to the dogs as she removed her headscarf. "I just stopped in on our walk. I can't stay long."

Phoebe took a seat opposite her. Her grandmother was tall like Phoebe and her hair was silvery white and tied back at the nape of her neck. Even though she was walking the dogs, she wore a Chanel tweed jacket over her cashmere sweater and double row of pearls. Riding boots and jodhpurs completed her outfit. She had occasionally been mistaken for the late queen. She ran George and his estate with effortless ease and would probably fight to the death before relinquishing that control when George got married.

"George thinks you have outsmarted him."

"That makes a pleasant change," Phoebe said lightly. "Normally he's far too busy interfering in my affairs to notice what an arse he's being."

The dowager sighed. "Can you please be serious for once? I simply wish to know one thing."

"I'll do my best." Phoebe met her grandmother's fierce gaze with a calmness that surprised her.

"Do you intend to leave this country in the immediate future?"

"I haven't decided yet."

"Isn't having tricked your brother into giving you what you wanted enough for you?"

"I'm not sure, and to be fair he only gave me what was rightfully mine in the first place," Phoebe said thoughtfully. "I became so fixated on winning that I forgot there is always a price to pay."

"That's hardly an answer," The dowager sniffed. "But I suppose it's what I should've expected from you."

"May I ask you something?" Phoebe said. "I didn't realize your health had deteriorated so badly."

"*What?*" Her grandmother sat up straight. "Who told you that? I'm hardly in my dotage."

"It's quite all right, you can confide in me." Phoebe tried to look sympathetic. "George said I needed to be here to care for you in your . . . rapidly approaching declining years."

"Did he now."

Her grandmother's lips thinned and there was a militant spark in her eyes that made Phoebe want to smile.

For the first time her grandmother looked directly at her. "I am perfectly healthy and quite able to look after myself for the foreseeable future, dear."

"That's a relief," Phoebe said. "Then you can have no objection to me making my own decisions as to where I plan to live, and whether I stay married to Max."

The dowager glared at her. "I suppose you think you have bested me, missy."

"I'd never think that for a moment." Phoebe rose to her feet. "Now, if you will excuse me, I have an appointment with a hot carpenter."

Her grandmother stood, too, her expression slightly shocked. "George said you had changed."

"For the better?" Phoebe bent to pat the dogs before walking over to open the door. "I've certainly decided I'm no longer going to allow myself to be walked all over. It's remarkably liberating."

"That's what happens when you take up with Americans." Her grandmother swept past her, dogs at her heels, nose in the air. "Far too independent. Good afternoon, Phoebe."

"Good afternoon, Grandmother."

Phoebe went back to the kitchen where she helped herself rather liberally to the cooking sherry because besting her grandmother *and* George on the same day required celebrating.

*   *   *

Later that day, her cell buzzed, and she took it out of her pocket to see a text from Jen.

Incoming.

She was still puzzling over what Jen meant as she cleared the tea things and rinsed the teapot, leaving it to drain on the side of the sink. Her doorbell rang and after wiping her hands she went to answer it.

"Hey, Feebs."

Max stood there grinning at her.

"Why are you . . . here? W-what is happening?" Phoebe stuttered.

He swept her off her feet in a giant hug. "Nice place you've got here. Can I come in?"

"Yes, of course." She stood back and let him into the hall. "How . . . how did you get here?"

"By plane? I got an upgrade to first class at the desk from this awesome flight attendant and let me tell you those lying-flat beds make the trip so much easier." He looked around approvingly. "I can see why you wanted this house. It's got your personality all over it."

She gestured at the kitchen. "Would you like some tea, I mean coffee, or something to eat?"

"Coffee would be great if I want to stay awake for a while." Max held up his backpack. "Anywhere I can dump this?"

Reason returned to Phoebe along with an intense feeling of gratitude that just maybe she'd been right all along.

"You can put it upstairs in my bedroom if you'd like."

Max took a breath and met her gaze. "You sure about that?"

She smiled, and the joy flowed out of her and surrounded him. "If you plan on staying at least a night."

He nodded and slung the bag over his shoulder. "Lead the way."

"I do have seven other bedrooms you could occupy if you'd prefer." She went up the stairs ahead of him smiling like a fool.

"I'd prefer to be near you, Feebs, but I'm not going to force you into doing anything you're not okay with."

She paused at the bedroom door to stare up at him. He looked remarkably refreshed for a man who had been traveling all night. "I should warn you that I still snore."

He nodded gravely. "Me too."

"Then that's okay then." She gestured at the large sofa at the foot of her four-poster bed. "You can put your bag on here. If you'd like to unpack and take a shower while I prepare you some food, it's through there." She pointed at what had once been the dressing room between the two main bedrooms.

She turned around and he was right there. His arms came around her and she leaned against his chest and sighed like she was coming home.

"I missed you, Feebs." He kissed the top of her head, his voice rough. "I can't believe I was stupid enough to let you go again."

She cupped his stubbled chin. "We certainly have a lot to talk about, do you—?"

His mouth collided with hers with a pleasing urgency that pushed all other considerations from her mind. She slid her fingers into his hair, knocking off his Stetson and kissed him back with a ferocity that should have startled her. His answering groan was music to her ears as she fought to push off his jacket and unzip his fleece. After several frantic moments when they were both breathing hard, he eased away, his expression intense.

"Last chance to stop me before I get you naked and under me, Feebs."

She nipped his throat. "Not if I get there first."

When they were undressed, he picked her up with an ease that still astounded her and tossed her onto the middle of the bed. She sank into the feather mattress and let him climb over her. His knee pressed between her thighs pushing them wide. She didn't offer any resistance as he cupped her mound, his fingers already seeking out the slick evidence of her desire.

"God, Feebs, sweetheart, darlin', I've missed this so much." He kissed her in the same rhythm as the drive of his fingers and she came almost immediately. "That's my girl. That's what I want."

She scraped her nails down his back demanding more. He didn't argue, and with a single, hard thrust, and a twist of his hips he pushed home, filling her completely, making her moan his name. He didn't mess around, and she didn't want him to, both fighting each other to the finish, and both winning as they came together in a thunderous burst of pleasure that left Phoebe laughing, crying, and holding onto Max for dear life.

He pressed kisses down her throat and along her shoulder.

"I had this big speech planned out, and one look at you, and all I can think about is ripping your clothes off."

"You can still give me your speech," Phoebe said. "But this was important, too."

"Yeah?"

"Because sometimes words aren't enough."

"Especially when it's us doing the talking," Max murmured against her skin and rolled onto his back bringing her with him. "Want to try that again just to make sure we're on the same page? I'll even let you be on top."

Much later, after he'd taken a shower, Max let himself out of Phoebe's bedroom and made his leisurely way downstairs, pausing to admire what he assumed were family portraits, landscapes, and people on horseback hunting various animals. The fragrant scent of coffee came from the kitchen, and he went toward it, stopping at the door in his bare feet to look at Phoebe. Her skin was flushed, her expression serene and he'd never seen anything more beautiful in his life.

"Hey."

Her smile as she saw him struck him hard in the heart and his breath caught. For a second, he wondered what the hell he'd done to deserve to be looked at like that by anyone, let alone Phoebe.

"I made you coffee. I hope it's acceptable." A little frown appeared between her brows. "And pancakes, the American kind, but I don't have maple syrup, so will golden syrup do instead?"

He went past the pine kitchen table, wrapped his arms around her waist, and kissed her neck. She melted against him like butter on a hot pancake and he immediately wanted to put her over his shoulder, march up the stairs, and make love to her all over again.

"It's all good," he murmured. "I'll take anything you've got."

He sat at the table and waited for her to join him.

She wore a soft pink shirt over her jeans. Any make-up she'd put on that morning had disappeared in their shared first shower. There was a slight bruise on her throat where his teeth had caught her. He stared at it, astounded that his dick was stirring just thinking about doing it again.

"How are you feeling?" Phoebe asked as she joined him.

She'd gone a little shy and he didn't blame her. He was feeling the same way himself, which was a first. He just didn't want to screw this up.

"I'm good. How about you?" He paused to pour himself some coffee from the glass carafe. "Were you surprised to see me?"

"Flabbergasted." She poured her tea. "Jen did send me a text, but I didn't understand its meaning until it was too late."

"What did she say?"

"Just 'incoming'. Which was correct but perhaps a little cryptic."

"Jen's retired military like the rest of us, she probably thought that was enough information for anyone." Max helped himself to a pancake, a slab of butter, and the syrup which was lighter in color than his usual choice. He took a cautious bite and then another one. "This stuff is awesome!"

"It makes an excellent treacle tart and flapjacks, too." Phoebe doused her own pancake.

Around the house, what sounded like fifty clocks started chiming the hour. Phoebe didn't appear to notice, but Max did.

"That's a lot of clocks."

"Don't you like them?"

"I like some clocks and if they all chime at the right time, I'm good with it," Max said carefully.

"I'll ask George if he will give me the name of his clock winder at Creighton Hall," Phoebe said.

"George has a clock winder?"

"Creighton Hall is quite large. If you're planning on staying, I'll take you up there to meet my grandmother. This house is on the edge of the park surrounding the estate."

Max looked at her. "I'd like to stay—but only if it's okay with you."

"We do have a lot to talk about," Phoebe said. "That alone will take some time."

"I dunno about that, Feebs. I think we've already established the important stuff."

"That we can't keep our hands off each other?" Phoebe was blushing but her gaze was clear. "There has to be more than that, Max."

"I guess I was thinking more about myself—that I was miserable without you and kicking myself for trying to be noble rather than digging in my heels and thrashing everything out with you in real time."

He met her gaze. This was not the time to shy away from the truth, he really had to lay all his cards on the table.

"I didn't understand what had happened, Max. One moment you were suggesting we had a future together, the next that I should leave early." She grimaced. "I felt horrible."

"I'm sorry about that. I was so intent on not letting George tell me what to do, I forgot to have that discussion with *you*. It was your decision to make, and I should've been more honest. I guess I didn't want to make trouble between you and your family."

She sighed. "And I thought I'd been too forceful and scared you off."

"You'll never do that, Feebs."

She reached for his hand, her fingers sticky with the syrup. "*Why?*"

"Why what, sweet pea?"

"Why did you agree to marry me in the first place?"

He held her gaze. "Because I fell in love with you the moment I saw you. You were so damn *brave* standing there in that casino asking for the impossible."

"Max . . . that's ridiculous." She was blushing now.

"It's the truth. You're funny, you're sweet, you're sexy as hell, and for some crazy reason you believe in me, and make me want to be a better person." He took a breath, wanting to get the words right. "And what I'm realizing right now is that I don't care where I live as long as you're there because you light up my world and I'm miserable without you."

Her eyes filled with tears, and he smiled.

"Hey, that's not how I thought my declaration of undying love would go, but you do you."

"These are happy tears, Max, but . . ." She hesitated. "I've also realized something. All this." She looked around the kitchen. "Everything I fought for means very little when it's just me enjoying it."

He tightened his grip on her hand. "How about we build something special here together, Feebs? Something new for both of us?"

"But wouldn't you miss your old life at the ranch?"

He paused and reminded himself that he was being honest. "I don't know, sweetheart, but I'm willing to give it a try."

"For me?"

"Yeah, because I love you."

She swallowed hard. "I don't want you rushing into things. Will you let me show you around the house, and the stables, and explain what I'd like to do here before we decide whether we're both all-in on it?"

"Sure, and I'd like to meet your family." He sat back and forked another pancake onto his plate. "There is one more thing, Feebs."

"What's that?"

"Any chance you could tell me you love me back?"

"Oh, for goodness' sake." She rushed around the table so fast that her chair tipped back on its legs and knelt by his side, her eyes shining. "I love you more than anything in this world Max Creighton-Smith-Romano. We'll find a way to make this work even if we have two homes."

He nodded even as he wanted to grin like a fool. "Good to know Mrs. CSR, I mean *Lady* CSR. Good to know."

Epilogue

Two years later . . .

Being married to a lady millionaire wasn't a bad deal, Max reflected as he drove their rental down the driveway to the Nilsen ranch. He got to travel in style, first class, find the best horseflesh for their charity, and spend time at his first real home whenever it suited him. This time Phoebe had come with him. She was currently dozing in her seat, her cheek smooshed against the glass as she gently snored.

Max touched her arm as he drew to a stop. "We're here, princess."

She woke up and smiled at him. "That was quick."

"Jen texted to say she's been in our house and made sure its aired and the heating is on."

"She's so kind." Phoebe stretched out her back. "Our first Christmas at the ranch." She pressed a hand to her rounded stomach. "I think I might be stuck at home next year."

"Then everyone can come to us." Max got out and the freezing cold hit him. He didn't miss it in the slightest. "Although leaving a working ranch with no personnel isn't ideal. The cows get ideas."

He opened Phoebe's door and helped her out. Though the baby wasn't due for four months, she still looked as if she'd just stuck a soccer ball up her sweater. He drew her back against him and cupped her stomach.

"How about Althea?"

"Have you been talking to grandmother?"

"Yeah, actually. She's a hoot and it *is* a great name."

"She absolutely adores you because you charm her to pieces." Phoebe acknowledged as they made their way to the main ranch, which was strung with multi-colored Christmas lights. "And I do like that name. I just don't like agreeing with her."

Max was still chuckling when Luke opened the door.

"You made it! Come in!"

Luke hugged Phoebe who went through into the kitchen to a series of whoops and turned to Max who had lingered by the door.

"Good to see you, bro." He grinned. "I guess we're both going to be dads next year."

Max wrapped Luke in his arms and slapped him hard on the back. "That's awesome!"

"Sky and baby Lee are going to have some play-mates." Luke said. "You'll bring your kid over here, right? Make sure they get their American on and can ride a horse western-style."

"You bet. Can't let them think they're all posh like their mama."

Max moved through into the kitchen and was soon hugging and kissing his found family, exclaiming over baby Lee's growth and likeness to Noah, and being talked at incessantly by Sky.

He took a moment to stand back and appreciate it all and felt a light touch on his sleeve. Sally, who had retired completely from her medical practice, stood beside him.

"You look happy, Max."

"I am." He smiled at her. "Thanks for helping me make the right decisions."

"You knew it in your heart. You just needed to believe that you deserved to be loved."

"Yeah," he looked over at Phoebe who winked at him. "I know that now."

"Are you going to tell your parents about the baby?" Sally asked.

Max had thought about it a lot. "I'm still not sure."

"Then wait until you see your baby before you decide." Sally smiled. "I hope they take after you, Max, because you deserve to be led a merry dance."

Max laughed out loud, and everyone looked at him.

"Sally's wishing the baby's just like me, Feebs."

Phoebe smiled right back at him. "I can't think of anything I'd love more."

And that, right there, was why they were married.

She got him.

She really did.